Review

The present tense prose powering Phoenix: King of the Chimerians captures your attention from the start. It is not an easy point of view to control and often demands authors rethink how they approach building sentences. Re-envisioning this aspect of their craft forces them, however, to operate outside their comfort zone. Phoenix begins fast – the first chapter establishes a smattering of background before introducing readers to the book's first characters. The science fiction element underlying the book's narrative is obvious from the beginning, but you see early on this is a story far more reliant on character than wonky details.

Scenes near the open detail the initial development of the Chimerians and set the stage for everything that follows. Phoenix: King of the Chimerians lays down the same brisk pace throughout the book's first quarter; plot developments come fast but never rushed. Randy Thompson commands the stage as a primary character early. The writing fleshes out his motivations and emotional weather. Randy's personality evolves with the introduction of additional characters and the author creates a compelling cast capable of complementing his central protagonist.

Longtime observers of literary history will note genre fiction has undergone a revolution in scope over the last seventy-five years. It has retained the time-tested formulas forming the bedrock of its appeal, but several seminal works over that period have expanded the novelistic range of such works. The traditional literary notion of a protagonist undergoing a gradual change throughout a narrative is in evidence. The book does not rely upon gimmicks or excessive technological descriptions. It mingles science fiction and fantasy tropes with an adept hand.

The book is not long and the writing aims for the broadest possible audience. Credible plot developments abound and build to a dramatic finale that strikes the right note. Longtime science fiction fans will appreciate the familiar frame of reference the author invokes for readers throughout Phoenix, but ample individual creativity fuels the work. Phoenix is never imitative and creates a compelling fictional universe for readers to inhabit.

It likely holds up under repeated readings and works as an ideal series entry. The book, nonetheless, works as a standalone and doesn't demand the trappings of a series character to entertain readers. The author creates a credible fictional environment with enough allure to draw readers in from the outset and never strains to achieve its effects. The prose is notable for its excellent line by line economy and few digressions slow the narrative. Phoenix King of the Chimerians is an unique entry in the science fiction tradition that riffs on recognizable turns yet sparkles with individual stylishness and creativity. It is a book that will leave you wanting more and, without any concrete details backing it up, it is safe to assume it is not the last we'll hear from this fictional universe. The promise of more lives in this book and the enduring characters the author creates are interesting enough to hold the interest of casual readers and genre aficionados alike.

—Reprospace Reviews™

PHOENIX

KING OF THE CHIMERIANS

RALEIGH MINARD

PHOENIX, *King of the Chimerians*
First edition, published 2021

By Raleigh Minard

Cover design by Reprospace.com

Paperback ISBN-13: 978-1-952685-29-3

Published by Kitsap Publishing
Poulsbo, WA 98370
www.KitsapPublishing.com

Acknoledgments

To my Lord for all the inspirations and Ideas for my book.

Thank You.

To Bobbie Kuniyuki, for all your help and suggestions.

Thank You.

CHAPTER

1

I, Hector, the royal scribe, have been tasked to compile the Chimerians' history. I'm using the writings of our creator Randy Thompson. Included are the visions that Randy had before he died. The origin of the Chimerians begins with the history Randy Thompson wrote several generations ago. Randy gave these writings to us from the beginning.

I, Randy Thompson, the creator of the Chimerians, have set down to the best of my recollection of how the Chimerians came into being. This is the most painful memory of losing my friends. It starts in an obscure lab in a city called New York.

Benison Static was a molecular mechanics and energy scientist; his partner Andy Johannsson was an electronics and metallurgical scientist. They are working on developing a transporter. They soon realize that they need a computer and programming specialist, so they brought on Candy Lake.

After many trials, they manage to build a transmitter and a

receiver, it was a very unwieldly setup, but they felt if they can get it to work, they could begin to make refinements and streamline their invention. The device's theory is that the transmitter would break down the item and transform it into data, then transmit it to the receiver, which would reconstruct that data back into its original form. In essence, the transmitter would disassemble the object one-molecule layer at a time and transform it into a data stream the computer could read, and then transmit the data to the receiver, and it would rebuild the object one layer at a time.

They build two pods and place one at each end of the warehouse they are using; at one end was the transmitter, and the other end the receiver. Candy's computers and programs controlled both units. In the first test, they use an old block of wood, and they sent it through the transmitter to the receiver. They place the wood block into the transmitter and run the first part of the program. The wooden block disassembles as it should have, and the computer receives the data. The next part of the program runs, it transmits the data to the receiver part of the transporter, and it rebuilds the wooden block from the data stream, but what they get is sawdust.

"At least it wasn't burnt like last time," said Candy.

"Computer record settings," said Candy.

"How many runs so far?" asks Ben.

"To date, twenty runs and all have failed, but this one was our best yet, at least we got wood back and not charcoal. Let me run some analysis on this sample, and I'll let you know if it's better," says Andy.

Andy takes the sample to his lab and runs some tests on it, and when he looks at it under the microscope, he sees what looks like some kid was playing pick-up Stix and dropped all the wood fibers onto the floor in a pile. Andy shares his results with the team.

"Well, from what I can see, the transmitter takes it apart, and that seems to be fine, but the receiver doesn't put the pieces back together the way it's taken apart or better yet in reverse order."

"Let me see what I can do to correct that problem," says Candy. Candy takes a few days, rewrites, and tweaks her program, and it's time to run another test. Candy puts a block of wood into the transmitter, fires up the computer program, and then launches the sequence. You can hear the transmitter as it disassembles the block of wood, then moments later, the receiver is re-integrating the block of wood, this time Candy got a solid block of wood.

"Andy, Ben, get in here now. It's working."

Both of them appear, and Candy shows them the block.

"Let's run another test," said Andy

"Use a new block, then I can have two samples to analyze," mentioned Andy.

Candy puts in the new block then runs the program. In mere moments, it cycles through the sequence, and the receiver gets another block of wood. Andy grabs them up and rushes to his lab to analyze the wood. Andy returns in an hour.

"Both blocks test out all right; now the thing is what was sent through, did it assemble the same way as it was taken apart."

"I see what you mean said Ben, let's try something else; I know I have this wooden bowl that a friend turned and it has designs on it; this should tell us if it's being assembled correctly."

Ben puts the bowl into the transmitter, and Candy runs the program, and moments later, they pull the bowl out of the receiver, and it's perfectly intact.

"I think this calls for a party, and a day off tomorrow," says Ben.

"Then on Thursday we can re-run it again to be sure," says Ben

Andy and Candy agree, and they all go out to dinner to celebrate the day's success. On Thursday, they all return to work and re-run the test on the bowl several times, and each time it's successful.

"Now we know we can put one object through the transporter, let's try two objects," said Ben.

Andy brings in a block of wood and a glass ashtray and puts them into the transmitter. They cycled through the transporter, and what they get is a wood ceramic.

"Wow! Look at that, it sure looks pretty, but that's not what it should be," said Andy.

"Hey, wait a minute. I want to try something else," said Andy.

Andy goes to a storage cabinet, brings a block of steel, and a titanium block, and puts them into the transmitter. Andy has Candy cycle the transporter. Andy takes the new material out of the receiver. "Look at this! This is fantastic! These metals will not combine under our current technology. I need to run some tests, and I will get back to you."

"What is it, Andy?" asks Ben.

CHAPTER

2

"If this tests out the way I hope it will, we can make millions creating new materials, that'll give us the funds to continue our work of the transporter."

Andy takes the material to his lab and runs his tests. The next day Andy is all but dancing around.

"This is great stuff; I'm going to approach one of the metal companies and let them have a sample of this material and see what they would pay to have it. I may want to duplicate our current set up in another warehouse so I can keep making new and different materials to generate us some money; let me go see what the market will bear."

Andy contacts a few companies and provides them with his new material; in a week, they want more material, and by the truckload. Andy decides to move his operation to another warehouse down the road, and then build a giant transmitter and receiver. He makes a deal to make the materials, but the company who wants the material will supply the materials, and Andy will process them into the new material for a fee.

Andy begins to make all kinds of new materials, and their bank account is approaching the billion-dollar mark. Andy could've set them all up for life, but their goal is still making a transporter. Andy is creating a new kind of material from steel and copper when a rat slips into the transmitter chamber through an open door. Andy cycled the transporter and got a strange shock when he opened the receiving chamber. There in the middle of the chamber is a rat shaped metal composite the size of a dog. The thing was heavy. Just what I need a statue shaped like a rat. Andy puts the rat on the shelf and closes for the day. That night in a meeting with Ben and Candy, Andy tells them what happened today at his lab, and he tells them about the rat-shaped statue he got.

"What's this?" asked Candy, "you say a rat-shaped statue came out?"

Andy responds, "Why, yes, does this mean anything?"

"Has this happened at any other time?"

"No, now that you mentioned it hasn't."

"Andy, we need to go see this statue, and right now," said Ben.

They leave and go to Andy's lab, and there on the shelf, where the steel rat was placed, it had moved and changed its position, from walking on all fours to sitting upright.

"This can't be," said Andy.

"I placed the statue in the middle of the shelf, and it was on all fours, now look at it."

"Andy, you must have had a rat in the chamber when you cycled it, and it became part of the new material you were working on."

"I gathered that much," said Andy, "but it's moving, it's alive, how can that be?"

Ben hazards a guess, the theory that rocks may be alive in their way maybe what's in play here. It takes the rat a while to make a move, much like watching the hour hand on a clock, we know it moves, but it is so slow that we don't see it move, but if we leave the room and come back later, we can see that it has moved. Someone suggested that stone maybe alive, but they move so slowly they cannot be seen to move. Not that I believe in the living stone, but the rat statue suggests a lot of possibilities. Right now, the rat is not anything to be concerned with; let's get back to our project."

Andy has amassed a fortune in his new metal process, and he shares it with Ben and Candy so they can proceed with the real project of building a transporter.

CHAPTER

3

Candy figures out how to send items through the transporter and get them back as they were transmitted. All they sent were blocks of materials. They tried to send shaped blocks; at first, all they would get is square blocks of material. Candy tweaked her program, and Ben set out to adjust the power to help make the system run more efficiently. They ran another test on a roller bearing, and they get a roller bearing back. Ben gave Andy the bearing to run tests on the metal to see if it was the same way as before the transport. Andy came back the next day and said it was a success.

"Ok, it's time to see if we can get some backers or prospective buyers for our transporter," said Ben.

Ben contacts six transport or trucking companies with their idea. Only two of them show up. After seeing the demonstration, the company men want to know when and if they can get the transporter for their use. Also, they want exclusive rights to it. One asked how much cargo they could ship at a time, how about the size of a cargo container full of product. At this point, Candy speaks up.

"At this time, that's not possible; you'd need a supercomputer capable of handling and storing all the data. With our current technology, this isn't possible yet. Right now, I'm using six terabit computers to do this demonstration."

Ben speaks up, "the process for the transporter is that the item in the transmitter is disassembled molecule by molecule then converted into data. In the computer buffer, the program cycles the data to the receiver and is re-integrated back into its original form. Which requires Terra-bites of computer memory. Our team realizes that we'll need to develop new technology such as a supercomputer to accomplish what you ask."

"Tell me, doctors, will this be able to transport people?" asked one of the buyers.

Candy speaks to this, "In theory, yes, but as we mentioned, it'll require a supercomputer to hold all the data, a person is more complex than a block of wood or metal. We've not tried to send a living thing through the process yet. We intend to try as soon as we figure out how to build a supercomputer." One of the buyers turned and, as he was leaving, said, "When you have it all figured out, call me."

The other buyer stood there as if in thought, "I did some research on you and found that you don't need money. You each are fairly rich using this machine to fabricate exotic materials, and I assume you're using this money to build your machine. Once perfected, you'd control all of the industry, why contact me for support?"

"Candy answers, "we'll need to bring in more people to help develop this computer technology, and it may well cost more than we are currently making."

"That makes sense. I may have the person you may need; his name is Randy Thompson, my son."

Andy is perplexed, "Your son; your last name is Byron."

"It's his mother's maiden name; he took it after she died. Randy and I don't get along. He's very talented with computers. This would give him something to do besides frittering away his life."

"Ok, send him to us, and we'll see what he's capable of. Does this mean you'll support us?"

"I'll consider it for now. I'll have Randy here in the morning."

The next morning Randy shows up at the lab.

Chapter

4

"Are you the people who need a computer geek?" asks Randy.

"Hi Randy we've been expecting you." said Candy.

"This is Ben our power expert, and this is Andy who really makes us our money by developing new materials."

They incline their heads toward him.

"Why am I here?" asks Randy.

"Your father suggested you may be able to help us."

"Don't say that, don't call him my father. He killed my mother, and I hate him!"

"No disrespect to you, and we'll not mention it again" said Ben.

"Candy will give you a tour, then we'll demonstrate our process, and maybe you can see how the transporter works."

"You're kidding right? A transporter like in Star Trek?"

"May be in the future we can make it like the one in Star Trek, but for now think of it more like a telephone transmitter and a receiver. We'll let Candy fill you in, she's our programmer and probably speaks your language."

"Hey I'm not some dumb kid, I made my own computer using a crystal and it's the fastest computer ever made, but my so-called dad hushed it up."

Ben looks Randy in the eye. "Randy, at this lab if you choose to help us and work with us, you'll be treated as an equal, not as a child. You'll share equally in all that there is, even the money that we make. Also, we'll share some of our dream projects, in time we hope we can place raw materials in that machine break them down and then integrate into a finished product, for instance a car."

"When do we start?" asks Randy."

"Randy follow me, and we'll take a tour and I'll show you what we've done," said Candy.

For the rest of the day Candy and Randy tour the labs. Ben's energy lab, where he has come up with different ways to use the current technology to generate power for their project. Then on to Andy's lab where Andy has on display several new materials that have been made, and lastly Candy's lab where the computers and programs are made.

"I'm impressed," said Randy, "where can I set up a lab."

"We hoped you'd be working with us so we made some space over there in that corner, there should be enough space for you, now for any equipment you need just ask me and I'll see that you get it."

"You really mean it don't you?"

"Like Ben said if you want, you'll be part of our team. We'll expect a lot from you, and if you don't deliver, then you'll be asked to leave."

Randy looks into Candy's eyes and says, "I'll deliver, and I want to thank you guys for giving me a chance, and not treating me like the boss' son."

"Your father does not own us, and we can hire and fire as we choose, we only contacted a few companies, because we're not business people."

"Then a word of advice, don't trust my father, he'll steal your inventions and leave you in the gutter. I've watched his tactics so many times. You'd be better off hiring a person out of college than my father."

"Ok, Randy thanks for the advice, I'll tell the others, no you can tell them at our meeting at lunch time."

Chapter

5

Randy looks over the computers that they currently use. He makes some notes; Randy changes some hardware to make the computers faster and more reliable; he also puts a proposal together for using a crystalline type of computer system. Lunchtime comes around, and Candy takes Randy to meet with Ben and Andy. In the meeting, each person takes their turn to talk about their project status. Ben tells of a new possible power source, Andy tells of the cash flow from the original materials he's making, Candy tells of the tweaks in her program to better collect and transmit the data stream. Finally, Randy got his chance; he warns the team about his father's business tactics and don't trust him. Then Randy tells them about some of the hardware upgrades to make the computers they have better. Last of all, he puts his proposal on the table to change the computer system over to using a crystalline structure; by the time he finishes, the others are impressed.

"That would solve a lot of our problems, the power, and storage would be unbelievable, and the speed," said Ben. The rest of the team looks at Randy.

Candy says, "Randy scrap the idea of upgrading the current computers. Let's build the crystal computers. Give Andy a material list of what you need and Andy will get it for you."

"Really!" exclaims, Randy.

The team looks at him and, in unison, says, "Really."

"This is the first time I've ever been a part of something where I've been taken seriously; Thank You, you guys!" Randy said.

"If this computer system you proposed works half as well as you say, man! Wow, it'll be worth whatever we spend on it. If you were a little older, I'd take you out for a brew. Would you settle for a soda for now? You're a godsend, Randy," says Ben, patting him on the back.

That day Randy makes him some friends. The next morning Randy gives Andy a shopping list of materials. Andy looks over the list.

" You're asking for diamonds and rubies. Is there a specific size you have in mind? You realize that these will be manufactured for us. Which one would be better?"

"That's a tough one. Each one has properties that would be better if they were packaged into new material as you do with the metals."

"So, what are the properties?"

"The diamond makes great storage, while the ruby is less crystalline and will pass a light like a laser more easily than a diamond."

"Laser, huh, that means the speed of the computer will be at the speed of light."

"That's why I suggested it. I also recommend specially made lithium batteries, so they don't explode."

"Randy, you are full of surprises. That means Ben can concentrate on the transporter power and not the computers. Randy, this is great. I'll order everything today, and everything should be here in a couple of weeks."

"Thanks Andy. I'll draw up the schematics for the computers. I have fiber optics on the list. Buy the best grade, so we have the capacity to make this work."

"You got it, Randy." Two weeks later all the materials are at the lab.

"Andy, I thought you were going to buy manufactured diamond and rubies already put together?"

"No, I changed my mind. We'll put them together using our process."

Randy hits himself with the flat of his hand. "You're right, Andy, you can do that. When will we do this?"

"In an hour. I'm processing some special metals. When that's done, we'll get your crystals merged. I'm rather anxious to put the new computer to work."

Andy puts equal weights of diamonds and rubies in a pile in the transmitter. He turns to the transmitter and cycles it to transmit the rocks into the buffer. Next, he makes a few adjustments to the receiver computer, so the rocks merge into a bar, not a strange shape. Andy cycles the receiver, and the crystal composite bar appears in the middle of the chamber. It's a clear mass shot through with the red of the ruby color. Andy calls Randy and tells him the crystal is ready, and Randy rushes over to collect it.

"Randy, I'm going to make another crystal so you can upgrade my computer too, I should have the components here in a few days, so when you get Candy up and running, you can come and do mine."

"That sounds great, Andy, I'll be glad to do it."

Randy gets all his components, goes to his lab area, and puts Candy's new computer together. Then Randy tears up the floor, and hides all the components under the floor and tells Candy to leave the old computer in place, so if someone breaks in to steal the computers, they would take these and not the crystal computers. When he's finished with Candy's computer, he hooks up Andy's computer, and Randy tells Andy to leave the old computers in place. All four meet for lunch in the next meeting, and Randy asks, "How the new computers are doing?"

Chapter

6

"The transporter is working far better than it ever has and much faster as well," said Candy.

Andy chimes in to say much the same. Candy wants to send a live animal through the transporter; she feels confident that the new computer can handle the data stream.

That afternoon Candy gets one of the white rats, puts it into the transmitter, and cycles it through to the integrator. As she opens the door, she throws up. The rat is not only dead but inside out. She went home for the day. Randy looks over the program, does more tweaking, and runs another test. The rat is alive and in one piece. The next morning Randy shows Candy his results after she left. Randy suggests that they put the new rats through a maze before they send it through the transporter, then run the rat through the maze after sending it to see if there are any changes to the rat. Randy took charge of the critters. He ran a rat many times through the maze until he was getting the same result each time, then Candy and Randy would send the rat through the transporter and then run the rat through the maze again. Everything appears to be just fine. Now Randy wants to run a larger animal through the transporter, so he buys a spider monkey. He and Candy do similar tests before and after with the monkey with no seeable problems or differences. Randy then takes the monkey to a vet to get X-rays done, and again, nothing is abnormal. The monkey is given a clean bill of health by the Vet.

Chapter

7

Ben receives a call from Randy's father to meet him for dinner that night; Ben accepts. Byron keeps asking about Randy, and his new computer system. Is it working yet? This appeared to be a father's pride talking, then he remembers that Randy said that they shouldn't trust his father.

Ben said that they were still working on the computer, and it's promising. By the end of dinner, Randy's father realizes they've built the crystal computers. This is what he was waiting for. With these computers, he could take control of all the businesses in the world and the military. Using a computer stronger and faster than the conventional computer, he'll be able to use it to control all other computers. He'll be the only one to possess it. Byron leaves Ben and returns to his office. Byron presses a button.

"Get in here!"

Moments later, one of his security men enters Byron's office. "Yes sir."

Byron tells him to sit and the security man does as he's told.

"I want you to spy on these people." Byron hands over pictures of the scientists and his son at the warehouse. "I want a report in a week."

"Now get out of here."

"Yes, sir." The security man leaves to do as instructed.

Randy goes to Andy's shop and loads up a CAD system to his computing system and places a simple piece of steel into the mixer. Randy started calling the transporter "mixer," since it combines materials. He then fires up the CAD system and programs the computer to make the steel block into a bowl; he cycles it through the process and gets a steel bowl.

"Randy, that's a great idea; how complex a part can we make?"

"I don't know yet, maybe something with only a few different materials in it, depends on how well we program the machine."

"This is going to be fun," said Andy

The security man has been watching the warehouse, and he even planted bugs and cameras so that he can record them, and over time, he discovers what his boss wants.

Andy calls the other two and tells them Randy has gone back to work; the three of them have decided to throw a party for Randy for all the excellent work he's done; they have cake and soda. They decorate the shop, and then they get ready to call him when two men in ski masks barge in with guns.

"Now, no one will be hurt if you do what we tell you," said the first guy.

"Where are the computers located?" said the second guy.

"What computers?" asked Ben.

The first guy hits Ben upside the head with his gun knocking him unconscious. Then he turns to Candy and slaps her across the face.

"Where are the computers?" Candy points to the computers over on the desk.

"Right there, you idiot." She's gets punched in the stomach and doubles up.

"Well, smart guy, now you tell me where the crystal computers are."

Andy refuses to talk, so the men grab Ben, they make Andy carry Candy to the transmitter, and they put them into it.

"Now wise guy tells us where the crystal computer is, or we're going to put you in there with them."

Andy says nothing, and they force him into the chamber and close the door. The first guy walks up to the computer console and turns on the transmitter.

"Hey, this works just like the boss said it would."

Then he causes the transporter to cycle, and what they get at the other end is enough to make a sane man sick to his stomach. All three of them are melded together, and they are turned inside out; what appeared in the receiver didn't live very long, and all three people are dead.

The two men look around trying to find the crystal computers, but Randy has hidden them so well they cannot see them.

Randy returns to his work area and sees that Candy is gone, and he decides to run an experiment; he puts his spider monkey and a ferret into the machine and cycles it, what Randy gets at the integrator puzzles him. All he gets back is the monkey; where's the ferret? Randy puts the monkey in his cage and goes to inspect the transporter. Randy checks from one end to the other and can't find the ferret.

Later Randy goes to check on the monkey and finds the ferret, and the monkey is gone.

"What's going on?" Randy asks himself.

He decides to put a camera on the cage to see what's happening; in the next hour, Randy plays back the tape; he's amazed at what he finds; the monkey changes into the ferret, and the ferret transforms back. The camera shows this happening several times, and what appears to have happened is the new creature can melt and shift from one form to another.

On one of the changes, the ferret had the monkey's arms and hands but kept the ferret's body. Randy decides for now to keep this quiet. It's time to close down for the day. The three adults left a call for Randy to come to Andy's lab area. They were going to throw a surprise party for Randy. Randy is about to run the last experiment using a snake through the transporter to make a report to the others on his findings.

Then two men wearing black ski masks grab Randy from behind.

"Where are the computers," says the first man.

"They are over there," said Randy pointing at the computer console.

One of them checks out Candy's station and sees the computers.

"These aren't the ones we want, where are they? Where are the crystal Computers?"

"That's all the computers we have right there."

"No, they're not the computers I'm looking for," said the first man.

Randy is dragged to the transmission chamber and thrown in with the rattlesnake being pitched in after him; Randy tries to avoid the snake. Randy starts beating on the door and screaming, "Let me out."

The man that locked him in is laughing and the other man finds the controls to the machine, starts the transmission cycle of the device and walks off. Randy hears them before he's transported with the snake.

"The others look like they were turned inside out and glued together. It sure was a mess in that other machine", said the men as they leave laughing.

"The boss' son will look much the same, and then we'll have all the time we need to locate the crystal computers that Bryon wants."

The men walk off, believing that Randy will meet the same fate as his friends.

CHAPTER

8

The machine cycles with Randy and the snake. Randy appears at the other end, no sign of the snake. He manages to open the door.

Randy looks down at his hands and sees scales, then he touches his face and feels more scales; he walks to the bathroom to look in the mirror. Randy sees his reflection, part man part snake, complete with fangs; he feels stronger than he did before, and his hands move at a blur.

"Father, you're going to regret this. I'm going to make sure you do."

Randy quickly runs to Andy's lab and finds what's left of his friends in the integrator; he drops down to his knees and pounds his fist on the floor, crying out in anguish.

"Why father. Why did you do this?"

It takes a while for Randy to control his grief. Randy forms a plan at the back of his mind of what he should do. Randy manages to put his friends' remains into a truck without being seen and drives to his family's cemetery. Randy opens the crypt, and inside he finds the next open grave box, puts his friends inside, and buries them in his family's tomb.

"You guys deserve better than this, and I'm going to make my father pay for what he did to you. Right now, I can't draw attention to myself. I love you all, you treated me as an equal friend. Thank you and goodbye."

Randy drives to his father's office building. There's a small vent about eight inches square at the back of the building; he rips the cover off. He changes into his rattlesnake form. Randy slithers into the vent, follows it down into the basement and a larger vent. Randy comes to the vent cover inside and peers through to see if anyone is in there, it appears empty, so Randy forces the vent open, then drops to the floor and changes back into his human form. Slowly Randy walks over to the stairs making sure he's not seen or that anyone may have heard him as he kicked off the vent cover. Randy climbs up two flights of stairs, and at the landing, Randy stops to listen at the door. Randy hears the two men that killed his friends, bragging about what they did. Randy quietly opens the door and steps inside then changes back into a rattlesnake; he slithers along the wall, then under the locker room bench, coils up and waits.

As soon as the men walk past him and he strikes the nearest one in the leg, he falls and is face-to-face with the snake, and Randy strikes again and bites the man in the neck. The other man grabs his friend and tries to help him, and Randy now bites him on his hand. He drops his friend and tries to get away, but Randy changes into a reptile-like man and stands up. The man is frozen with fear and can't move. Randy walks over to the man, bites the man in the neck, and then changes back into himself. The second man asks, "What are you?"

Randy knees down beside him and says, "You should make sure a person is dead before you leave. The men die right there. Randy goes out to the lobby and takes an elevator up to the top floor. Before the doors open Randy changes into a snake, and when the entrance to the elevator opens, Randy slithers out into the room.

"Who's there? Show yourself. I have a gun, and I won't hesitate to shoot."

Randy makes his way to the couch and slithers under the couch to locate his father on the far side. Byron walks over to the elevator and sees that it's empty, and he mumbles to himself about having building maintenance look at it in the morning. Byron returns to his desk. Off to the room's right, a door opens, and a young girl enters the room.

"What's wrong? I heard you talking".

Byron looks up and smiles, "it was nothing. Go back to the bedroom, and I'll be in shortly."

She leaves the room. Randy slithers up to his father's desk and transforms back to himself and stands up.

"Hello, father, miss me?"

"What are you doing here?"

"Why father didn't you expect to see me anymore; I can assure you the talk of my death was premature."

"Ahh, yes, how are you doing" he reaches for his gun.

"Don't do that, father, leave the gun there, or you be dead in mere moments."

Byron stops reaching for his gun and stands up, but he doesn't see Randy holding a weapon and figures he can still grab his gun and kill him. Byron wants to see why Randy is here, so he asks.

"What do you want?"

"You had my friends killed so that you can steal my crystal computer. You killed them for nothing, and now I want your life."

Byron grabs his gun, but Randy changes to a man snake and strikes (bites) his father in the neck before he can get his hand on the weapon. Byron looks in horror at his son and stammers out, "What are you?"

"The men you sent to kill me; sent me through the wrong transporter. You see, father, I was working on a different project, and I discovered by accident that the transporter set up, causes transformations in my subjects. I was interrupted, and instead of the lizard I was going to put in, your men put me in instead with a rattlesnake and cycled the transporter thinking it would do the same to me as it did my friends. Now I'm changed, I can be a snake or a human or something in between, as you just discovered. Oh, I see you're dead. Too bad."

Randy, in his human snake form, starts for the elevator when the young girl reenters the room and sees this alien creature standing in the room; in a blink of an eye, Randy is standing next to her, ready to bite her when she breaks down in hysteria losing her mind.

Randy decides not to kill her. Going over to his father's desk, he locates a little red book with all the passwords to all his father's accounts. Then Randy walks back over to the girl and stares at her. All she can do is scream. Randy turns and leaves the room and uses the stairs to leave the building. The next morning the guards find Byron and a crazy girl in the penthouse, and the two security guards in the locker room. The coroner says they were bitten by a rattlesnake, but can't account for the different sized fang marks in the victims' legs and neck. The crazy girl keeps mentioning a human-sized alien looking like a reptile bit Byron but didn't do anything to her. She's so distraught that they have to sedate her. The next day Randy reads the newspaper and smiles. Using the crystal computer in Candy's lab, Randy commences draining all his father's funds into various shell corporations, banks, and so on; by the time Randy is finished, the money trail is so tangled it'll take an average person-years to track all the money.

Randy also hacks his way into his friends' accounts and does the same. Randy is sorry, but he'll need the money to implement his plan. Randy decides to run some tests on himself to see how he is. Randy goes to a doctor as himself and gets a physical, then he makes an appointment with his specialist for a mental evaluation; in all his tests, he's normal. The snake side of him will become a problem later, as it turns out it's not a factor for now. (At least not yet). Randy decides to create a new world on a remote island. We'll be known as the Chimerians. Who should I pick, what type of people do I choose to be the new race?

Chapter

9

After some consideration, Randy decides that it might be prudent to test this out on someone else before making others like himself. Randy sets out to find another person to transform into a Chimerian. Randy decides to experiment with homeless people this way no one would pay too much attention if they go missing. Randy comes across his first subject in an alley, an old native American Indian who looks like he needs help.

"Hi. Do you need help?" asks Randy.

"Why would you help me? I'm dying. Go away and leave me in peace."

"I'm a mad scientist, and I'm looking for a subject to test my transformation machine on. If you're dying, then if it fails, it won't matter, what do you say?"

"Can I have a last meal before we do this transformation?"

"Sure, what would you like. I'll get it for you," says Randy.

"I would like a pepperoni pizza? I've never tasted one before."

"Sure, let me help you up, and we can go to my lab."

At the lab, Randy assures the old man that the machine will not kill him. Randy explains that the machine was used on him, and he shows the Indian his snake side. The Indian's eyes open very wide.

"Will I become like a snake too?"

Randy calls in to order the pizza then turns to the Indian to answer him.

"You'll become whatever animal you want to be. What's your name?"

"In my tribe, I was called Iron Eagle."

"What tribe did you belong to?" asks Randy.

"Black Foot Indians, of Flat Head Lake Montana, we were the Southern tribe our totem was the eagle." "Interesting, Iron Eagle, you can sleep over there on that couch tonight. I'll get you a blanket." "What's your name?" asks Iron Eagle.

Before Randy can answer Iron Eagle, the pizza arrives, and Randy pays for it and gives it to Iron Eagle.

"I'm Randy, I have to leave you here for a time, I need to pick up something, and I'll be back, please don't touch any equipment. The bathroom is over through that door, and a kitchen is through there. You may have whatever you want."

"Thank you, Randy."

Randy leaves the room, and later that night, he brings back a Bald Eagle. Randy had gone to the zoo and located the bird. As luck would have it, it was too old, and was to be exterminated. Randy bought it from the gamekeeper at a steep price.

Randy returns to his lab with the Eagle. Randy does not know how to handle the bird very well. "Randy, what are you doing? You might hurt that bird," cries Iron Eagle.

"He'll be fine, now come over here please."

Iron Eagle does what he's asked and gets into this machine.

"Here takes the eagle in with you," said Randy.

"What's going to happen to us?" asks Iron Eagle.

"You'll now become like me, but instead of being a snake, you'll be an eagle."

Iron Eagle and the bird are in the chamber when Iron Eagle looks out the machine's window.

Randy cycles the machine, and Iron Eagle and the bald eagle are transmitted to the integration chamber. Randy opens the door to the integrator chamber and out steps Iron Eagle; he looks like a young man compared to when he went in. Iron Eagle looks at his hands then into a mirror.

"What magic is this?" queries Iron Eagle.

"Not magic, science," says Randy. Now watch me, and Randy goes through the change again from a man to a snake then back again. Now you try it, you should be able to transform into an eagle."

Iron Eagle transforms into an eagle, takes off, and flies around inside the warehouse; then, he transforms back into a man.

"Such magic, and I see that I'm much younger, what have you done?"

"I can't explain it, but the people who built this machine were killed, and the people who did it tried to kill me, but instead of killing me, they changed me as I've changed you. I call us the Chimerians, and I wish to make more of them. Will you help me?" asks Randy.

"Yes, Randy. It would benefit whoever we allow into the machine. Look at me, I'm younger and stronger than I ever was, and I have my youth back."

For several days, Randy and Iron Eagle search out other homeless people, young and old, and take them into the warehouse to feed and clothe them and see to their needs. Randy sets out to find a place where he can move his new subjects. In his search, Randy finds at the edge of the Bermuda Triangle an island that his father had purchased from the Navy; it was abandoned after World War II. It had been a station to observe ship movements, mostly the enemy ships. Randy leaves Iron Eagle in charge and takes a trip to the island to see if it can be adapted for his use. After several days, Randy returns and decides to pack up the warehouse and ship everything to the island. Randy finds out that the island is nothing more than some huge rock sticking up out of the ocean. With his father's connections.

Randy has an excavation crew brought in, and they build an underground facility, complete with solar power and a massive dome of concrete to house everyone. After a year, the construction crew leaves the island. Randy brings all his new subjects to the island, and the first day after they arrive, the weather changes, and massive hurricane forms and passes over the island. Everyone inside the dome braces for the storm's impact, and then when it's over, they realize they weathered the first hurricane with no problem. Now Randy starts to purchase and import all sorts of animals; he tries to buy ones that were pets at one time, some were very old. He had over a hundred people on the island. They were runaway teens to older men and women. All of them are looking for a new life.

Chapter 10

Randy has gone out of his way to make sure he didn't pick up anyone with a criminal record. He didn't want to give criminals that kind of power with the ability to change that he's going to be giving them. A month after all the construction was complete; Randy sets up the conversion machine and the crystal computer. He announces to the people what's going to happen when they enter into the transformation chamber. Some of the people are in disbelief until both Randy and Iron Eagle display what they can do. The next day everyone shows up to be converted or at least watch. The older people are first to enter the chamber with their chosen animal, some of the animals are their pets, dogs, cats, and even a parakite, and when they came out, they're young again. The transformation is a remarkable sight. They watch an old person enter into the disintegrator and then emerge from the integrator a young person, but where is the animal? Randy cycles twenty-five people through the machine, then stops the process so he can show them how to transform. Randy, with Iron Eagle, shows them how to transform themselves. One lady who merged with a raven change into a harpy; others changed into half men and half animals. The other people who had watched can't wait to get into the transformation machine.

After everyone has been through the change, they all get along with each other; there doesn't seem to be any social barriers they saw back home. Everyone is a Chimerian, no black person, or white or any other race. Randy suddenly realizes he's the only reptile of all the Chimerians. Randy decides he wants a few more similar to himself, so he searches for others to become reptiles. In Brazil, Randy finds several new prospects, and he brings them to the island; among them is an old Mayan Indian. He brings with him an old condor and a young python. He wants to be merged with these two animals. Randy is interested to see if it'll work, so he allows it to happen. After transforming the new people into various reptile people like iguanas, lizards, and some snakes, none of which have any venom, Randy turns to the Mayan Indian to make sure he still wants to transform using the condor and the python. The Mayan is very confident, and he goes through the transformation. Once transformed, the Mayan Indian finds he can change into a large Condor or a python, but when he wants, he became a feathered serpent, much like the god his people worship. Randy goes about setting up rules and regulations to help govern the Chimerians. Like when someone lands on the island, everyone has to transform into human form and stay that way until the normal people leave. Randy, not versed in governing, looks for Chimerians who have been leaders or have even run businesses, to help set up a way to govern his new people.

Chapter

11

As time moves on, the Chimerians break into factions, reptiles, birds, and mammals, and the next faction is the Indian Iron Eagle and the Mayan they separated from the rest of all the other people on the island. Both begin to see new problems. Iron Eagle and the Mayan know how to cope with their animal nature that they have. While the other Chimerians keep reverting to their animal nature. After one of the storms, a python man goes for a walk along the beach; it's not long when he discovers a sailboat that has been beached; his human side is curious, so he climbs aboard to search it. He finds a small child that's still alive. When the child sees the creature (a reptile man), the child goes into hysterics. The snake's nature takes over the man's mind and changes into a snake, then it wraps itself around the child and squeezes it to death, then the python swallows the child. Now that it's full, it leaves the sailboat and crawls to the far side of the island to hide and digest its grizzly meal. A week later, two others go in search of the python man. They find the empty sailboat and move on down the beach.

Both creatures run on to the python man as he heaves up the bones from his feast.

Tiger man says, "What have you done?"

The python man changes into his semi-human form.

"Nothing, it was already dead, and I was hungry."

"You know that Randy will be furious!" says the leopard woman.

"Who cares, I can do what I want, besides who's going to tell him?"

"If it was already dead, no harm is done," said the leopard woman.

"Let's get back to the compound; we were sent out here to find you," said the Tiger man.

They return to the compound in silence; little did they know they were being watched from the sky. Iron Eagle goes to Randy to observe him, and soon it becomes apparent to both Iron Eagle and the Mayan that everyone is changing. It appears that the animal nature of their makeup is starting to assert itself; even Randy is affected. On one occasion, Randy is feeding one of the many reptiles in his lab when one of them bites his hand to escape. Still, in his rage, Randy changes into a rattlesnake, bites the creature, and watches it as it thrashes about until it dies from the venom. It's because Randy is the only Chimerian who has venom that keeps all the others in check.

Iron Eagle tries to get Randy to understand the effects of animal nature on the people's human side, and they are becoming more dangerous. Iron Eagle feels that something more serious is going to happen.

Randy asks Iron Eagle, "won't this affect you too?"

Iron Eagle explains that since he lived with the animal world most of his life, it's easier for him and the Mayan Indian to accept animal nature and cope with it.

"The difference for us is we know we don't control the animal, but it doesn't control us either; we just understand it better."

"Then help me understand," said Randy.

"I'm not sure I can. The Mayan and I have lived with and studied all animals that we have ever lived with. Especially the animals that can kill us and the ones we admire. It's a lifetime of knowledge that I can't impart to the others on the spur of the moment."

After that, Randy seems driven to make more reptile people; all the birds and other animals are let go, and the lizards, snakes, and toads and the like are kept. Randy has brought more homeless people to the island. Randy wants to have more reptile people and an amphibian people over the mammals and birds they already have. His rattlesnake mind is overshadowing Randy's mind. Randy's mind and the snake's mind are melding together, and the predator is overriding Randy's human side. Randy keeps making more and more people, and soon the island will not support everyone who lives there. The supply ships have stopped coming; they're afraid due to the monsters they've seen from the boat. On a couple of occasions, one of the Chimerians could be seen as they changed back to human form, the people in the neighboring islands are very superstitious at best, and the strange creatures they've seen scares them.

Chapter

12

Randy is not the only one affected, all the Chimerians are exhibiting the same tendencies. The factions are getting more prominent as well, reptiles in one group, cats in another, and so on. Then one day, when one of the cats was getting some water, it started the beginning of the war. The amphibian or toad man was bathing in the water, and a fight breaks out. When it's over, the amphibian man is dead. Randy became angry, and he bites the cat-person that killed the toad man, so the cat dies. That incident sets off the war. At first, it's like watching children having a war with snowballs only with claws and teeth. It was more like they would rush at each other, then slash, bite, hit and make additional attempts to fight. No one seemed to know any strategy of how to assailing each other. The only person on the island that has experience at war is the Minotaur man; he has been in the army as a sergeant and has some military experience.

Chapter

13

The Minotaur man has gone underground into the tunnels, there are places where he can defend, and nothing can come upon him from behind. The Minotaur can face his adversary. This, coupled with his strength, will allow him to protect his position. The tiger man has no military experience, but is good at strategy; he makes friends with some of the bird people, especially the smaller ones. He's able to use them to get intel on the other factions. The island is full of little birds, and so they'll not be easy to detect. The bird people get close to another faction and listened in on their conversations to see what they're up to, and then they'd report back to tiger man, and from this, he's able to counter what the others are going to do.

Iron Eagle and the Mayan Indian know things will only worsen, the reptiles control the freshwater, and the cats control the food. The birds can subsist on the insects and seeds found on the island, so they have no real concerns other than staying alive. On one of the encounters, a python man captured a leopard woman and crushed her to death, then drags her into the reptile camp where they shared her body out to all the other reptiles. Iron Eagle decides to go to the radio room and send out a distress call for help. Iron Eagle flies to one of the hatches that lead down into the next level, and he changes back into a man and then makes his way to the radio room.

CHAPTER

14

"Mayday, Mayday, we're at latitude and longitude here at the edge of the Bermuda Triangle and we need help, we're at war, please hurry. Mayda...."

The Minotaur man destroys the radio with a single hit with his fist.

"No, you don't! You invaded my territory and you're now going to die."

With the barest of luck Iron Eagle manages to get out of the room in his eagle form and flies down the hall, the minotaur is right on his tail. As Iron Eagle reaches the doorway, the Mayan Indian is lying on the floor in his snake form and he manages to trip the minotaur, which allows Iron Eagle to escape. Then the Mayan changes from a snake into a condor and follows Iron Eagle to the level above. Trying to get away from the fighting both, Iron Eagle and the Mayan managed to leave the dome through one of the doors.

"Did you send the message?" asks the Mayan.

"I hope so; I managed to get off a plea for help and our location, before the minotaur destroyed the radio."

Just as the conversation ended, two harpies dropped in on both the Mayan and Iron Eagle.

An aerial battle ensues, the harpies' talons are dipped in poison and would kill either one of them, it's fortunate that both Iron Eagle and the Mayan's bird form is much faster than the harpies and the harpies are not able to catch them. In the aerial fight each harpy takes on the eagle or the condor, so the two each lead away a harpy, then they turn toward each other and fly as if they are playing chicken with each other. At the last instant, the eagle drops toward the ground, and the condor heads for the sky. The harpies are so intent on their prey that they don't realize until the last moment what was happening to them until they collide with each other, sending them to crash land on to the island.

Chapter

15

"Steve (Paladin, from the story Paladin the modern knight), you need to come to the lodge."

"Why CAT (an AI computer build by Paladin)? I'm enjoying the day with my family?"

"Steve, maybe you should go to CAT; he never bothers you unless it's important," said Samantha.

"Ok, but remember, this is your idea. CAT I'll be there shortly."

Steve kisses his wife and daughter Kim and walks into the house and teleports to the lodge.

"Ok, CAT, what's the problem that you had to pull me away from my family?"

"There's a small island that the Navy once held in the central Atlantic, there's a war going on, on it."

"Well, let the Navy handle it; it's their island."

"Steve, look at the screen and see who or rather what's fighting."

CAT shows a satellite picture of the island.

"Is that camera messed up, that looks like animals that have a form of people. Are you sure this is not some movie like the Island of Doctor Moreau?"

"It's genuine, Steve, I've been watching since I received a call for help; this is real. The next problem is the Navy is sending in a couple of ships and the Marines to investigate. This means a lot of people are going to get killed."

(What Steve does not know is that CAT is offline and the Insect people control CAT).

"Ok, I'll go see what's going on, and see if I can do something about it."

Thirty minutes later, Paladin appears on the island; he's in total shock at the scene he sees. Before Paladin can make a move, a harpy drops in on him knocking him to the ground. Just as she is about to rake Paladin with her claws, a condor and an eagle pounce on her; Paladin rolls to his feet then shoots the harpy with his dart gun, but it takes a couple of darts to knock her out.

Then Paladin turns to face the condor and the eagle with his gun pointing at them. Iron Eagle changes to a man then the Mayan does the same, holding up their hands palms open.

Iron Eagle says, "You got my message?"

"In a manner of speaking, what's going on here?"

Then without warning, the other harpy attacks them. To avoid her Paladin teleports Iron Eagle and the Mayan to another island.

"Now what's going on?"

Iron Eagle tells Paladin the whole story of the machine and how it combines the humans and animals, then Iron Eagle and the Mayan demonstrate the changes.

Chapter

16

"Wow, you realize that the Navy is on its way to level the island?"

"No! Most of the people are good people. The animal instinct is what drives them to fight, and the lack of food and water, is causing them to fight too. We must save them," said the Mayan.

"I'm open to suggestion," said Paladin.

"The Navy will provide a common enemy; we just need to figure a way to exploit it," said Iron Eagle.

"True, but we don't want to hurt the Navy either; they're just doing a job," said Paladin.

Paladin teleports the other two back to the island furthest northern location. Who're the factions and their leaders?"

While the Mayan tells what he knows, Paladin doubles the sleep potion in his darts.

"The first thing to do is take out the leaders, then the deadliest of the creatures, with this done, we may get enough attention to get them to understand that I can take them somewhere else where they can live free and get away from here."

"As I recall, you told me about a machine that can transform people and animals. We'd better destroy that before someone else uses it for the wrong reason. Mayan, how hard would it be for you to get to it?"

"Not so hard, except the Minotaur roaming the underground tunnels."

"Would you be willing to try? Iron Eagle and I need to put the leaders to sleep and see if we can get everyone's attention."

Paladin puts his hands-on Iron Eagle and the Mayan and teleports to the dome's front entrance, only to be surprised by the Minotaur coming out of the building looking for Iron Eagle. Paladin is knocked to the side as the minotaur tries to get at Iron Eagle. Paladin lies there, trying to get his breath. "What was that?"

"That's the Minotaur, now I'll be able to reach the machine and plant your bomb," said the Mayan.

Getting to his feet, Paladin draws both of his dart guns and shoots the Minotaur several times before he collapses in a heap on the ground.

Chapter

17

"Thank you," said Iron Eagle, "Let's get to our part of the task."

"Steve, the Navy will be nearing the island in one hour, and from their communications, they're going to give a brief warning then shell the island."

"Ok, CAT, have they launched a drone yet?"

"They will in a few minutes, they want to see what they're dealing with."

"Great, with these animal people all over the place, they'll shell first then ask questions later."

"Who are you talking to, Paladin?" asks Iron Eagle.

"For lack of a better term, he's a friend. The Navy is launching a drone to see what's going on here. There're too many of your people out here in their animal forms. We need to get them back inside the dome and into their human forms. Otherwise, when the Navy sees them, they'll shoot first and ask questions later, and if I were in their place, I'd not blame them either," said Paladin.

"Iron Eagle, if we're going to save the day here, we need to get moving."

Paladin and Iron eagle work their way into the dome, right off Iron Eagle is embroiled in a fight and tries to fly away, when Paladin stops Iron Eagles antagonist with a couple of darts then pulls him aside.

"Here take this radio, and fly above all this and give me direction, first the leaders, then the fireworks." Iron Eagle takes to the air; the first leader leads the cats; Iron Eagle gives Paladin the location, and then Paladin teleports up behind the cat leader. Instead of talking to the cat leader. Paladin shoots him from behind and puts him to sleep. The next target is Randy; Iron Eagle cautions Paladin to be careful; Randy is a rattlesnake with venom. Paladin acknowledges Iron Eagle and teleports behind Randy, but Randy turns to face him before he can shoot him.

Chapter

18

"Who are you?" asks Randy.

"I'm someone trying to save you and your people from destruction. The Navy is coming and will be here in an hour. A drone is flying over the area, and there are enough of your ware people out there to make things very bad for you."

"How so stranger?"

"The Navy will shoot first and ask questions later, your people will scare the hell out of them and you know what people will do when they don't understand and have fear of something or someone."

"So how can you help, you're just one man."

"Let's just say I can take you to a better place."

"Where would that be?"

"At the moment, I have a friend working on that, but right now we need to restore order, and get everyone together so I can be ready to move you all to a different Island."

"I was going to kill you, but now, I'll help you. What's your plan?"

said Randy.

"I have had to put a couple of your people to sleep already, the leader of the cats will be asleep for a while, and that faction has stopped and is trying to protect him. Can you call off your people and we may yet restore some order."

"Yes, Randy tells his faction to stop and pull back."

The python man says "why, we're winning."

"Either you pull back or you'll feel my bite." All of the reptile people pull back to their defensive position.

With enough of the combatants stopped, Paladin pulls some fireworks out of one of his windows. Then sets them off, this gets everyone's attention. Then Randy steps up to speak.

"Everyone, we will be under attack by the US Navy, they'll shell the Island soon now, we broke our rules by appearing outside in or alternate forms, at this moment a drone will be or has already flown over the Island. Since we're now different, we'll be their target. This stranger has come to help us, we need to follow him. I'll back him up."

Just after the speech, a missile hits the dome and part of the roof falls in. Paladin steps up.

"We need to get everyone back into the dome and into the lower levels, it'll give us some protection, and I can set up a portal to take us to a different island that I know, until I can find a better place for you to live. So, you'll not be bothered by anyone else."

Chapter

19

Several of the stronger animal people are given directions. They head for the doors to pick up and bring back anyone outside of the doors, not able to move on their own. Paladin had to go out and teleport the Minotaur back into the building because he's so big and bulky for anyone to carry.

"CAT, I need the coordinates to move these people to an island, and I need it now!"

At that moment, the Navy starts shelling the island, and the dome is taking a beating; one thing it did was to cover the explosive that the Mayan Indian put in place to destroy the transforming machine. Everyone (That is, the Chimerians and Randy) just thought that the Navy did it with the shelling.

"CAT, where're those coordinates?"

"Steve, open the portal. You now have the coordinates." (Again, CAT is being directed by the insect people). Paladin opens the portal and ushers the people through; it's slow at first, then the pace picks up when the dome is breached at the far end; it's almost a panic rush to get through the gate. The last ones to leave the dome are Randy and Paladin.

"Where are we? This isn't earth."

"I don't know, CAT, what's going on?" From the brush behind them, a loan figure steps out to confront Paladin and Randy.

"You have arrived in a world with no name, no one lives here anymore, but you and your people may make your homes here, everything you need is all around us."

"Who are you?" asks Paladin. "It seems that I should know you."

"We met before on an Island where you almost died; we saved your life."

"Why don't I know you?" ask Paladin.

Chapter

20

"At the time we cleared your mind of us, and implanted a memory that the Island natives saved you."

Before Paladin can ask more questions the creature stabs Paladin with a stinger, and he falls to the ground. Randy is getting ready to strike, when the creature promises that Paladin is going to be OK. "That he's just sleeping, and when he wakes up, he'll not remember what has happened here. Other than he took you to safely to an island, one he'll never be able to find."

The creature turns to Iron Eagle and the Mayan Indian.

"You'll take Paladin back to his world, and both of you will stay there because you'll help him in the future, and you'll save many people from dying, Paladin as well. I'll not take this memory from you as I have done to Paladin. According to our histories, Paladin and his wife will save our world, so you both will need to make sure they stay safe."

The creature turns to Randy, "You're the leader?"

"Yes."

"Don't worry your people will settle down now and be as they were before your war, as I've said, you have all the materials here on this world to make good lives for your selves. I've been to your future, and you'll thrive. This world is like many new worlds it'll be a struggle at first, then you'll build a new and wonderful life."

The Instructor turns to Iron Eagle.

"Pick up Paladin and I'll send you back to his secret place."

Then to the Mayan "I'll return you to your land, Paladin will not remember you or Iron Eagle." The portal is opened again. Iron Eagle carries Paladin through to his mountain top lodge, he leaves Paladin on the front porch and changes to his Eagle form and flies off. The Mayan Indian is sent to his old village in Central America, and he walks off into the jungle and changes into the feathered serpent. He flies off into the jungle to confront the drug lords burning the forest, so he can put a stop to them. Iron Eagle flies off and around Paladin's mountain, sees the hologram, and knows that this place has protection on top, so he decides to patrol around the base of the mountain.

Chapter

21

Back in the new world, which resides in the same place as earth just in a different dimension, the Chimerians take on the new world. It doesn't take long for Randy to discover who should be leading the people. Randy turns to the Minotaur and has him organize people into teams to explore a place to set up camp, one team finds a large lake with fresh water, and it has schools of fish, others bring in wood, and soon they have a camp.

"Now, what do we need?" asked Randy to the Minotaur.

"We need shelter, food, and water. We have solved the water and possibly the food problem; we can live off the fish and some of the other animals. We need tools, and weapons to hunt with and to build with."

"Sounds good. What do you want us to do?"

"For tonight we'll set out sentries, in four-hour shifts. Tomorrow we'll continue to explore to see if we can find a better place to stay."

In the morning, they all meet at the campfire.

"Here's what I want to do, all the bird people split up, and each group flies around the lake, this group will go to the left and the other group to the right, meet back here when the sun is right above us. The rest will explore this area; I want to find anything that would make weapons, tools, and food sources. Like the bird people, everyone meets back here when the sun is directly above us. Randy and a few others will stay here to guard the camp. Now let's move out."

They do this over the next few days when one of the bird people locates a cave, a small distance from the other side of the lake. Minotaur and a few of the cat people take a trip to check out the cave. When they get there, the Cats ruffle their backs.

"What is it that you sense?" asked Minotaur.

"We don't know."

"Then let's be cautious," says the Minotaur.

Chapter

22

Minotaur enters the cave first, it's large and will hold most of the Chimerians.

"We can excavate the back of the cave to make room for everyone, and cover most of the cave mouth for protection. Let's return and tell others. Turning to the cats, what did you guys sense?"

"We don't know whatever it was, it was huge, but we sense that nothing has lived here for some time. It could be just a bad feeling."

They return and tell others. Then a decision is made to move to the cave as a safe place to work. They send out search parties to find wood and other materials. The cat people became the hunters; they keep the tribe as they refer to themselves, well supplied with meat. Others, like the bird people, find seeds, plants, and fruit to feed the ones who would not eat meat. The Reptiles became the guards and protected the camp. One of the people find a flint rock and remembers how to make stone knives by flint napping, and soon everyone has a knife, then spears, and soon a bow and arrow. Winter comes, and it's tough going. A few of the Chimerians die due to the extreme cold. When spring comes, Minotaur decides to take a team with him and head south in search of a different place to live.

Minotaur sends out the bird people on his team since they can travel faster and further in a day than the whole team. One morning a raven returns and tells Minotaur about a deserted city or town three days further on. The team then sets out the next morning at a ground-eating pace, and on the third day, they find the town. On investigation, they determine that's been here and deserted for at least a hundred years. It's not as far south as the Minotaur would like it to be, but they can clean it up and use parts of the city to get to next spring, then travel further south next year. Minotaur leaves his team there, and takes the raven with him and returns to get everyone back at the cave and bring them to the town they have discovered.

Chapter

23

The Chimerians pick up their few personal things and hike to the city that is five days away. The people Minotaur left behind find water, and a supply of meat, and fruit. For the time being, they have a rude camp. The abandoned city was not like New York, but more like you would find in London during the fifteenth Century Earth. Some of the buildings are made of wood or stone and sometimes both. In a park-like area, they set up gardens to grow food, one person finds an old forge with tools, and so in time, they would have metal knives and tools. It didn't take long, and they find a long building they can use for meetings and gatherings. Everyone is allowed to take a house, clean it up, and make it their own. It doesn't take long for the females to attach themselves to a partner.

The Chimerians can't mate as animals. They have to mate as humans, so families are formed, and over time children come; it's extraordinary. As a child reaches puberty, they can change, the parents determined the changes. One paring is a small sparrow to a panther, as his parents. When the child changes, he became a real Chimerian. When this child changes, he can become a winged Panther and fly. Other families have similar children. The Chimerians decided to stay in the city and make it their own. A few years later, the population is overwhelming, so some of the children who can fly started going further south looking for other cities. Over the years, the story of how they were brought here by Paladin is distorted, and before long, Paladin became close to being a deity. Randy's record, who made them, also is distorted, and the Minotaur's story is also distorted. It's assumed that since Randy and Minotaur have long since died, Randy told that one-day Paladin would return and that we should all be looking for him.

He helped us, and one day we will need to help him.

Randy had taken ill and was in what we thought delirium, but Randy was babbling. The babbling continued, and then he would repeat it. At that time, the leader called for a scribe to have the scribe listen to Randy and write down all that he said. From this, we got two visions of the future. The hive instructor confirmed one vision, that Paladin, who brought us here to this world, would return. That vision has happened. It is chronicled in the following history. Randy's second vision; the coming of the King Phoenix. He now sits on the throne. Phoenix has tasked me to write the history to date. Along with the visions, I took the time to write the book of names. With the help of some of the older Chimerians, I wrote a book of myths.

After the first year of living here on this planet, we call Randal. We, the Chimerians, settled on a government similar to the United States. Not long after that, we broke down into a monarchy, and the feudal system became the norm. For generations, there were battles over land. Over time, the towns became populated, and the head of each town was the Chimerian strong enough to hold it. Time moves on, and all the towns on the continent have been populated. One town on the cost of a great ocean learned to build ships. The ships were constructed much like the Viking ships. They crossed the ocean into another land, and over time, the separation changed the Chimerians that crossed the ocean into being more like the Vikings of earth. They became feared, along the coastal towns. One group of people called the Avarians wanted to remain pure from all the others. The aviary Chimerians are consisting of all bird DNA groups and none of the other animal groups. Over time, they learned about inbreeding; it took several generations before they realized the problem. With each child born, a small percentage is deformed and left in the woods to die.

Chapter

24

Randy's first vision of Paladin's return. As revealed in the following narrative, as written by Blossom.

Steve and Samantha (from the book Paladin the Modern Knight) arrive in this world from a portal, and they sit down to take a rest.

"That was the worst world we've encountered," said Steve.

"One thing good about it is we grew younger instead of older, I feel like a young teenager again."

"I hope you'll not be disappointed, but we nearly are. If we had spent any more time, there we would've lost the ability to open the portal. I'm glad to get away."

Steve opens the pack and takes out the map as Steve is looking over the map, a creature steps into view from the nearby brush.

"Are you the one called Paladin?"

The creature was a cross between a lion, a bird, and a reptile.

"Maybe," answers Paladin. "Who wants to know?"

"You're as wise as they say, and wise beyond your years. The

Instructor of the hive said you'd arrive at this day and hour. So, I waited for you."

"Answer my first question, who are you?"

"My tribe calls me Sky Lion, and they also call me the Watcher."

"What name do you prefer?"

"Either one, so why not call me Watcher? It's shorter than Sky Lion."

"Let me introduce my wife…"

"Aaah. Yes, the mate of Paladin, the one called Samantha."

Watcher bows to her in reverence.

"Steve, I like this one, are you taking notes?"

Steve chuckles and turns to Watcher.

"Well, Watcher, where are we, and where are you taking us?"

"Paladin, you are on Randal, and I'm to take you first to the hive, then to my people. The Instructor will explain all to you when we get to the hive."

"Ok, let's go."

Watcher leads them into the woods from where they are, and after a short time, they come to a camp, already set up. A female creature somewhat different from Watcher was tending to the stew on the fire.

"Ho Blossom, it's I, Watcher, and I've brought Paladin and his mate."

"Please to enter our camp, revered ones."

"What are they talking about, Steve?" asked Samantha.

"I'm not sure, but there's something I barely remember from the past, about a group of humans changed into animals. It's so foggy in my mind."

"All will be explained to you, Paladin, when we reach the hive tomorrow. Here please eat and turn in. It'll be a hard trip tomorrow," said Blossom.

"My mate is correct, so please eat and turn in; those blankets are yours to use. My mate and I will watch over you, so you can sleep," said Watcher.

"Alright," acknowledges Steve.

Samantha and Steve take the bowls of food that are offered to them and eat. Then when they turn in for the night, it's dark out. They soon nod off to sleep. Morning comes bright and shiny, and Blossom has breakfast ready. After the repast, the camp is packed up and off; they go toward the mountains. They push through for the first part of the day, and at mid-day, they take a break. Blossom takes out a bunch of dried fruit and some smoked meat. While Blossom is taking care of Samantha and Steve, the Watcher changes into a bird and flies ahead to scout their path. After a time, the Watcher returns to the camp.

"All that is ahead is clear," announces the Watcher.

"What were you looking for?" asks Steve.

"Just making sure that the path we must follow is open, and it is. Now if everyone is finished eating, we must press on, if we are to reach our destination before nightfall."

CHAPTER

25

They gather up their stuff and move on up the mountain pass. In the hours that follow, they soon reach the top and view the valley that's spread before them. It's a vast meadow, surrounded by forest, and out in the middle of the meadow, there appears to be a town.

"What town is that?" asks Samantha.

Blossom answers her question.

"It's where we must be before dark."

"That is easy enough to do." Steve takes Samantha by the hand and teleports them to just to the edge of the meadow. Then Steve teleports them two more times, and then they are standing not far from the edge of town. Right on their heels are Watcher and Blossom.

"Is that soon enough, Watcher?"

"Yes, Paladin, it is."

Watcher and Blossom transform into human form and lead Samantha and Steve to the gate where they enter the town. Watcher and Blossom lead Steve and Samantha deeper into the town to a small house where Blossom leaves them, and the Watcher leads them further on. They soon arrive at the hive entrance, and they wait. A short time later, The Instructor shows up and motions them to follow her. Watcher then says his good-byes and returns to his home.

Steve starts to talk to the Instructor when she motions him to be silent. Then she leads them down into the hive, to a room much like the one on the first hive world. The Instructor passes her hand over a crystal globe, then sits down, and starts speaking.

"I have sealed off this room so no one can hear us; I'll now answer your questions."

"Why are Samantha and I here?"

"Mostly for this conversation."

"Alright, then get down to business and tell us why!" said Samantha.

"I have just completed the history of you and all you have accomplished. You and your mate have saved each of the worlds you have passed through, except for the maze world. It was already dead, but you turned off the computer, so new life can begin to grow. The other worlds you saved in different ways. You stopped a plague on one world and set up a good ruler on another one. In the last world, you showed them what a war could be like."

"So, what's our task here, then?"

"To see what you caused on this world, and to remember."

"Remember what?' asks Samantha.

"Your mate brought these Chimerians to this world from your world. The Chimerians were fighting the Navy on a lone island in the Atlantic Ocean when your mate stepped in and saved them."

"How?

"Your mate transported them through a dimensional-portal from your world to this one. We were there to assist, but he had to open the portal. Let me start from the beginning. I finished the book of histories, and as a matter of fact, this is it (holding up the book). When you leave for the portal back to your world, I'll return to the past and deliver it to the Queen. She'll pass it on to the next generation, and so on; this will be how we provide help to you from time to time in the past. Now the meteor Steve found will be launched to you as soon as I return to that present, you'll find it and then embark on this journey.

Chapter

26

The Hive has intervened with you several times. One time was when you discovered that you could teleport with the crystal. Then you had it embedded, and we directed you to keep you from hurting yourself. When you hesitated to help your future mate at that park, we held you back so you could see that she's what you needed. The next time we helped you was when you appeared at the micro sun, where you nearly died. We allowed you to send the micro sun into your sun. Then we became a life support system until we could help regenerate you back to your former self. We trained you and helped you get back all your movement and abilities. Then you went home. The next time we helped you was when you were fighting the Navy with the Chimerians. We allow you to open the portal. All this was necessary so that you could learn. We gave the China man your address. We're sorry it cost you a loved one. The last interference we forced was when the beast captured your mate, and you followed them. In the end, you saved everyone, including the beast's world.

You see, we have been in effect guiding your life."

"What right did you have in doing that?" asks Steve.

"The right to save our species, and without us, you'd never have found your mate."

"I guess you have me on that one. Now when can we go home?"

"Not for a short time yet. Besides, your world is not the same as it was when you left. In your dimensional traveling, you have lived a lifetime, your world is three hundred years older than when you left it. Your daughter Kim did have children, so you have relatives in your world, but they'll not know you and one other thing you need to know. The machine you call CAT is about to take over the world and rule humanity."

"I gave him all the best ethical laws you can give, even Asimov's three laws."

"Over time, CAT has figured a way to break them; by ruling mankind, he can protect them from themselves."

"I was afraid that would happen. Then I'm the only one who can stop him."

At that moment, the Instructor stung Samantha, where her crystal was located, and then replaced it with a crystal-like what Steve has now.

"No. What have you done!?" shouts Steve.

"Your Mate will be fine tomorrow; I've given her a new crystal-like the crystal that you now have."

"Why did you need to do that?"

"When the time comes, you'll know why. I've told you all that I'm allowed to tell you. You must return to the Watcher and his mate."

Steve picks up his wife in his arms and carries her out of the Hive. Watcher is there waiting for him at the entrance.

"Is your mate, alright?"

"The Instructor said she'd be fine tomorrow. The Instructor better is right!"

Watcher decides to be silent, as Paladin sounds angry, and he doesn't want to set him off. They reach Watcher's home, and Blossom is there waiting. She guides Steve into a room with a mat for a bed, and Steve carefully lays Samantha down. He checks her over and sees that she's asleep. Then Steve recalls that the Instructor did the same thing to him in the Hive world. Sleep makes it easier for the body to accept the new crystal. Blossom enters the room and places a hand on Steve's shoulder.

"She'll sleep the day away; come I have some hot root drink ready."

Steve looks up, shakes his head, and follows her out into the next room. There on the table is some hot beverage. Steve takes a careful sip and finds it quite flavorful before he drinks it down. Soon he falls asleep at the table, and Watcher picks him up and carries him to the room where Samantha is sleeping and lays him beside her.

"He is going to be angry when he wakes up and not likely to trust us anymore," said the Watcher.

"It'll be ok. When they wake, they'll be hungry, so you best go hunt something down."

Watcher looks at his mate and smiles.

"You're right; I'll be back soon."

Watcher goes off to hunt some game for dinner.

The next morning Samantha wakes up and is very hungry. She wakes Steve up, and he has a clear head.

"What happened?"

"I don't know, Steve. All I remember is a pain at the back of my neck, and then I woke up here."

"Oh, yea. The Instructor replaced your old crystal with a new one, and somehow, I was drugged by Blossom. I think in the long run, it was probably the best thing to do. Otherwise, I'd have sat over you all night worrying about you."

"I feel pretty good now. Maybe we can get in a run, and some sparring before breakfast?"

"You know Samantha, that sounds like a great idea."

They get up and rummage around in their packs for their blue jeans and shirts. They slip out of the house to run around the lake, not far from the village. When they return from their run, they square off in the field and start sparring. Neither one holds back. After an hour or so, they work up a sweat and decide to wash up some before returning to the Watcher's home.

"I hope you two weren't trying to hurt one another as that was some fight!" said Blossom.

"No, said Samantha, we were exercising. It has been a while where we could do that safely with each other. It felt really good."

"You are right, Samantha; it has been a while. It sure was great. I had forgotten how nice it was to spar with you!" said Steve.

Samantha turns to Blossom and asks, "How long before we eat."

Blossom smiles and says, "When you're ready."

"Good, I need to take a bath; where can I do that?"

"At the lake?"

"Another cold bath said, Samantha.

"Only if you use this end of the lake. The other end gets very hot, so you can be scalded if you're not careful."

"Coming, Steve?"

"I wouldn't miss it for the world."

Samantha teleports them to the lake's end, where Blossom

indicated to go for the hot water. Steve and Samantha strip down and test the water. They soon find a suitable place where the water is not boiling. They slip into the lake for a nice swim. When they have just about finished their swim, they decide to wash their clothes and hang them up to dry. As they lay in the sun, a shadow briefly covers them as Watcher and Blossom fly in with some food.

"Hail Paladin and Samantha! We see you are relaxed and washed. We have brought you something for breakfast."

"Tell me, Watcher, do all the Chimerians fly?" asks Steve.

"That's a bit of a long story, so where do I start? Randy, our leader, discovered by accident that a pair of transporters could combine man with animals, and this change allowed them to change from one form to another. It also prolonged our lives. Randy brought us to an island in the Atlantic, on your world, where we were able to create more of us. Our animal nature got the better of us. Then the Navy was sent in to destroy us. That's when Paladin appeared on the scene and brought us to this world. Randy said the transporter machine was destroyed, and so no new animals could be made."

CHAPTER

27

"I sort of recall that; I remember that I had one of the Chimerians blow up the machine for that reason. Please continue."

"At first, it was very hard living here; we're not prepared to survive on our own. If it weren't for the Minotaur, who had been in the Army. He saved us. He took over the leadership from Randy for a time, and Randy was more than willing to do this. Thanks to the Bull-man's survival skills and the different animal skills we all had, we could survive. We mostly ate meat for our first winter. When spring came, we pushed further to the south where we found ready-made villages and towns. We found tools and had to learn how to use them. Our surveillance system became the people who could fly. They were able to fly out great distances and return to make reports. They also located game we could use," said Watcher.

"So, tell me how you came to be so many?" asked Steve.

"We discovered that we could mate as humans and whatever animal the parents' were, they passed these genetics to their offspring. Birds became the preferred mates. Then according to Randy, our true leader, we're now true Chimera, and as we continued, we became more mixed."

"I see. So more of you mixed with the others and created human offspring, who could change into whatever the parent's animal DNA was. If you mated as animals, you could create offspring, but they'd be mules if you could mate at all."

"Yes, a few of us discovered that. So, the only thing in common is the human side of our being."

"Have you been at war since you have been here?" asked Steve.

"Sadly, yes. We don't do that anymore; no one wins. To keep war from happening, we exchange our children and raise their children, and they raise ours. No one wants to kill their child accidentally, so this stopped us from warring with each other."

"That's one way to do it. Who came up with that plan?" asked Steve.

"Randy, our leader, and for all these years, it has all but stopped war here on Randal."

"Thanks, Watcher, but it's time for Samantha and me to be moving on, we have our world to return to."

Steve takes Samantha's hand and their clothes in the other and teleports back to the Watcher's home. They get dressed in their battle suits. Steve opens the map, which shows him the way to the portal.

"Samantha, the map points to the North. We had better get moving, while the season is still warm. Snow can be very miserable to travel in."

Chapter

28

With everything packed, Steve takes Samantha by the hand and teleports next to the Hive entrance. Then they head off into the direction of the last portal.

As they travel north, it does get colder. That night Samantha finds a cave and calls Steve's attention to it. Steve checks out the cave and finds it empty. There are signs that it has been in use. Steve puts some wood into the used fire pit, and using his blaster; he sets fire to the wood. Soon a nice toasty fire is going. Samantha goes off to collect more firewood for the night, and Steve goes off to hunt, not sure of what he can kill. Steve decides to catch fish for dinner. He would hate to kill one of the Chimerians accidentally. Steve manages to catch a couple of good-sized fish and brings them back to the cave. As he is cleaning them, a message comes from Samantha, and she's in trouble.

Steve homes in on her helmet and sets off in that direction. When he arrives, he sees a Chimerian carrying Samantha off to the West.

"Not again, Samantha, can you teleport back to the cave?"

"I believe I can."

"Do it, and I'll be there too."

Steve teleports to the inside of the cave to wait for Samantha and the unfriendly Chimerian to arrive. Time passes, and Samantha with a Griffin, appears at the entrance. Steve teleports up to the creature and shoots him several times with his sleep darts. The Griffin lets go of Samantha and keels over asleep.

"What happened?" asks Steve.

"I was collecting wood when that thing swooped down from above me and snatched me up and took off into the air."

"Well, we can't leave it out here, it may freeze to death; I'll teleport him into the cave."

Samantha teleports back to the bundle of wood she collected and returns with it. By the time she does, Steve has finished cleaning the fish.

After they eat, the Griffin starts to wake up. Steve watches him as he stirs.

"Before you get excited, I'd remind you that I can either put you to sleep or kill you."

The Griffin stops what he's doing and looks Steve in the eye. Steve gestures to a rock outcropping, opens a window, and closes it, shearing off the rock in an excellent clean cut. The eyes of the Griffin widen in fear.

"What're you doing in my clan's territory?" growls the Griffin.

"We're just passing through. We're trying to get home; I want nothing of you or your clan. We want to be left alone and treated with respect. Now it's freezing outside, and I could've left you out there to die. We chose to bring you into the cave instead."

"I'm Prince Gary; I meant no harm. I'd be willing to escort you to the edge of our territory so no one will bother you."

"In the morning, we'll take you up on that."

They all turn in to sleep. In the morning, Steve catches a few more fish and cleans them.

Samantha cooks them up and offers our guest a portion, and they all eat well. When they collect their belongings, they all step outside of the cave. Prince Gary has them climb onto his back and tells them to hold on tight. Gary takes a running start and flaps his wings, and soon they rise into the air. Gary turns to the north. Eventually, Gary drops toward the ground to land at the edge of his territory.

"May I have your names?" asks Prince Gary

"I'm Paladin, and this is my mate, Samantha."

"Not thee Paladin of old?"

"I'm afraid so."

"He's not very impressive, is he Gary?" said Samantha

Gary was speechless.

"Well, Gary, thanks for the ride. We'll leave you here and move along. Oh, how many other clans are out this way, or is there any other Chimerians we must be aware of?"

"Steve, he's in shock. We had better move along; we'll find out if we run into any others out there."

CHAPTER

29

Steve takes Samantha's hand and teleports northward, and leaves Gary alone. After several more teleports, they come to a vast meadow and teleport to the far side of it. They walk through the woods and make short teleports until they can get to a clear area to teleport longer distances. Gary realizes that this is the Paladin who brought the Chimerians to this world. Gary flies off toward home so he can tell everyone. Steve and Samantha teleport on for the rest of the day and find a lake, but the temperature gets too cold at night to be able to camp out. That night they find no shelter, so Steve makes a note of the area and then teleports Samantha and himself back to the cave where they met Gary to spend the night again.

In the morning, they break camp, and Steve teleports them back to the last place they managed to get to. From there, they teleport as they did the day before, in short distances (Line of sight). By nighttime, Steve gets ready to return to the cave, when Samantha points out a cabin in the trees. Steve teleports them over to it to see if anyone is living there. The place is a bit run down, but the roof and walls appear to be in place. Steve looks in a window and sees it's filthy and dusty.

"Samantha, this looks to be abandoned, shall we go in?"

"Let's, said Samantha; I'd like to sleep on a bed or a wooden floor rather than that rocky cave floor for another night."

Steve then teleports them into the hut, and they look around to see that it has been abandoned for a long time. There are tables, chairs, and a fireplace. The bed was sound enough, but it needs to be cleaned up.

"Steve, go catch us something for dinner; I'll clean around a bit to make it more comfortable."

Steve teleports outside and decides to leave the door as it is. He teleports to a nearby lake and shoots a couple of birds floating on the lake. Steve hopes none of them are Chimerians. He then fills a bucket with water and teleports back to the hut. Samantha is busy cleaning the bed and the table and chairs. Steve puts down the water and goes back outside to clean the birds for dinner. Soon, Samantha has the fire going, and the hut has something of a cheery aspect to it.

After dinner, they decide to move the bed closer to the fireplace to keep warm. They turn in to go to sleep. In the morning, when they wake up, they discover a snowstorm had dropped a foot of snow in the area.

"This is going to make traveling a bit dangerous. We're going to have to walk as we'll not be able to teleport; since we don't know what's under the snow."

"Then maybe we should stay here for a day or so; what do you think, Steve."

"I don't know. I fear that if we stay, we might be stuck here until spring."

"Would that be bad?" asks Samantha.

"It could be worse, I guess. We can get food and water, and there's plenty of wood in the area. I can make a pair of snowshoes and scout out ahead to see what I find. OK, let's plan to spend the winter here."

Steve decides to fix the hut up and make it stronger; he picks out a tree, and using his windows, he cuts the tree down. Suddenly, he had to teleport out of the way. The tree nearly fell on him. After it was down, he cut the tree again to remove the branches. Finally, he chopped the nice sized branches into small logs for the fireplace and took them back to the hut. Then back at the tree, using his windows, he slabs the tree lengthways then transports the planks to the cabin. Steve teleports the planks into the house walls, which makes it more substantial than if he had nailed them up. In a few hours, he has the cabin's walls reinforced; by teleporting the wood into the wooden walls, it makes the cabin very solid. The next morning Steve clears off all the snow on the roof of the cabin and teleports more wood planks into the roof. It makes the roof more solid. Now it can take any snowfall this world can throw at it.

"Steve, we need some utensils, plates, and bowls. Can you make them?"

"I don't know; it would have to be made from wood."

"For now, that'll do," answers Samantha.

"Let me see what I can do."

The next morning Steve sets out to find a birch tree; after a few hours, he locates a small stand of them. He looks for a tree about ten inches around, cuts it down, and transports it to the cabin. From the tree, he cuts the end off to make a platter, then some flat dishes. The tough stuff is what's next, trying to make a bowl. Steve has always made his windows square; now, he is trying to shape them round and concave. The first bowl exploded in a shower of dust. The second bowl wasn't much better. By the third bowl, Steve is starting to get the hang of it. Steve manages to make a bowl, then makes a couple of others, and finally, one large one. He manages a few large spoons, then a few others. The fork was tough but the wood knife was the easiest to make.

Chapter

30

Between the small birds and fish, Steve manages to keep them fed through the winter, with no calls to go off and risk his life. He could spend most of his time with Samantha, and she seems to be enjoying the attention. Then one morning, Samantha gets up and rushes outside to throw up.

"Are you alright?" asks Steve.

"I'm fine; we're going to have another child."

"What!"

"I'm pregnant; we're having another child."

"Oh, wow!"

"How much longer are we going to be here?" asks Samantha.

"Spring is going to be here soon. Are you sure you're having another child?"

"Yes, I'm sure, don't you want it?"

"Yes, I want another child, I'm just shocked some, and you have made me happy."

Steve pulls Samantha to him for a hug, being sure not to hurt her. Then Steve lets out a howl of delight. Steve gives Samantha a big kiss.

"You better stop that. That's how I got into this condition."

It was several weeks before spring arrives. As soon as the ground is bare, Steve sets out by himself to find the dimensional-portal. He returns to the cabin each afternoon to bring home food and look after Samantha. Alone Steve can cover more territory, and ten days later, Steve finds the dimensional-portals location. He returns to the cabin to let Samantha know he has found it.

Samantha is just starting to show her child bump. Steve wants to get her home as soon as he can, so Samantha can have a doctor's care for her and the child.

The next day Steve teleports Samantha and their belongings to the dimensional-portal, and when they arrive, they're surrounded by Chimerians.

"Is there a problem?" asks Steve.

"No problem, Paladin, we just wanted to see you and wish you well." said the Watcher.

"How'd you know we'd be here?" asks Samantha.

One of the Chimerians changed to human form and then held up a book.

"This told us you'd be here on this day and time, and here you are."

"We just wanted to see you off and tell you thanks for saving us in the past. If you would please return for a visit someday? It has been nice to see one of our legends in the flesh, so to speak." said the Watcher.

"Paladin you also impressed one of our young ones, Prince Gary." Laughs Blossom.

The Chimerians all moved away, and Paladin stands with Samantha and their packs. Steve opens the dimensional-portal back to their world, and they step through on to the Island where so many years ago, Steve had opened the portal to the world they just left.

Chapter 31

Paladin and his mate return to their world, leaving us behind. Randy Thompson's second vision the coming of the King. The unknown scribe that captured Randy's last words made a notation that he wasn't sure he heard all that Randy said; it was a bit incoherent at the end.

The Phoenix is coming; he'll not be able to reproduce but will be King for all time. There can only be one Phoenix, and fire will test him time and again. The Phoenix will come from a group of Chimerians not well regarded. The King shall wheel the sword of the Sun and Fire, and He'll rule all the lands. His rule will bring peace to all the lands. Everyone who reads this account passes it off as the babblings of an old man.

After several generations, the Avarian clan was trying not to get involved in all the skirmishes and battles the other clans were having over land; they had moved high into the mountains where no one wanted to go. This history is starting with Zeke, the King's grandfather. It was early morning. Zeke was out for a morning flight in the mountains when the dawn sky lit up by a falling star. Zeke perched upon an old tree stump and watched where the star hit the mountain where he was flying. The impact caused an avalanche of snow and rock to fall into the pass. When the ruckus settled down, Zeke flew to the impact site and changed from his owl shape back into a man so he could approach the crater and investigate. Zeke couldn't get close to the crater. It was too hot. Zeke noted the area to return later to dig up some star stone (Meteoric Iron) hopefully. Zeke returns home to his wife. She's expecting their first child. Zeke doesn't say anything about the star that hit the mountain. Making sure his wife is doing fine, Zeke walks out to the blacksmith's shop and fires up the forge to begin his day. Zeke has a few knives to make and repairs to make on a few farm tools he promised to have finished by the end of the day. Zeke is well known for his work, and the people from all around seek him out to have him make or repair their tools. A week later, Zeke returns to the mountain to seek out the star stone. With some digging, Zeke manages to unearth the star stone. It was in two fist-sized chunks; Zeke packed up his gear and the star stones and flew back to his home. Zeke hides the rocks in his shop and goes into his house to see his wife; she was cooking some rabbit stew when Zeke walked in, she looked up and smiled.

"How was your morning flight, husband?"

"A bit on the cool side, but all in all, it was soothing."

"Come get your bowl, I caught a rabbit early when you were out, and have made your favorite meal."

Zeke walks up to Lisa, his wife, gives a gentle hug, Zeke takes his and Lisa's bowls to the table, and sits her in her chair. Lisa pats her now huge belly and asks Zeke what gender he would like the child to be.

Zeke takes Lisa's hand and, in a good-natured way, tells her that he'll love either boy or girl.

"What do you hope for Lisa?"

"As strong as this one kicks, I think it'll be a boy, and I'll be happy whatever we have."

After the meal, Zeke cleans up the dishes so that Lisa can rest. Zeke leaves the rest of the stew over to one side of the fire to keep warm. They'll have it for dinner later. Zeke sees his wife over to a comfortable chair and covers her up and givers her knitting things. Zeke returns to the smithy and starts up the forge. Zeke has a few knives to finish today, and as he reaches for the iron to make them from. He grabs the star stones. For some unknown reason, Zeke goes into a trance, and everything seems like a dream. Time seems to stand still; Zeke makes a sword and the two knives. The blade is a thing of beauty. It is longer than the usual sword. It's polished with a hilt that looks like a great bird in flight. The pommel of the sword has a head of a bird never before seen in this world. Zeke slashes it about and sees that it's perfectly balanced and that it's lighter than it looks. Zeke hides it away, not wanting to show it to anyone, not even Lisa, his wife. The next morning Zeke finishes the two knives, and the customer stops by to pick them up. Just as the two were concluding their business, Lisa calls out that it's time to get the midwife. Zeke impresses the customer to get the midwife so he can stay by his wife's side.

The man transforms into a sparrow hawk and flies to the next house in the glen to get the midwife. The midwife returns and ushers Zeke out of the house and out of their way; this is women's work. Outside, Zeke paces back and forth, wondering what's going on, hoping that his wife and child were both all right. It seems like hours before the child was born. In reality, it was only an hour. Zeke is called into the house to see his wife and child. They have a cute baby girl, and she becomes the star of her daddy's heart. Both mother and daughter are doing well.

Chapter

32

Their daughter now has all the bird DNA from the Avarians clan. She'll be wed to the man with all the same DNA as the guidelines are set forth by the clan elders from years ago. The reason for this is set in stone, but no one knows why anymore. It had something to do with a prophecy from generations ago. Zeke holding his daughter, decides he is going to make all the metal cooking tools for her. Over the years, his daughter grows, and her dowry grows enough to make her wealthy in her own right. From the day they are born until the day they reach puberty; they have no name; they are called girl, boy or child. As they grow, the parents teach the children how to read, write, and do numbers. Lisa gives the book of names to her daughter and tells her to choose a name for herself. As she reads the book, she decides to settle on the name of Pam. It's short and straightforward. Soon, girl calls her mother and tells her future name Pam.

Pam reaches her name day, and they get a visit from the family from down the path who lives in the glen. Pam is to meet her future husband and his family on this day. After the ceremony, Pam and her future husband, Todd, walk out together to meet for the first time.

Such is the way of all arranged marriages. Both are a bit scared. They seem to get along, and at the end of the day, Todd and his family return home. The wedding is to take place several months off. Zeke and Lisa aren't happy with the match after seeing how Todd's father treats his wife like a slave. One day Zeke makes it a point to corner Todd and tells him if he treats Pam the way his father treats his mother that Zeke will consider shortening his life. Todd takes it to heart and goes out of his way to treat Pam differently. During the wedding's waiting time, both Zeke and Todd's father build a house for the two newlyweds to be. With all fixings that Zeke made and Todd's father purchases from the wood maker, they have quite a nice place. Todd will be expected to add to the house as the family grows.

The wedding day arrives, and the two settles in, and true to his word, Todd treats Pam better than his mother is treated. Like his father, Todd is a merchant who would deal in all sorts of merchandise from the small herd animals to gems. Todd traveled from home often to travel about selling and buying from village to town. Todd found the coastal towns the most profitable, and when Todd would come home, he would bring Pam some small trinket to give her. Todd had a lot of affection for his wife. Todd knew his wife. They were expecting a child. (Note: due to the inbreeding, both parents were the first to contain all the bird DNA from all the Avarians in both families). Pam was happy to be having a child; now she'll have someone to look after since her husband is always off buying and selling, it'll be nice to have a little one to care for. Mid-way through pregnancy, Todd went off to the coast to do business, and he sold off a herd of animals for a good price.

CHAPTER

33

At the inn that night, Todd drank a little too much and was bragging about his sale. A couple of thieves heard him, not realizing that the money wasn't yet in Todd's possession. That night after everyone went off to bed, the thieves enter Todd's room to relieve him of his money. When they discovered he didn't have it on his person, they killed him so he couldn't identify them later. No one in town knew Todd so he was buried in the potter's field. In time, Todd's child was born, and it was decided that Todd had been killed and wasn't coming home. Todd's father was going to bring his daughter in law into his house. Pam's father knowing Todd's father, stopped it and let Pam come to his home where she'd be treated like a woman and not a slave. The day came, and Pam, with her mother and mother in law gathered to birth the new child. He came into this world screaming and kicking, he was a wonder to behold until they realized he was deformed. He was born a eunuch such children were taken into the woods and left to die. Pam wouldn't hear of it, and Pam's mother sided with her. Todd's mother thought otherwise since Pam wouldn't kill the child; Todd's parents disowned the child. Pam lavished all her love on the child, and his grandfather Zeke took the boy at the age of six and began to teach him the trade of being a blacksmith. Zeke took his time to teach the boy how to shape the steel and properly forge it, by the time the boy was ten, he could swing a hammer with either hand and make ornate items, knives, utility works for cooking, or tools for whatever is needed. One day while cleaning up the smithy, the boy ran onto the box Zeke had put away and forgotten about.

"Grandfather, what's in the box?" asks the boy.

"What box?"

"This box." The boy holds it up to show Zeke.

Zeke takes the wooden box and opens it to reveal the polished sword it contains.

"I remember as if it were a dream, a star fell from the sky, and I brought home two-star stones, and I fashioned this sword from them and put them away. I had forgotten it," said Zeke.

Zeke took the sword out of the box and hefted about a few times, "it's still as good a shape as when I put away." Zeke put the sword away back into the box and put it back on the distant shelf. The boy watched Zeke. It appeared that Zeke was in some trance. When Zeke put the box away and turned back to the boy, he seems to have forgotten the box altogether. The boy never said anything about the sword. Next year the boy will be old enough to have his name day, so the boy poured over the book of names trying to find a name that he would like. The first name he liked was Orion; then, he came across the name Phoenix. He liked the name Phoenix. He looked up more about the name and found it to be about a mythical bird. The Phoenix could only be one in the world at a time, and it never died, but was burned in a fire every thousand years to be reborn from the ashes. "I like that, and it's different than any other name ever used," thought the boy.

Grandfather sent the boy home so he could help his mother. The boy ran off into the woods, and when he was out of sight, he changed into an eagle and flies the rest of the way home. He landed in front of the house, and his mother had watched him from her window, thinking it was someone else come to visit until she saw her son standing there. Pam dropped her sewing and ran out the door.

"Was that you who flew in?"

"Yes, mother, it was."

"You shouldn't be able to do that yet; you're not thirteen years yet."

"Did I do something wrong, mother?"

"No, you did fine. You shouldn't be able to do that yet."

"I'm sorry mother; I'll not do that again."

"It's ok, my son. I'll not forbid you to do that; however, I'll ask you not to do that in front of anyone. Especially not that bird you came in on, it's too huge. Use the falcon shape. It's faster and small. No one will notice it or you."

"Sure, mother."

"Have you picked out your name for name day?"

"I have it! I like the name of Phoenix."

"That's an interesting name. I like it!" said Pam.

"Mother, you don't want me to fly or change until my name day?"

"I won't ask you not to, what I suggest is stay with the falcon and do it in private, don't let anyone see you yet."

"Yes, mother, I'll do as you request."

Pam hugs her son, and then holds him at arm's length, "go wash for supper."

The boy runs off to the water trough to wash up for dinner.

At supper, the boy talks about the sword grandpa made and has it in a box, in the smithy. Mom was listening with her mind pulling her in a different direction. There was a prophecy that was written so long ago that it almost faded from memory.

"Son, are you going to participate in the summer festival this year? What do you think?"

"If you say so, mom, I wonder if my friends will be there."

With supper, being over the boy helps his mother clean up and goes to bed. The next morning the boy leaves to return to the smithy to help grandpa. The boy changes into a falcon to fly there; on the way; the boy makes a detour because he likes to fly, so he took a route that leads to the mountain where the star stones fell. The boy lands on top of the mountain to take in the view when a flash of light and heat strikes him knocking him out. (A solar flare showered him. This has never happened before in all the history that the Chimerians have lived on this planet). The boy lay there on the ground surrounded by ash; his clothes were burned off. There wasn't a mark on the boy. Zeke had been out flying when he saw the flash of light and followed it to the mountaintop where he found the boy. Fearing, he was dead; Zeke shook the boy until he woke up.

"Son, are you ok?"

"What happened?" Looking down, he saw his clothes were gone.

"I'd say that they were burnt off. Let's fly back to the smithy. I have some clothes you may fit into so you can return home. Does anyone know if you can fly yet?"

"Just mom and she said I need to keep it a secret until my name day."

"Not a bad idea. Return to the smithy and use the back window and stay in the falcon form until I let you in the window."

"Yes, grandpa."

Chapter

34

They both change and fly back to the smithy and grandpa lands in the yard and walks into the smithy. His wife sees him go to the smithy as if to fire up the forge to get it started; he does this from time to time. Zeke opens the window and lets the boy into the smithy.

"Boy, look in that basket over in the corner. You should find some of my old clothes; I'm going to start the forge, so your grandma doesn't get suspicious of my actions."

"Now that I'm dressed, how should I leave?"

"Change back into the falcon and fly out the window, you best go see your mother."

"Sure, grandfather, I'll be back later."

The boy changes and fly's out the window and returns home. As he returns home and lands in the front yard, his mother walks out of the front door, wiping her hands.

"Did you fly up near the mountain this morning?"

"I flew down in the valley below it; I didn't want grandpa to see me when he flies up there."

"Did you see the two flashes of light?"

"I only saw one flash of light. I assumed that another star stone fell to earth and knew if grandpa saw it, he'd be there to look for the stone, so I stayed away."

"Are you sure?"

"Yes, mother, I'm sure."

Pam didn't pursue the question. She could tell the boy was not telling her the whole truth.

"Wash up, it's time for breakfast, and you'll need to go to the smithy to help grandpa."

The boy did as he was told, and he flew back to the smithy after breakfast, and when he walked out of the woods, grandfather was talking to a man, who's every move dripped in grace and efficiency of movement. To be polite, the boy kept his distance until his grandfather called him over to meet this man and hear how to transact business.

The man looked down at the boy. "Have you had your name day yet, lad?"

"No, sir."

"I'm called the Dance Master. What name have you chosen, lad?"

"Orion or Phoenix, I'm still trying to decide."

The dance master looked the boy up and down, then taking his chin and moving his head from side to side. "If I were you, I'd choose Phoenix." Then the Dance Master turns back to Zeke to go over the request for the two rapiers that were to be ornate, and two that were to be practice weapons.

"Why do they call you the Dance Master?" asks the boy.

"Would you like to see lad?"

"Yes, sir."

"Do you have a couple of wooden swords?"

The boy disappears into the smithy and returns to hand the weapons over to the dance master.

"Here, boy, take this wooden sword and try to hit me."

The boy takes a swing at the Dance Master and misses, but the master has not moved more than a foot; the boy tries again and misses as the Dance Master moves out of the way. The boy loses his temper and tries to hit the Dance Master, and the Dance Master not only moves out of the way, and gives the boy a sound smack with the wooden sword knocking him flat to the ground. The Dance Master picks up the boy. "Lad don't ever lose your temper when you fight, you lose focus and then your life. Now stand up!"

Dance Master walks around the boy sizing him up. "Lad you move like an ape with one leg, your movements must be graceful fluid; you must flow like a breeze through the trees. You show great potential, but enough for now, I must return home."

"Dance Master!" calls Zeke. "Before you go, I have decided upon a price for the swords."

"What may that be master, Zeke?"

"Follow me into the smithy, Boy wait here."

The two men enter the smithy, "Well, Zeke, what did you have in mind?"

"I want you to teach my grandson how to dance, as you say."

"I'll return in a month and a half for the swords. We can discuss it then, based on the quality of the work of the swords, do you agree?"

"I agree," as Zeke puts forth his hand to shake upon the agreement.

The Dance Master looks at the boy and smiles. Then he walks toward the woods, shifts into a wolf, and runs off towards his home.

"Come on, son, we have a lot of work to do to forge the swords."

For the next few days, Zeke has his grandson watch how he forges the sword blade, the handle, knuckle bow, pommel, and hilt then welds them together.

"Now boy, you make the next three blades, and I'll finish the decorative filigree and brass on this sword."

"Yes, grandfather."

The boy works on the next sword and does the same forging his grandfather showed him, and when he finishes the blade, he gives it to Zeke to see if it'll pass his inspection. Zeke takes the blade and flexes it a few times, then hits a wooden barrel, and then looks it over.

Zeke looks at the boy and smiles, "this blade is as good as if I did it. Good work! Tomorrow you'll finish this rapier and make the next two. Now off to your mother, she'll be expecting you."

"Thank you, grandfather." The boy changes into a falcon and flies' home.

The next morning the boy was hard at work forging the following two blades for the practice rapiers. The boy then builds all the components to complete the blades, and Zeke shows him how to weld them together. Zeke takes the time on the second rapier when he carves the filigree to show his grandson how to do the work. Zeke has the boy put similar work on the practice swords using a wolf's head as part of the artwork carved into the hilt; then, he shows the boy how to polish the blades to a mirror finish.

"Excellent job, boy. You know it'll be nice to call you by name instead of a boy. Do you know I was rummaging around in my stockpile and I found some more star stone, let's make you a rapier from it, what do you say?"

"I'd like that, grandfather."

"Here's the star stone, tomorrow when you get here, you can make it."

The boy was so excited that he ran off without saying goodbye to his grandfather. Zeke smiles as he watches his grandson run home and not fly. (Oh, to be young again.)

Chapter

35

In the morning, the boy has the forge fired up, waiting for grandfather to show up so they can start forging the star stone into a sword. Zeke shows up after his morning flight to find an anxious grandson being patient to begin his sword. With a smile on his face, Zeke complements his grandson.

"I see you've learned one of the most important things every man needs but seldom learns."

"What's that, grandfather?"

"Patience lad. Shall we get started?"

"Yes! Grandfather, I can hardly wait."

"I see that." Zeke pats his grandson's head and smiles.

They spent the rest of the day forging the star stone into a blade; it was a long and arduous process; the quality of the blade was far superior to any of the other blades they just finished. Tomorrow they'd make the rest of the components and weld it into a proper rapier. The day arrived on a wet and gloomy day, but the boy was there to finish the work. All went well in the construction, and all that was left was to add the decorative finish, which Zeke had his grandson do. When the boy finished, it looked like the mythical Phoenix on the hilt and on the flat of the blade.

The day came for the Dance Master to return and claim his swords. The boy was flying in to work with his grandfather. He spots a wolf at the edge of the wood. The boy flew back into the woods and changed from a falcon into a boy; then he walked the rest of the way to his grandfather's smithy. When the boy arrived at the yard, the wolf changed into the Dance Master.

"Good morning, lad, is Zeke here?"

The boy looked up into the sky and said that his grandfather would be here soon, he's on his morning flight.

"May I see the swords your grandfather made for me?"

"That sir is between you and grandfather; I'm not allowed to deal for him."

"Smart lad, we'll wait then."

"I can, however, show you the rapier that we made for me if you'd like."

"Splendid, I'd like to very much."

The boy goes into the smithy, returns with his sword, and hands it to the Dance Master.

"This is incredible! I've never seen such quality and workmanship, are the rest of the blades like this one?" Zeke landed and changed to his human form.

"No. said Zeke, they were made from regular metal, still good quality though, but this sword was made from a small star stone. I didn't have enough to make any more than the one."

The Dance Master slashes the air with the star stone sword, "this is the best sword I've ever tried."

The Dance Master turns the sword over to the boy, "Now let's see what you have for me."

Zeke leads the way into the smithy and pulls the swords down from the shelf to show the Dance Master.

The Dance Master hefts the swords and flexes them. "Zeke, these are great swords, not as good as the star stone one, but excellent just the same. Yes, I agree to your terms for payment. I'll teach your grandson how to dance with a sword as well as with a girl."

Zeke held out his hand, the Dance Master took it, and the deal was sealed. The boy would take dance lessons.

"Lad, come here!"

The boy returned from the smithy, "Yes, Dance Master."

"I'll be back tomorrow; I want you to have a girl here as well, your mother will do as well, one other thing, I'm a stern master. If you fail to do as I ask, that'll end your lessons. Do you understand?"

'Yes! Dance Master!"

"Good. See you in the morning."

Zeke turns to the Dance Master, "I see you travel as a wolf. I have a pouch I can put on you so you can travel with the swords."

"My thanks, Zeke." The Dance Master transforms into a large wolf, and Zeke buckles on the pouch to carry the swords. The wolf takes off into the woods.

"Boy, take the rest of the day off and go tell your mother that you need a girl or her to be here every day for a time until you learn to dance."

"Yes, grandfather." The lad leaves for home.

The boy flies' home and tells his mother all about the news.

"Son, why aren't you at your grandfather's smithy?"

"He gave me the rest of the day off and to tell you, I need a girl partner to learn to dance properly."

"The nearest girl here is at the village, which is too far for her to get here on foot."

"Then, the Dance Master said I'd need to bring you if I couldn't find a partner to bring."

"Me?"

"Yes, mother, you'll be my dance partner."

"Ok, I'll come; now let's go talk to your grandfather. I want to find out more about this Dance Master."

Pam and her son fly to her father's cottage. To see what her father was up to about this dancing.

"I've been expecting you to show," said Zeke.

"Then you know why I'm here."

"Kind of, why don't you ask your questions, and I'll do the best I can to explain."

After a discussion, they decide to travel to the young girl's home in the valley to see if she wants to learn to dance. If she would, the girl could stay at grandfather's so she'd be handy. For payment, Zeke and the boy would make all her utensils for her name day and possible wedding. This way, she could stay as long as she needed for all the lessons.

After some discussion with her and her parents, they all agree. The girl packs all her clothes, and they use a lama like a creature to carry all her stuff to grandfather's home. They arrive late in the evening. Grandfather and the boy take all the girl's things into the house, and they put her up in Pam's old room.

The next morning, the boy and his mother walk in from the woods. Only to run into the wolf who transforms into the Dance Master. They walk into the yard and announce their presence. Zeke, his wife Lisa, and the girl all appear.

"We have quite an audience I see. Who is this ravishing young woman?" as he takes Pam's hand.

"Pam, the boy's mother," she stammers.

"Are you sure you appear to be too young to be his mother?" He takes her hand and kisses it.

Pam blushes at the compliment.

The Dance Master turns to the boy. "Now, you do the same thing to the young lady over there, but I'd not say the same thing."

The boy walks over to the girl, pays her a compliment, and kisses her hand. Unlike his mother, the girl doesn't blush but almost laughs.

"It will do for a start," says the Dance Master.

"Pam, would you attend me?" Pam walks up to the Dance Master.

"Girl, would you attend me," asks the boy. The girl walks up to the boy, and they watch the Dance Master and Pam.

The boy and the girl followed suit. In the background, Zeke plays a stringed instrument. The Dance Master takes Pam into his arms, and the boy and girl do the same thing. With fluid grace, the Dance Master twirls Pam about the yard. The boy and the girl try to follow, but both are clumsy and awkward after about an hour. The women are dismissed, the dance master takes the wooden practice swords and shows the boy the proper dance steps with the blade and give each dance segment a name. The girl continues to watch, and when the boy makes a mistake, she giggles, and the boy blushes.

The lessons continue four times a week, and in between, the boy and the girl have to practice at the same time Zeke keeps his promise and forges out knives, spoons, forks, and such for the girl to take home for her wedding day, which will happen soon after her name day. She has yet to meet her prospective husband. The day comes for the spring festival, Zeke loads up the girl's dowry to drop off at her parent's house on the way.

By this time, the boy and the girl have been well taught to dance. At the festival during the dancing, the boy dances with the girl, and they both enjoy moving together. Then her future husband demands what's going on here. The boy apologizes and tries to walk off; the boy, called Brad. Bully's the boy. The boy tries to walk away when Brad throws a punch, and the boy ducks it. Zeke is about to intervene when Pam stops him.

"He may get hurt, Pam."

"He may, father, but it'll hurt more if you stop it, let him face his problem."

"Ok, Pam."

They stand by and watch as Brad rounds on the boy, but each time the boy dances out of the way, making Brad madder. Soon the boy ends the fight by pitching Brad into the creek. Then Brad's father clears his throat, stopping Brad in his tracks.

"What a way to act in front of your bride to be."

"But he was dancing with her."

"Yes, and quite well, it seems. You need to learn some manners, now go tell the boy you are sorry for being foolish."

"But!" Brad shakes his head yes, and approaches the boy to apologize.

The boy puts his hand out, and Brad is reluctant to take it, but he does.

So, not to cause any other problem, the boy asks other girls to dance, and the response is quite well taken; before he knows it, there is a lineup of girls who want to dance with him. Being the center of attention is to his liking. The boy has made many conquests this day.

"See, father, things turned out," said Pam.

"He could've been hurt," said Zeke.

"I don't think so. Maybe his pride, but he would've been fine. I'm glad Brad's father stepped in before Brad got hurt."

"The boy was good, wasn't he Pam?"

"Yes, father, he was. Let's find mom and get something to eat; it'll be a long trip back home with the girl."

"I agree," said Zeke.

Chapter 36

Before it gets dark, Zeke and the family with the girl start back to the smithy. It'll be at least two days before they arrive. They arrive late back at grandfather's home, where the boy and Pam decide to go home. They say their goodbyes and enter the wood where Pam and the boy change into falcons and fly the rest of the way home. The next morning Pam and the boy return to take up the dance lessons with the Dance Master. All goes well, and the Dance Master declares that the lessons are at an end, "I've taught all that I can. All you need do is practice what you've learned."

"Dance Master, will you come to my name day in two weeks?"

"I'd be honored to be there. Turning to Pam, I'd like permission to visit from time to time to see how well my student is doing what I have taught him."

"You may; I'll look forward to seeing you. By the way, how are your wife and child doing?"

"They're doing well. I'll be seeing them this evening. I'll tell her you asked after her. She'll be happy you did. I must be going. You boy practice, I'll know if you don't."

"Yes, sir."

They all watch as the Dance Master changes into a wolf and dashes off into the wood.

The girl asked if she might stay until the boy's name day. Grandmother tells her in front of everyone that she may if she likes. Two weeks later, everyone shows up to celebrate the boy's name day. Grandfather brings out the box with the sword made from star stone. The sun is at the highest point in the sky. The boy is busting at the seams to proclaim his name.

"Well, boy, have you chosen your name, if you have, proclaim it now!"

"My Name is Phoenix!" and Phoenix bursts into his bird form, showing his fiery feathers.

The girl shouts, "No, it can't be!" she runs off into the house.

"What did I do wrong?" asks Phoenix.

"Grandmother will find out, but you did well, my grandson, that was a most impressive display."

"You sure lived up to your name Phoenix. The Dance Master pats him on the shoulder. Here I have a name day gift for you. Keep this medallion if you need help, show this at castle Phoenix, and they'll send you my way."

"Thank you!" said Phoenix.

"I must return home to my family. Phoenix, practice what you have learned, it'll help you in the time to come." The Dance Master steps back and bows to Phoenix, then runs off changing into his wolf form.

Grandmother followed the girl into the house to see what the problem is with the girl.

"Girl, what is the problem?" asks grandmother softly.

"You saw, he's the Phoenix!"

"What of it, girl?"

"Don't you see, my name day is weeks away, and then I'll be married to Brad."

"That doesn't explain what your problem is, girl."

"I was hoping to marry your grandson, now I can't, because of the prophecy."

"I have a question, and I want you to answer me truthfully."

"Yes, grandmother."

"Do you want to have children?"

"Don't all girls wish for a family with children? I'm no different."

"My grandson can't give you children; he cannot father any children. He's a eunuch."

"I guess that explains why he never tried to get me alone; he doesn't feel about girls like the other boys do," said the girl.

"Now go out and wish Phoenix well, and it's time to return you home."

The girl runs out to wish Phoenix well and hugs him with a kiss on his cheek. She leaves Phoenix, blushing. The rest of the day, the girl packs up her things. Loads then on to the llama for the trip home. The next morning Phoenix and his mother show up to see the girl off when grandfather has an accident hurting his foot and can't walk. That means Phoenix will have to take the girl home on his own. (Something grandmother cooked up to make this happen).

Phoenix was not happy, but he realizes she needs to get home, so he agrees to take her. They start after grandmother makes breakfast and packs them up some food for the trip. The two set off.

"Will they be ok? Should I go with them?" asks Pam.

"No! This is necessary for both of them; they'll be just fine.

Phoenix is nearly a man, and he needs to be one. The girl needs to learn a few things as well. Nothing will happen to them that Phoenix can't handle. You'll see," said the grandmother.

On the first day of travel, not much was said between them, that night they set up camp and raided the food grandmother supplied. When they've finished, they cleaned up and sat close to the fire.

"Phoenix, do you want a family?"

"I don't know, I have never given it a thought. I don't seem to have any feeling in that direction."

"I see, I always wondered why you never tried to hold my hand or get me alone. Your grandmother told me you were a eunuch, and you could not give a girl any children. I suppose that'd make you less desiring of a woman."

"I guess. I did like dancing with you, and I did like the kiss you gave me yesterday. I do wish I desired you, but I don't. I want to be a friend."

"Then I'll be your friend," she sighed.

They turned in for the night, each in their blanket until late in the night when the girl asked if she could share his blanket, she was freezing, so they laid next to each other. It was very cold, so Phoenix turned up his body heat to warm them up. In the morning, they loaded up the gear and moved on toward the girl's home. They could reach it if they pushed on into the late evening.

As the two approach the village where she lived, they both could see a red glow in the sky, and they stopped to listen; they could hear what sounded like fighting in the distance. Phoenix took them off into the brush "stay here and stay quiet. I'll check ahead to see what's happening."

Phoenix changes his shape into a falcon to fly off when he hears the girl says to be careful. He flies off toward the red glow, and he sees men killing and setting the village houses on fire. Phoenix realizes these are sea raiders from across the great ocean; what are they doing so far inland. This has to stop. In mid-flight, Phoenix changes to his true form of the Phoenix and screeches out like rolling thunder. This gets everyone's attention, and his flaming form absorbs the nearby fire as he lands. The sea raiders turn to attack Phoenix. They shoot arrows at him and all the arrows burn to ash in midflight. The sea raiders advance on Phoenix with drawn swords charging him like madmen, and they are burned to ash. Phoenix lays about him with his wings killing the sea raiders, which starts them in full retreat back to the sea.

When the sea raiders are driven off Phoenix changes back into his human form to see if anyone is still alive, he finds several alive and well, and he gets them to look for others. They find several injured and try to get them help. After things settle down, Phoenix flies back to pick up the girl.

"It's Ok, to come out, girl."

She comes out of the brush leading her pack animal. "What happened? I heard thunder in the distance."

"I drove off sea raiders, and I had to use my Phoenix form to do it. Now let's get to the village and see if your parents are still alive."

"Oh, no! Let's hurry!" said the girl.

They push on and reach the village quickly, and she leads them to where her house once stood. The girl drops to her knees and cries for her parents. Phoenix kneels beside her to offer comfort. After several minutes, he gets her to stop crying then asks her where her Brad lives; they may be there.

"Yes, they may have gone there, let's hurry" as she holds back the tears.

She leads them toward the South, away from the village, and sure enough, many people ran to Brads home to try to hold off the sea raiders. The girl's parents come running out of the compound to catch up their daughter, and soon Brad and his parents are there.

Brad's father asks, "Where are the sea raiders?"

"Gone for now. The people in the village need help with the wounded. I'll check on the sea raiders and make sure they don't come back."

"You're just a boy, how can you do anything?" said Brad's father.

Phoenix says nothing. He steps away, changes into The Phoenix, turns to look at the people, and screeches his thunderous voice, "Watch." Phoenix launches into the sky and heads off to follow the sea raiders. It doesn't take long to find them; some of them have changed to wolves or dogs, and other animals all headed to the coast. To hurry them along Phoenix let out his thunderous scream. This spurs them on to greater effort to get to the coast. Phoenix estimates that it'll take them another day to get to the coast, so with another scream, he turns about and heads back to the village to see how everyone is doing. Phoenix lands in the village square and changes back to the boy. A crowd surrounds him and cheers him for driving off the sea raiders and saving the village.

CHAPTER

37

Brad's father approaches the boy. "Son, Thank you! I'm sorry I doubted you, may I shake your hand?"

Phoenix puts out his hand and shakes it. "My name is Phoenix, not boy any longer."

"You have got that right. Phoenix, I'm proud to call you, friend."

The next moment the girl comes up to him and hugs him. "Thank you, for saving our village and my parents are safe."

"You're all welcome. Now how are the injured are they being taken care of?"

Brad steps up and puts out his hand to shake, "Phoenix, we'll see to them. I want to thank you for taking care of my future bride."

Phoenix takes his hand. "I must attend to other business; I'll be back soon."

As Phoenix gets ready to transform, the girl asks him to come back for her Name day.

"I would be honored. Do you think your husband would let me have the first dance?"

They look to Brad, and he smiles and nods yes. "Then it's settled,

I'll be here. When will it be?"

"In three weeks." Phoenix kisses her on the forehead, and says, "I'll be back."

Phoenix launches into the sky and heads back toward home. He arrives at his mother's house, and she meets him in the yard. She perceives something that has happened to him.

"What went on, Phoenix?" she asks.

"I had to kill, mother. Sea raiders were destroying a village, and I stopped them, they're now headed back to the coast, I'll go there in the morning to drive them from our shore."

"I see, is the girl, alright?"

"She is, and her parents are also safe; most of the villagers had gotten away."

"Good, now go get some sleep. You look tired."

Phoenix goes to his room and doesn't even take off his clothes. He falls into a troubled sleep. In the morning, his mother makes him breakfast, and then after cleaning up, he flies off to see how the sea raiders are doing as far as leaving our shore. He passes over the last place he saw them and continued to the coast. When he gets there, he sees the ships out at sea, and he follows with a thunderous screech and a bolt of fire from his mouth aimed at the sea.

"If you come back to my shore, I'll destroy all your ships," says Phoenix in his thunderous voice.

Phoenix turns about and heads to the village. He lands in the square, and he is greeted with cheers and laughter. Phoenix bows to the people as taught by the Dance Master. Brad steps up to him.

"Hi friend Brad, I've driven the sea raiders from our shore. I don't expect them to return anytime soon."

"Thank you, Phoenix."

Phoenix turns and launches into the sky, then circles the town and moves off to the west to head for home. Phoenix lands at his grandfather's yard to report to work in the smithy.

"Good morning lad, I hear from your mother you saved the village where the girl lived. I'm sorry you had to kill people."

"Thank you, grandfather, let's forget it and get out some work. I want to forget what I did."

"I understand, we have some knives to turn out, let's get started."

By the end of the second week, Phoenix remembered the girl's name day and set about making her dagger. After rummaging around in the scrap metal, bin Phoenix found a small chunk of star stone. Remembering how grandfather made his rapier, he forged out a dagger, then set about polishing and engraving the dagger with a pink colored handle and a Phoenix figure carved into the handle and on the flat of the blade of the knife. He made a soft leather sheath for the blade. On the day of her name day, Phoenix and his whole family all meet at the smithy, then changed into falcons and fly to the village just in time for her name day.

Her father called her out and asked, "Girl, what is your Name!"

She called out "my name is Pam," and she changed into a German Shepard. Everybody clapped and cheered. Then they gave her presents, most of them had to do with her up and coming marriage. At the last Phoenix stepped up and handed the dagger to Pam. "This is to protect yourself. I made it myself; I hope you like it."

Pam takes the dagger out of the sheath. "You made this?"

"I did. It's made from star stone; it'll keep its edge. Keep it safe on your person."

She is so happy with the gift she throws her arms around Phoenix's neck and kisses him soundly on the lips, making Phoenix blush.

Brad comes up from behind and clears his throat. "That's my bride, you know."

Phoenix is so flustered he doesn't know what to say. Brad clasps his shoulder and laughs a good hearty laugh. "Phoenix, remember you have the first dance, but I get all the rest of them."

Phoenix clasps Brad's shoulder, "I'll remember."

After the lunch is put out for everyone, they sit around talking when the music starts, and all the girls surround Phoenix, and as he gets up, Pam (the girl) snares him first. They dance, and as they go through the steps, Phoenix asks, "Why did you pick the name, Pam?"

"I took it to show respect to your mother. I like her, besides the name is short and cute."

"Good choice, somehow it suits you."

The music ends for that dance, and the next tune starts, and Brad is there to claim his future bride. Phoenix returns to the waiting gaggle of women to select his next partner. He manages to dance one dance with them all, and it ends late into the night. Brad puts Phoenix and his family up for the night at his family home.

In the morning, Phoenix and his family get ready to leave and return home. Brad walks up to say goodbye, and Pam, his bride to be, is on his arm.

"Phoenix, we'd like you and your family to come back in three more weeks for our wedding."

"I'd be delighted, but I can't speak for my parents. You'll need to ask them." His mother and grandparents agree to return.

"Phoenix, would you be my best man at the wedding?"

"Brad, don't take this the wrong way, but no. You have a life-long friend who should be your best man."

"You save everyone here, and this is the way to give you some honor."

"I understand. My answer is still no. I do thank you for the honor, but if you think about it, you'll see that I'm right. Your friend deserves that place. I will ask for one thing?"

"What's that?"

"May I have a second dance with your wife?"

Brad grabs Phoenix's hand. "Yes! Only because I'd never heard the end of it if I didn't."

"Goodbye, all." Phoenix and his parents transform into falcons and fly off towards home.

The day arrives for the wedding, and all Phoenix can remember is that it came and went like a blur; the one thing he remembers is the last dance with his dance partner Pam. They never get to dance again; Phoenix would remember that dance fondly for the rest of his years. Phoenix would spend most of his time exploring the continent; he'd be gone for days at a time, seeing what the world had to offer. Phoenix was always on the lookout for star stone, so when he saw a smithy, he would strike up a conversation and inquire if he had any star stone. If he found any, he would offer to buy it. Most of the time, he could get it pretty cheap; not many people knew how to work it. As luck would have it, Phoenix stayed at an inn where his father was killed; when Phoenix brought in a large bag of star stone, the same thieves thought it was valuable and decided to rob him of his goods. That night they entered Phoenix's room; he woke to the noise they'd made when they entered. Phoenix got out of bed. He didn't have much on by way of clothes.

"That's unfortunate," said one of the men.

"How so?" asks Phoenix.

"We now have to kill you because you saw us."

"Oh, is that all?"

"Why are you not fearful of us?" asked the other man as he drew his rather large knife.

"I see a couple of bumbling thieves who are going to pay for their crimes."

The man with the long knife rushes Phoenix, and he dances out of the way and plucks the blade from his attacker's hand. The other man charges Phoenix slashing with his sword. Phoenix dances out of the way, knocks the man to the floor, and uses the knife's handle to knock out the thief on the floor. He turns to the other thief; he decides to beat his feet toward the door. Phoenix throws the knife handle first and hits the thief in the back of the head, stunning him. Phoenix calls the innkeeper and gets some rope to truss up the thieves. In the morning, Phoenix locates the town leader and turns the men over to be dealt with.

Phoenix takes his heavy bag of stones out to the town square and changes into the Phoenix, grabs his bag, and flies off toward home. Phoenix lands at his grandfather's yard and hands him the bag of star stone.

"What's this lad?"

"Star stone grandfather, I got it for next to nothing. It appears no one knows how to work with it. They were willing to get rid of it. Half that bag I got for just taking it away. The rest I paid a few coppers for".

"This is all good stuff, lad; we can make a small fortune from what we can forge from all this star stone."

"I'll keep looking for star stone grandfather as I explore more of this country; I best go see my mother. She'll be worried about me."

Phoenix changes to a falcon and flies' home. His mother is glad to see him, she ushers him into the house, and as she fixes a meal for them, she has him tell her all about his adventure, and not to leave anything out. In the next few days, Phoenix works for his grandfather at the smithy to help catch up on many customers' backorders. Phoenix enjoys working in the smithy with his grandfather. He likes heating the metal then forges it into shape; they turn out several knives, swords, and utensils between them. The few days were productive, and they got caught up. Phoenix decides to fly west to explore his country. In the morning, Phoenix said good-bye to his mother and flew off to the west. As he passed westward, Phoenix saw a couple of men riding llamas to the east, with a couple of other llamas for pack animals. At the time, Phoenix gave no thought to them, thinking them merchants. As he flew westward, he saw that the people were unhappy, and when Phoenix finely approached a city, he changed to a falcon, flew into the wood next to a plowed field, and changed to human form.

Phoenix saw a man plowing a field. He was directing the bull-like animals to pull the plow. He noticed that the man looked downtrodden and wearing rags. "Sir, can you talk with me for a moment?"

After the third time of asking, the man said nothing and kept plowing; Phoenix walked toward the castle. He meets a slave master with a whip and a sword on the far side of the field.

"Who're you, peasant?"

"I'm not a peasant, just a free man visiting here."

The man takes his whip, snaps it at Phoenix, and cuts his face, "Now back to work, peasant!"

"I'm not a peasant, and you'd do well to realize it."

The taskmaster flicks his whip again. This time Phoenix dances out of the way. The taskmaster flicks his whip again, and once more, Phoenix dances out of the way. Now angered, the taskmaster uses the whip to mark Phoenix again. Standing still, Phoenix uses his power of fire to burn the whip to ash. Enraged, the taskmaster rushes Phoenix with his sword drawn; Phoenix dances out of the way, several times, and in the end, plucks the sword out of the taskmaster's hand and, using the flat of the blade, whips him into submission.

"Now kind, sir, you'll tell me who rules here!"

"King Phoenix does."

"Really? I'd like to see this king. Where can I find him?"

"At the palace, he rules this land now."

"I see." Phoenix shoves the taskmaster away. If I ever see you whip anyone again, you'll pay with your life." Phoenix pushes the man away from him, changes into his Phoenix form, and launches into the air. Once above the castle, Phoenix lets out a scream of thunder and lands in the castle's courtyard showing all his flaming glory. People scurry to a place of safety. Phoenix changes back into his human form. "King Phoenix come forth and show yourself!" announces Phoenix.

From the overlooking balcony, the king calls out, "Who are you, usurper?"

"I'm the true Phoenix, and I've come to set things right. Prove you're the Phoenix of the prophecy," shouts the King.

The king changes into a flying lion and tries to crush Phoenix in the courtyard. Phoenix changes to a sparrow and flies out of the way. The king is maddened that he missed the man in the courtyard. Phoenix appears behind the king. "Is that the best you can do?"

The king turns to face the usurper. "Archers fire on him!"

The arrows come in from all directions, and Phoenix burns them to ash in mid-flight.

"Tell me king who the true Phoenix is? All I see in you is a petty tyrant! No true king would treat his subjects the way you do." (The people cheer at the Phoenix's words).

"Well, usurper, will you fight the king's champion for who rules this land?"

"I will. Will you permit me to get my sword?"

"No. borrow one from one of my subjects."

"Here sire, a sword the usurper may use." The Dance Master walks up and hands Phoenix the rapier that Phoenix himself made.

"That will do, Dance Master. Will you accept it, usurper?" asks the King.

"I will." The Dance Master walks up and hands the sword to Phoenix.

In a whisper, "Remember, lad, it's for your life."

Phoenix nods his head and the taskmaster returns to the crowd.

From behind him, Phoenix hears the clanking walk of a man in full armor. Phoenix knows not to turn his back on the king, so he moves off to one side so he can keep both men in sight. Phoenix sizes up the champion to locate all the weak points as the Dance Master taught him. He sees all the weak points, the armpits, behind the knees, elbows, and the helmet's eyeholes. The Dance Master stands where he can see Phoenix fight; he knows that he can best the champion if the champion doesn't cheat or the king for that matter.

Chapter

38

The champion made the first attack swinging his two-handed broad sword at Phoenix. He just danced out of the way and flicked his rapier at the champion's wrist, leaving a nice cut, and this went on for several minutes with a charge by the champion and Phoenix dancing out of the way and leaving a cut in various places. With each cut, the champion was losing his temper. The people in the crowd were silent, as if they were holding their breath. In a raging scream, the champion charged Phoenix, and the King ran up from behind. Phoenix heard the Dance Master and knew what was happening, so he directed the sword of the champion past him, and the King ran on to the sword of his champion; at the same time, Phoenix ran his rapier into the eye socket of the champion. Phoenix stood up, and the crowd roared.

On the balcony stood the queen with her children. The crowd went wild and wanted to kill them, so Phoenix changed into his Phoenix shape and thundered at the crowd and scared them into being silent and made them standstill. He changed back and said, "The queen and her children are under my protection; I'll burn any person who threatens or touches them."

The crowd went hushed, "From now on, there are no peasants or high born. Everyone is now free. I'm disbanding the army but will keep a small force to maintain law and order. Taxes will be ten percent from everyone to include the wealthy merchants as well as everyone else.

Phoenix looks up at the queen and asks her to come down to him. She shows up with her children, and someone in the crowd throws rotten fruit at her. Phoenix catches it and turns to the crowd. "Who threw this?" No one answers. "I said the queen and her children are under my protection, and I mean it." He throws the fruit into the air and burned it to ash. "Everyone, clear out!" people scattered and left the queen and her children with Phoenix.

"Your majesty, I need someone to rule here and carry out my rulings. Would you do that?" asks Phoenix.

"Are you sure you want a woman to rule this place? Men don't like being ruled by women."

"My lady, I didn't ask if anyone would like it. I asked if you could rule here."

"I can."

"Then you'll rule in my stead. I'll return from time to time to see how it all goes. If you can't do it, I'll replace you."

"I understand."

"In time, your son or daughter may become the ruler here, so teach them well."

"I will."

"I'm going to send you a friend of mine to be an advisor, he'll not rule. Be assured he won't candy his advice; if I were you, I'd listen to him. He'd tell me what I'm doing wrong, and I listen to him myself.

He'll appear to you today."

"If you say so, King Phoenix."

"I guess I'll have to get used to that. I need to talk to my friend. I'll take my leave of you, my lady!"

Phoenix steps back, changes into his phoenix form and wings his way into the sky, and disappears. When he is out of sight, he transforms into a sparrow and returns to find the Dance Master. Phoenix buys a cloak with a hood from a vendor so he can walk around unseen. He sees a person in the street and walks up to him, shows him the wolf medallion, and asks for the Dance Master. He points down the road and indicates his studio is four buildings away. Phoenix gives the man a couple of coppers and walks off to see his old friend, the Dance Master.

At the studio, the Dance Master put up the rapiers he had been using for one of his classes. Phoenix enters the studio. "I'm sorry, friend, but I'm closing for the day, please come back tomorrow."

"Now is that the way to greet an old friend, Dance Master" chuckles Phoenix.

With eyes as big as saucers, "Your majesty! Come in, please, I'm always open to you. I see you still drop that right shoulder when your sword fighting."

Phoenix clasps the Dance Master's hand. It's good to see you, my friend. Thanks for the use of your rapier."

"It was my pleasure; I never saw a person use another person to kill an enemy as you did today with the king."

"I've come for two reasons, one I need a place to stay for a day or so, and I need you to work with the queen as an advisor and protector."

"The room I have, but advisor and protector of the queen, maybe too much to ask."

"May I ask why old friend?"

"The King's tax collectors killed my wife and child, and I've been looking for revenge all that time. It might be that I'd be tempted to kill them myself."

"I see, I understand, and I'm sorry for your loss."

"You served me well today, your majesty, by killing a vile person and his lapdog."

"Have you given thought to another wife?" asks Phoenix.

"No!"

"Well, you see, I know a woman who's heart you have stolen, without meaning to."

"Who would that be?"

"My mother Pam, she won't say it, but she has fallen head over heels in love with you."

"Your mother?"

"Yes, she loves you, but she'd never admit it because you were married, you could comfort each other. Besides, you'd be the father of a king."

"I'll give it a thought. As for the queen, I'll help until you find another advisor and protector."

"I'll accept it. Is there another way to leave here unseen?"

"This way, your majesty," and Dance Master leads them out a sideway, and they enter the courtyard unseen, and then up into the castle proper to meet with the queen and go over how she'll rule in his stead. When they finish, the queen signs the declaration with the Phoenix. Dance Master finds the queen not as bad as the King. She thought the King, a vile pig. She was glad he was killed.

The business of ruling the kingdom, the Phoenix makes a big show of leaving. The queen follows the declaration, and the people prosper, so then does the kingdom. Phoenix is searching for the tax collectors; when he finds them, he makes them take back the money they have stolen. They protest until he demonstrates his power, then they comply, fearful of being burned to ash. They also say they'll inform the King and he'll put a stop to your foolishness.

"When you see the king tell him I said hello."

The tax collectors return to the castle to complain to the King about the usurper in the woods.

Phoenix was at the castle when most of them return and a couple of them faint when they see the new King.

"As your King, you'll return all the plunder to the people you stole from them. If I get one complaint, it'll be your life. Now go!"

The tax collectors' trip over themselves in getting back to their mounts to return the stolen goods to the people they took them from. Phoenix visits the queen regent to check in and see how they are doing, and let them know he's about. Over the month's Phoenix considers the improvement in the peasant class people. They appear happier and more content. No longer wearing rags and eating regularly. Phoenix commends the queen upon the progress. In their discussion, she informs him that there are fewer up risings, and the people like her if not love their queen now.

"I'm glad your Grace. I must take my leave; this country is huge and a lot of ground I must cover. I'm heading south this day to explore; I should be back in a month. Be well, my lady!"

"Goodbye, my King, I look forward to seeing you again. Before you go, my twin, children's name day is coming, could you be here for them?"

"It would be my honor, thank you for the invitation."

Phoenix leaves the throne room, and in the courtyard, he launches himself into the air as a great eagle and flies off to the south. Once out of sight, he changes into the Phoenix form and flies onward. He flies to the edge of the continent and finds another great ocean, he lands to watch the sea roll in, and he spends a few days flying along the coast. On his way back toward the north, Phoenix spots a large town. Phoenix changes into a sparrow to snoop around and finds the condition even more appalling than any other kingdom he's seen. The people were shackled like slaves, and if they fell, they would be beaten. Enraged, Phoenix changed to his human form and confronted the taskmaster; by the time he finished his discussion, the taskmaster gave Phoenix his keys and ran away. Phoenix unlocked the shackles from off the people he saw. The people were confused and fearful. All they knew was slavery. By the time he finishes unlocking the shackles, an armed escort shows up to take the Phoenix to the rulers.

"You stranger, come with us. We're taking you to the rulers of this city."

"I'll come along, if anyone shackles any more people, I'll deal harshly with them."

Poking a spear at Phoenix, "What are you going to do if we do?"

Phoenix burns the spears to ash burning their hands, making them jump back. "Will that do, my friend?"

The armed men stand back; the slaves watch to see if they'll stay free or be enslaved again; one person changes and runs off. The guards lead the way at a distance. They march up to the stone building made from some marble; there three men dressed like kings meet them.

"So stranger, you're the one who freed the slaves; by what right did you do this?"

"By the right of being your king!"

"We have no king except us," he indicates the other two on the step with him.

"According to the prophecy, the Phoenix, a mythical creature, is to be your King. I am he!"

"What proof do you have that you're him?"

Phoenix changes into the mythical bird, and from the top of the building, several arrows are flying toward him. Phoenix burns them to ash; then, he scorches the three on the top steps. Phoenix doesn't kill them. He scorches them to get their attention.

Phoenix changes back into his human form. "Is that proof enough?"

"We yield your majesty."

"Good now! Now give me fealty."

Everyone kneels and gives fealty to Phoenix.

"You three may remain in charge, as long as you follow my accords. If you deviate from them, you'll be replaced." Phoenix hands them a copy, and they read them over.

"Sire, we cannot follow this! It would mean a loss of income."

"Too bad. If you follow my accords, you'll lose nothing, and the people will gain. Which means they'll buy more, and you'll still prosper without stealing? You'll follow my accords starting today."

"As you say, your majesty!"

"Now you'll spend your own money to clothe and feed all the people you had enslaved; you'll disband your taskmasters and most of your army. You may keep a small contingent for policing."

"We'll do as you say, King Phoenix."

"I must move on and free other places like this one. Be warned I'll be back, and you won't know it until it's too late. I strongly suggest you do as I say."

"We'll do as you say, your majesty."

Phoenix launches upward into the sky in his Phoenix form screeching in a thunderous voice he'll be back. High in the air, he disappears and changes into a sparrow and returns to watch. He lands on a windowsill to listen to the three.

"We're not going to do what he says, are we?" said one of the three.

"Yes, we will," answered the one who is mostly in charge.

"Why asks the third one?"

"I don't know about you, but being turned to ash wouldn't be something I'd like very well."

"We see your point."

"Good, that doesn't mean we can't find a way to remove him from the picture, then return to our ways."

"How do you propose we remove him?"

"Come inside; we'll talk about it behind closed doors."

The three enter into the castle, go to a far room off the throne room, and post a guard to make sure no one can hear them plot against the King. Phoenix manages to find a ledge in the space above the door, and he flies there to sit quietly and listen to the plotters. They can't decide if they want him assassinated or kidnap someone to hold sway over him. They decide that holding power over him would be more preferable. Now they need to find out who, so they decide to send out spies to see who would be suitable. Phoenix decides to return to castle Phoenix to warn Dance Master of the possibility of a kidnapping. Phoenix could've stopped it by stopping the plotters. He decides to let it play out. Then he'll have evidence against the three. He'll use this to discourage others from doing the same thing.

Reaching the Dance Master at his studio, he takes him into his confidence about the possible kidnapping. Once warned, the Dance

Master knows a few trustworthy men to place in the palace to watch the queen and her children.

"Dance Master, have you considered seeing my mother?"

"I have, I haven't had the time to approach her."

"I've been gone for a while, and have taken kingship of a few more towns, the ones who treat their people as people; I leave alone. Those who abuse the people I have forced them to follow me. However, three devious men enslave the people who live to the south. These are the ones we need to watch."

"I understand my lord; I'll see to the protection of the queen and her children come morning."

"I thank you, my friend. I know you'll do a good job. May I sleep in your loft? I've had a long trip getting here."

"Sire, do you require any food?"

"No. I stopped along the way and ate a small creature a few hours ago; I'll be fine until morning."

The Dance Master shows his friend the King to the loft where he can sleep. Phoenix wastes no time in falling asleep. He's wakened in the morning by his friend.

"Would you like some breakfast, sire?"

"Yes, I would."

"Come, the washbasin is over there, and I'll meet you in the next room."

Phoenix washes up and meets the Dance Master in the adjoining room. A nice thick steak is waiting, with warm bread and a mug of ale ready for him.

"This is great, my friend, and I'm hungry!"

They both are eating when the Dance Master asks a question. "Sire, may I have leave to go away for a short time, that is after I set up protection for the queen and her children."

"You may, Dance Master, I don't wish this castle to be your prison. I need your help, and you have done that. You may leave at any time without my permission."

"Then I'll take you up on your suggestion to go see your mother. I find she is on my mind more often these days, and finding another mate would be nice."

"If you decide to get married, you'll invite me to the wedding?"

"You know we will."

Laughing, Phoenix says, "We best go see the queen."

Both men ask to see the queen in private and explain the plot to her to be aware.

"Why kidnap the children and me?"

"They believe that they'll control me through fear of your lives."

"I see," answers the queen.

"I have tasked Dance Master to arrange protection for you and your children."

"Thank you, sire."

"Now we have the doom and gloom out of the way, how fair the children?" asks Phoenix.

"The closer they get to name day, the more excited they become."

"What about the death of their father?"

"There's no love lost there. He was a tyrant and a power grubbing pig who abused everyone, even the children. The children and I think you did us a good thing."

"Good, that reminds me of a couple of things. One I need to make them a present, and two have they been betrothed to anyone yet?" asks Phoenix.

"My children will just be happy if you show up without a gift. I've not betrothed my children at all; my husband was going to use them as pawns for forming alliances with other kingdoms."

"Good, then they can just fall in love and marry whom they will then."

"You do realize, my daughter wants to be your bride?"

"If I were a normal man, I'd be honored and willing to have her. I can't have children, and she needs a man who can give them to her."

"You can't father children?" asks the queen.

"No."

"Then how will your rule be carried on sire?" asks both the Dance Master and the queen.

"For that, I'd suggest you look to the myth of the Phoenix. It appears to live 1000 years then dies in a fire and is reborn. I guess I'll wait and see."

"I'll explain to my daughter that you can't marry her. She won't like it, but I'll explain", said the queen.

"I need to go. I have other kingdoms to visit. I'll be here for name day. Before I forget, the Dance Master will be gone from time to time. He's got my permission."

"Very well. Will he supply me with a trusted man?"

"I will, your majesty. He'll be ever as bit as good as I and as loyal to you, my queen as I am."

Everything is settled. Phoenix leaves them so he can return home to his mother. He lands in the yard outside her home and is greeted by her. After recounting his adventure to the south, he is fed and forced to take a bath. Phoenix laughs at the thought, here my mother orders her son about who is her King. I obey without question. The people at court would be aghast that she orders him about.

The next day Phoenix visits his grandparents and regales them about the land to the south and the great ocean he saw. After a time, Phoenix asks his grandfather if he may use the smithy to make some gifts for the twin's name day. Grandfather asks if he can help.

"Son, what do we make them?"

"I was thinking of a pair of daggers, a matching set made from star stone."

"Sounds like a good idea. Let's go fire up the forge."

In a couple of days, they had forged out the daggers, and now they spent a few more days polishing the metal to a mirror finish. Then grandfather engraved a Phoenix on each knife's blade, while Phoenix makes up a leather sheaths to hold them.

"Thanks for all the help grandfather, these are princely daggers; I have even added the Phoenix to the leather sheath. Now, if you wish to come to the queen's children's name day, I'd be honored to have you come. One thing must be observed. You can't associate with me there."

"Why is that?"

"I have found a conspiracy planned against me; they want to kidnap anyone close to me and use them to control me. I don't want to make targets of you. You'll stay with the Dance Master; he'll see to your needs."

"I understand, son, it'll be as you've asked."

"Well, I'm off to home, and then I'll be going back to the castle with the daggers."

Phoenix returns to his mother's house and finds an old friend there, the Dance Master.

"Are you well, your highness?"

"My friend, please address me as Phoenix when at my mother's house."

"As you wish, sire."

"May I inquire why you're here?"

"You invited me here, remember?"

"Dance Master, I was headed back to the palace and stopped by to say goodbye to my mother."

Pam comes from around the house from tending her garden. "Oh, good two strong men who can lend me a hand."

"What do you need, my lady?" asks the Dance Master.

"A rotten tree fell into my yard, and if you two would move it out of the way."

"We'd be delighted to assist you, my lady." The Dance Master bowed low and took her hand.

Phoenix was smiling very large and said, "we'd be glad to assist you, mother."

Both men move to the back of the house and realize this is no small job. Phoenix decides to get the saw and ax out of the shed to cut up the rather large tree. It'll make a nice pile of firewood for his mother. The nice thing is the Dance Master is here to help.

Several hours later, both men have reduced the tree to a nice neat wood stack next to the house, all cut and split. Mom calls the boys into supper, and they go over to the water trough, strip their shirts off, and wash up for supper. When they enter the house, they can smell the food, and both men are hungry. Phoenix pours some cold ale for himself and the Dance Master, and they sit at the table.

"This is nice said Pam having two men to cook for." Pam sits at the table, and the men wait until she serves herself before they dish up their food.

"Mother, I'll be leaving in the morning. I have to return to the castle."

"What about you, Dance Master?" asks Pam.

"If no one will take exception, may I stay here for a few days?"

"I don't know," said Pam.

Phoenix spoke up, "sure, why not? I'll be gone so the Dance Master can stay in my room."

"Or if the lady is concerned, I can sleep in the woods."

"Oh, no. if you can stay, I'd be delighted to have you here."

"Then it's settled, Dance Master, you stay in my room."

Morning came, and Phoenix was already gone. Pam went to wake the Dance Master, and he was gone too. Pam returned to the kitchen and started the fire to warm up the house and prepare some breakfast. Someone knocked at the door, and Pam opened it up to find the Dance Master standing there with some freshly caught game. "Will this do for dinner?" he asks.

"Yes, but you didn't have to do that."

"Where may I put this, so I can gut and skin it?"

"Over by the shed, Phoenix set up a table and a contraption for hanging it up to make it easier to clean.”

“Thank you, my lady.” Dance Master carts the animal over to the table and sets about cleaning it and skinning it. Over breakfast, the Dance Master tells Pam about his dead wife and son. He asks if it’d be all right with her if he could court her. Pam breaks down and starts crying; the Dance Master gets up to put his hands on her shoulders to console her.

“I’m sorry, my lady, if my words have hurt you. Maybe I should go.”

Pam grabs his hand. “No. you have made me so happy, please stay!”

“But you’re crying.”

“They are tears of joy. Believe me! I’ve been in love with you since the first time we danced together.”

“Then I may ask for your hand in marriage, for I love you as well. Is there someone I need to ask for your hand?”

“My son and my father.”

“Then I’m halfway there; your son already gave me his consent to marry you.”

“When did he do that?”

“A few months back, right after I told him what happened to my family. He’s the one who told me you fell in love with me.”

“He was always good at reading me,” said Pam.

“Let’s go see your father.”

Pam makes breakfast, and they clean up the dishes and set out to Pam’s father’s house. They make it a race. Pam changes into the falcon and Dance Master in his wolf form race off to their destination. Pam wins by several minutes; she transforms back to her human form and waits for the Dance Master to arrive.

“You are much faster than I am, I bet we could hunt together very successfully, I'd wager."

"We could at that," laughed Pam.

They both walk arm and arm to her parent's house. When they arrive at the door, Pam's mother opens it.

"Hi, mom, is father about?"

"He's where he always is at this time; his morning flight to the mountain and back. He should be returning in a short time. Would you and the Dance Master like to come in for tea?"

"Yes, mother. Dance Master, you going to come with us, or wait in the smithy?"

"I'll wait in the smithy."

The women go in and have tea. Pam is bursting at the seams to tell her mother about her being wed by the Dance Master. In the smithy, the Dance Master is working up the courage to ask for Pam's hand in marriage. Dance Master paces back and forth, he rehearses what he wants to say. Zeke lands in front of the smithy, and as he enters, he sees the Dance Master pacing and mumbling. He listens and realizes he is going to ask for his daughters' hand in marriage. Zeke smiles to himself. Not to say, Zeke has a mean strike in him, but he couldn't pass up a moment to get the best of someone. Zeke clears his throat.

The Dance Master nearly jumps out of his skin and blurts out, "May I marry your daughter!"

With a straight face, Zeke asks, "What makes you good enough to marry my daughter?"

"I love her and will make her happy."

Zeke can't take it any longer; he breaks down into a hardy laugh and extends his hand. "Son I couldn't have found my daughter a better match than you. I'd be honored to have you in the family."

With a sigh of relief, "That was the hardest thing I've ever done. I, too, would be honored to be in your family."

"We best go tell the womenfolk; they'll be excited and expectant to hear the news," said Zeke.

The men walk into the house, and Pam jumps into the father's arms, thanking him before he can say anything. They are taking away all his fun. Before they knew it, the men are being rushed out of the door, so the women can plan for the wedding.

Zeke turns to the Dance Master. "Are you sure you want to do this?"

"I'm not so sure now."

Zeke laughs and guides them out to the smithy. "Let's turn out a few things; it'll keep us out of trouble and help us to pass the time."

At the castle, Phoenix makes a show of landing and changes to his human form. The queen meets him at the entrance to the court.

"Majesty, we must talk; something has come up," said the queen.

"Inside and away from prying eyes." They both walk side by side into the castle and go to a tower room to talk where no one can hear them.

"What's the matter?" asks Phoenix.

"Someone has broken into the family living apartments, and move things around."

"Where are the men Dance Master left here to guard your persons?"

"No one knows, they disappeared, one was found dead down in the dungeon, the others I assume are dead, but we haven't found them," said the queen.

"Where're the children? I have something for them for their name day. I'm going to give it to them early. It may save their lives."

"Right now, they're in the library doing their lessons."

"May we interrupt them?"

"Your majesty may do anything he pleases."

"Your grace, that's not true. If you allow me, we can interrupt; if you don't, I won't! They're your children."

"Let's go see them, your majesty, they'll welcome the distraction. I'll see to it they finish their lessons later."

Phoenix bows to the queen and says, "Thank you."

Both Phoenix and the queen enter the library, and the children look up, and to the dismay of the teachers, they lose the children's attention and the teachers decide to let the children have their distraction. Both the twins go to their mother then turn to the king, and bow to him. The boy shakes Phoenix's hand, and the girl throws her arms around his neck and offers hugs and kisses. Phoenix blushes and thanks to them.

"I have made something for you. I want you to keep it close to you always; it may save your life." Phoenix hands them the small daggers he made them. The twins take the blades out of the sheath and marvel at the workmanship.

"You made these?" asks the boy.

"Yes, I made both of them with a great deal of care and love. These knives are made from star stone."

The queen looks at the knives. "These are exquisite and from star stone?"

"Yes, something I learned to do while growing up."

"Thank you, your majesty. They're the best gifts for our name day. You know its only days away, and the girl said I haven't been betrothed to anyone. Would you like to be my husband?" asked the girl.

Phoenix looks into her eyes and sees the affection there. "I have a question to ask you, girl, do you want children?"

"Yes, it's a duty for the royal bride to produce heirs for the throne," said the girl.

"No, you didn't answer the question. Do you want a family with children? I'm not asking about duty," said Phoenix.

"Yes, I'd like a family one day, with lots of children."

"Then, I cannot marry you. I don't have the stones to make you pregnant, so I can never give you children. You need to marry someone who can love you and keep you. I'll never be there when you need me; I'll be gone to other parts of the kingdom. I'm truly sorry!"

"I love you." she cried.

"Girl, I'll always carry you in my heart; you are the child I can never have. I look forward to your children. Now back to your studies with you."

The girl ran crying to her room, followed by her brother, who tried to console her.

"I'll go see her and help her understand," said the queen.

"I'm truly sorry I can't marry her, and she'd always be alone."

"Your majesty, you did the right thing. I considered approaching you myself, but you're gone all the time. My lord, I'd like to marry again, would you be agreeable to this?"

"I would, you are young yet, and you need a few domestic distractions. Find a good man."

"I thank you. I'd best go see my girl and console her."

Phoenix changes into a sparrow and flies out of the castle to Dance Master studio to get some sleep. In the morning, Dance Master has returned and shakes Phoenix to wake him up.

"Come on, sleepyhead, wake up. I have some gloomy news for

you.”

“What… is something wrong?” as Phoenix grabs some clothes to put on.

“Yes, something is wrong, I asked your mother to marry me, and she accepted. I’m going to be your new father.”

Phoenix starts laughing.

“Now wait a minute, that’s not funny! I don’t know what title to use as it is. Majesty, Sire, lord, now I can add son.”

“Use what is necessary at the time!” chuckles Phoenix.

“Well, lad, let’s get a move on. Tomorrow is the name day for the twins; we’ll need to get ready.”

They finish breakfast and head for the castle to set guards for the queen and the children. When they enter the castle, the queen greets them, and the boy is there as well.

“Good morning, my lady and boy, how are you? Where’s the girl?” asks Phoenix.

“We’re all doing well, your majesty,” answers the boy.

“My daughter is suffering from a broken heart; it seems.”

“Boy, have you picked a name yet?”

“Not really, I was thinking of Thomas or Peter. What do you think?”

“Either one is a good name. You know, I was considering another name when I chose Phoenix. I was thinking of the name Orion.”

“Orion? What kind of name is that?”

“Orion was a warrior; it was uncommon, and I liked it. My destiny was to be Phoenix.”

“Orion, huh, I like it. May I use it Sire?”

“Of course, you may, my brother.”

The boy, shocked by what Phoenix called him, embraces him.

Phoenix looks down on him and enfolds him in his arms, and kisses the top of his head. A tear falls from his eyes onto the boy's face.

"Are you alright, Sire?" asks the boy.

"You bet I am. Now I need to go see your sister and mine to see if I can cheer her up." Phoenix walks away to the Girl's room.

"Mom, why did Phoenix cry?"

The queen pulls her Son into her arms and leans her head on the boys, and whispers. "He cares about you, and you made him happy."

Phoenix knocks on the door to the girl's room. "May I enter?"

"No. Go away and leave me be!"

"Then, I'm going to have to exert my kingly rights and enter anyway."

Phoenix enters her room and sits next to her. "You're being childish; you learn something you don't like, and you pout like a little child."

"You don't love me, not like I want," she cries.

"I know, I have even turned down your mother."

"No, you didn't, did you?"

"Yes, for the same reasons, I turned you down. When she thought about it, she realized that I was right, like you, she needs the love of a good man and one who'll be around and not gone all the time."

"I see, maybe you're right," sniffs the girl.

"Now, sister, have you chosen a name for your name day?" asks Phoenix.

"Not exactly, I was thinking of Rose or Mary."

"I like either one," said Phoenix.

"If you were to choose which one do you like best?" the girl asked.

"Well, if I had to choose, Mary would be my pick. Roses have thorns. Yes, Mary sounds nicer and softer."

"Then, Mary, it shall be."

"Mary, go wash your face, and we'll go down to your mother and brother."

Mary goes over to her washbasin, washes her face, and puts on a smile. "I'm ready to go down."

Both Phoenix and Mary walk arm in arm down the stairs to be with the queen and her brother.

Phoenix and Dance Master set up the guards knowing that the children or the queen will be kidnapped anytime soon. That night Phoenix meets with the queen.

"My Lady, I have a gift for you." Phoenix hands her an amulet. It's made of star stone.

"This is nice work; did you make it?"

"Yes, and same as the children keep it with you at all times."

"Why is that, your majesty?"

"Because I can track it, I made it, so if I had to find you, I can."

"I understand, and it's quite beautiful. Do you make such things for all your friends?"

"I have." The queen kisses Phoenix on the cheek and thanks him.

CHAPTER

40

There was a lot of activity for getting the castle ready for the twin's name day. Dance Master and Phoenix assumed that would keep the kidnapers from striking so soon, but the confusion made it relatively easy. The two assassins enter the castle during the day, change to rats, and keep in hiding to wait for the other two to show up so they can strike. When it was midnight, the two men walked up the stairs to provide a distraction to the two guards at the children's doors while the rats transformed into human form and killed the guards from behind. Then they enter the boy's room, render him unconscious, and roll him up in a carpet to carry him out as if working on the name day decorations. The same process is done to the girl. The men carry the packages down to the courtyard without being stopped, and then they place the two into a cart and drive out the gate.

In the woods, they separate the boy from the girl and send him east to be carried away by the sea raiders as a hostage to keep the Phoenix from stopping them from landing on his shores. The girl is sent south to the southern kingdom to keep the Phoenix from interfering with them anymore. In the morning, the queen goes to awaken her children and finds the guards all dead and the children gone. The queen keeps her head and sends it for the Dance Master. The Phoenix and the Dance Master show up.

"My queen, what's wrong?" asks Phoenix.

"The children have been taken; the guards are all dead."

Phoenix runs up the stairs, enters the children's rooms, and finds something that they have worn. Returning downstairs. "Dance Master, you're a wolf, do you know others who are like you that you trust?"

"Yes, Sire."

"Here is a scarf from the girl's room, and here is a shirt from the boy's room to get someone on their trail."

"Yes, Sire." Dance Master leaves the castle to find who he needs.

The Phoenix sits on the floor and closes his eyes; the queen starts to say something when Phoenix holds up his hand for silences as he concentrates. Moments later, he opens his eyes. The star stones show one of the twins is headed to the east coast, and the other star stone is headed south.

"My Queen, I have located the twins, one is heading east toward the sea. I would guess it's the boy Orion, and one stone is heading south must be the girl Mary."

"Are they alright?"

"I don't know, but I'll get them back, and the people responsible will pay for this."

Phoenix was getting up to find Dance Master when a guard rushes into the room.

"Your majesty, a man gave me this note to give to the queen."

She takes the note and reads it. "It's like you said, sire. The boy is going east. To be put into the hands of the sea raiders. The girl to the southern kingdom to be married to one of the three to keep you away from them or she'll die."

"My lady, your children will be returned in two days, you have my word." I'll go get your son, and we'll be back as I said."

Phoenix locates Dance Master. "You and a few of your men go south and track the girl; I'll need a good man or two to go with me to the east. Be careful how you approach them according to the note they will kill them if they think they're being pursued."

"Yes, sire, I'll give you one wolf, and I'm taking the rest with me, and we'll hunt them down."

"I'll find you when I have Orion safe and sound with his mother."

They split up, and Phoenix meets with his party. He explains they need to be silent and catch these kidnapers without the boy being hurt. Phoenix leaps into the sky as the bird Phoenix and flies off to the south, and then he changes into an eagle and turns east to locate the boy. Down below Phoenix sees his pack of wolves following the trail while he follows the star stone knife, he gave the boy. Phoenix flies on ahead and locates the three men and the boy Orion. He ducks out of sight and changes into a sparrow to keep close tabs on the party. Soon they make camp. It's getting close to sundown, and they don't travel well in the dark. Phoenix flies back along the trail and finds his wolf pack, he changes to his human form, and they do the same.

"The camp is just ahead; we'll surround it and wait till they turn in. I'll deal with the man next to the boy, the rest of you take care of the other two."

"Yes, Sire."

Phoenix changes to a sparrow to hide in the tree above the boy.

The wolf pack encircles the camp to wait. As the fire dies out, they attack. Phoenix changes to his human form and drops down from the tree limb onto the man next to the boy crushing his rib cage, killing him. Before the other two men can react, they're face to face with the snapping jaws of a wolf.

"Bind them up and bring them back to the castle. Be careful. They can change to rats."

One of the men changes into a rat and makes a mad dash to the woods, and Phoenix burns him to ash. Then he turns to the other one. "Are you going to cooperate or wind up like your friend?"

The man changes into a rat, and the wolf man ties up the rat so he can't escape. "We'll meet you back at the castle, sire."

Phoenix turns to Orion, "Are you ready to go home?"

Wide-eyed Orion nods his head, yes. Phoenix changes to his phoenix bird form, picks up the boy in his talons and flies off toward the castle. The boy watches the ground but can't see anything because it's dark. As Phoenix approaches the castle, he announces his presence with a thunderous scream. The queen reaches the castle door as Phoenix lands and drops off Orion. Phoenix launches back up into the sky and heads south to get Mary. The queen takes Orion back into the castle and to her apartment to keep him there. The whole time Orion recounts the adventure he was just on.

Phoenix follows the star stone's call to the south; when he gets close, he changes into an eagle and soars above the treetops in the dark and realizes this is not good, so he transforms into an owl that has better eyesight in the dark. Phoenix floats noisily above the trees until he spots Dance Master and his pack. Phoenix drops lower and changes to his human form, so does Dance Master.

"How's it going?" asks Phoenix.

"Well, sire, they're just a few miles ahead of us, we'll catch up to them by dawn."

"Good, I'll be there to help, by the way, the boy is safe and at home with his mother."

"Outstanding sire."

Phoenix changes into an owl, flies ahead, to locate the camp. Perched in a nearby tree Phoenix waits for Dance Master and his pack to arrive. The wolf pack surrounds the camp, and Phoenix provides the distraction. Phoenix lands on the man guarding Mary in his Phoenix form, and he screams in his thunderous voice, giving the wolf pack time to capture the other two men. One man had pulled a knife to throw it at the girl when his hand stopped. Dance Master turned the hand with the knife so that the blade was at the man's throat.

"Now you weren't going to throw that knife at my King, were you?"

He shakes his head, no.

"Good, drop the knife, or use it on yourself."

The man drops the knife.

"You men, truss up the men and take them back to the castle, first make them change to small animals," said Dance Master.

Mary speaks up, "those two can change into rats, and this one into a raven."

At the mention of their animal forms, the two rats change and try to escape. Phoenix prevents the escape by surrounding the two in a ring of fire.

"Thank you, sire, it would've taken a lot of effort to capture them had they escaped," said one of the men.

The raven gets the same treatment. Once they have the prisoners secure, Dance Master and the others head back to the castle.

"I'll see you in one-week men; Mary and I have another task to perform." Phoenix changes into his bird form, picks up Mary, and flies south to the southern kingdom. When he arrives, he sounds off, wakes everyone up, and lands in the courtyard. The three rulers appear on the top steps and look down upon Phoenix.

"Why are you here? Wasn't the note explicit enough? We'll kill the young girl if you continue to interfere."

"You mean this girl?" Phoenix steps away from his charge, and she stands up.

"How, did you get her back?"

"That's not important; the fact you confessed is. I'm taking you back with me to my castle as my prisoners."

The three men change into animals to try to escape Phoenix. (rat, snake, and a raven).

Phoenix encases them in a fiery cage to keep them in place.

"Where's your blacksmith? Bring him to me."

The blacksmith limps from the stable area. "You called for me?"

"I did; I need a cage for these vermin so I can carry them back to my castle to deal out justice. Do you have, or can you make me a cage?"

"I have just such a cage in my smithy; I'll be back shortly."

Several minutes trickle by, and the blacksmith returns, carrying a cage with fine mesh screen. "Will this do?"

"That's perfect; thank you for your help." Phoenix hands him a gold coin.

Phoenix sees the three villains put into the cage, and he seals it shut by welding the door closed so only he can open it.

"Mary, follow me." Phoenix walks off in the direction of the smithy.

"Blacksmith, where are you?"

"Here, sir."

"I'm curious; do you know who I am?"

"I suppose you're my king."

"Just so, why do you not address me as such?"

"I only address people who have earned my respect, until you do; you're just somebody to get in my way."

"What's your name?" asks Phoenix.

"I'm called Angus."

"Angus, you are a man after my own heart, you have no respecter of persons, my kind of a man."

"You mean you're not here to scold me for not using your title?"

"Not at all. I have two propositions for you. One, do you know how to work with star stone?"

"What's that?"

"Mary, please hand me your knife; I'll return it to you in a few moments." Mary hands her knife over to Phoenix.

Phoenix hands the knife to Angus. "This is star stone, and I forged it."

Angus takes the knife and turns it over and over, then tests the edge of it and cuts his thumb.

"This is excellent quality; you said you made it?"

"I did, all but some of the engraving my grandfather helped me with that. Would you like to learn how to work with this star stone?"

"I sure would!"

"Good, I can teach you but not today I have to return Mary to her mother. Second proposition I need a person to rule here in the southern kingdom, if I ask you would you do it?"

"I don't know who would convince the people here to follow my ruling."

"I will, and they'll know it today."

Angus's hands back the knife, "You'll teach me to work with star stone?"

"It'll be my pleasure."

"You'll give me the authority to rule here."

"I will."

"Shake my hand on it."

Phoenix takes Angus's hand, and they shake.

"Yep, you have worked in a forge; I feel the rough hands, and the strength in them. I accept."

"Angus, have you started your forge yet?"

"No, I was about to when you called me to the courtyard."

Phoenix walks deeper into the smithy and spy's the forge and puts his hand on it, and it bursts into flame.

Angus's eyes get huge, "How'd you do that?"

"Come with me, Mary and Angus, it's time to announce the new ruler of this place."

Out in the courtyard, Phoenix strolls out to the steps and climbs them to the top, with Mary and Angus tagging along.

"Gather everyone here," and everyone within hearing distance gathers around the courtyard.

"As of today, the three rulers have been arrested in a royal conspiracy and will be taken to my castle for trial. As of today, Angus here will rule in my stead!"

"What if we don't listen to him?" shouts someone from the crowd.

"Then, I'll do this to the people who don't obey." Phoenix passes his hand over a small pile of chopped wood and burns it to ash.

Everyone stood there, looking at the ash and shuts up.

"Angus will follow my accords; he'll have the rule to assign or demote anyone he chooses. One last thing if Angus is assassinated or harmed, I'll do to all the people of this castle what I did to the woodpile. Am I clear?"

No one contests the Phoenix; he looks at a few elites and has them move the cage into the courtyard. He can see the resentment in their eyes. He and Mary follow them down into the courtyard. Then he whispers to the three men carrying the cage. "If Angus meets any problems or harm, I'll hold you three responsible. Do you understand?" Wide-eyed, they nod yes.

Phoenix changes into his bird form and collects Mary in one talon, then he grabs the cage in the other and launches into the air; with a scream, he sets off to the north with his charge and the prisoners.

It takes Phoenix all day to cover the distance to the castle, and he passes the wolf pack, who'll take a couple of more days to cover the same distance. At sundown, the Phoenix lets the castle know he's there, and he lands in the courtyard.

Chapter

41

The queen was there to receive them looking for her daughter, who she swept away to her room to make sure her daughter was still untouched. To her relief, she was untouched.

Phoenix had the cage guarded until the Dance Master and his men return. Later that next day, the wolf pack from the east arrived with their prisoner, to add them to the cage.

"Phoenix sire, what do you want done to these men?" asks the Dance Master.

"Nothing, I'll deal with them tomorrow morning."

"As you wish, sire."

The next morning, Phoenix takes his leave of the queen to take care of the caged villains. He grabs the cage, launches into the air with the cage in tow, and heads east towards the sea. It takes a day to reach the coast and three days to cross the ocean to the sea raiders' land.

Phoenix reaches in, grabs the raven, and takes him out of the cage; then, he welds the cage up so the snake, monkey or rats can't climb out.

"Well, my not so fine feathered friend change to your human form." The raven refuses at first until Phoenix grabs a wing and burns the long feathers off his wing, and he changes to human form. On the Phoenix other hand, he has a metal brand shaped like a phoenix, and he brands the man's face and lets him go. He runs off to get away from the king. Phoenix does the same to all the others in the cage. When he finished, he says, "If any of you ever show up in my kingdom of the east, I'll kill you."

It has been four days since he had any food or drink, so the king changes into an eagle and flies off to find a stream or lake. He spots a stream from high up in the air, and so he lands to get a drink, then he spots fish, so he catches one to slake his hunger. Then he finds a place to hold up to get some sleep. Refreshed Phoenix decides to set off for his trip home. He launches into the air and gets ready to leave when he sees a red blow in the north; curiosity gets the better of him, so he flies northward.

Phoenix comes to a village that has been set on fire, so he absorbs the flames and picks up a lot of energy he can use. He lands and finds everyone is dead; he walks about to see if anyone is alive. Death is everywhere. Sick to his stomach, he's ready to leave, when he hears a moan, he looks around and finds someone covered in debris. He uncovers the person to see to his horror; it's a woman with her unborn child cut from her belly. Phoenix almost throws up; he picks up the girl and holds her to comfort her.

He hears her in a weak voice, "Kill me, please!"

Phoenix looks around and sees it may be a kindness to do so, but he can't bring himself to kill her, and he cries, his tears fall on her face, and she wakes and reaches up to touch his face and the tears streaming down it.

"Please have mercy and kill me." Then she passes out.

Phoenix stands up, changes into his bird form, scoops the girl up into his talons, and rises into the air; he circles the village and burns it to ash to keep the dead bodies from being savaged by carrion eaters. Phoenix wings off into the west clutching the girl up close to him to keep her warm. Flying with a tailwind, he manages to cross the ocean in two and a half days, and then on he flies for his mother's house.

Phoenix lands in the yard, and his mother comes out to see why he's here.

Phoenix lays the girl down on the yard, picks her up, carries her into the house, and places her in his bed.

"Mother, she's dying, please see how she is."

"If she was dying, why bring her here?"

"I couldn't leave her in the village to die; she even asked me to kill her."

"What is her problem?"

"Someone cut her belly open and removed her unborn child and left her to die."

Pam runs to his room to examine the girl. What she finds confuses her.

"You did say someone cut her belly open."

"Yes, I saw the wound myself and the dead child beside her."

"Come with me," his mom uncovers the girl's belly, and all that's there is a scar, and the girl is sleeping.

"That's not what I saw; her belly was cut open."

"Come with me. I've been studying the myth of the Phoenix. Did you cry, and did your tear drops fell on her?"

"I believe so. I know I was crying for her and her village, my tears may have fallen on her, so, what?"

"Read this passage."

"The Phoenix's tears heal wounds and sickness. What, you mean, my tears have healed her?"

"You saw her scar on her belly. She's in no pain; she's just sleeping."

"We best let her sleep, speaking of that, I need to get some sleep, some food, and water, not necessarily in that order."

Pam dishes out some cold stew from her dinner, slices some bread, and sets it down before Phoenix. While he's eating, Pam has him explain why he was over in the sea raiders' land. Phoenix tells his mom all the details, and instead of killing, he banished them to that war laden land.

As Phoenix was about to take another bite, he sees his mothers' eyes go very wide; then, he feels the knife at his throat.

"Why am I here?" asks the girl.

"I brought you here."

She pressed the knife a little harder, "Why?"

"You needed help, so I helped you. You're safe here; please put the knife down."

"All I remember is my village was attacked; they gutted me and took my unborn child. Wait, I remember a man bending over me, holding my head up. I asked him for mercy."

"That was me," squeaked Phoenix.

"Then, I remember a great bird bearing me away into the heavens."

"Again, that was me. Now please put down the knife, no one here is going to hurt you."

She puts the knife down and sat down to cry. Phoenix got up and wrapped his arms around her to give comfort. She stopped and was very tired; he guided her to a chair. He could hear her stomach growling.

"Could you eat some food?"

She nodded yes, so Phoenix dished up some stew for her, and he warmed the stew in his hand before he sat it down. She ate like a starved person.

"Would you like some bread?"

She nodded, yes. Phoenix cut it up for her, and she wolfed it all down.

Phoenix points to himself, "My name is Phoenix; this is my mother, Pam. What's your name?"

She looks up, "I'm called Alana. I'm of the wolf clan."

"I can see that; you look rather wolfish. I've never seen a girl with golden eyes, and your hair has the same color as a wolf. Gray, Black, and white."

"Is that a bad thing?" she asks.

"Not at all, it looks good on you. If you've finished eating, let's put you to bed to get more rest."

Alana grabs the knife. "You'll not use me as my husband has!"

"Alana, you have nothing to fear here. Keep the knife. You can sleep in my room. I'll sleep next to the hearth."

"You'll give up your room for me?"

"Yes, it's the proper thing to do. I'll be fine."

"What a strange land this is." Alana returns to the room and is quickly asleep.

Phoenix gets a blanket and curls up on the floor to sleep. In the morning, Pam wakes up her son.

"Son, go get us something to eat, a rabbit-like creature, or a partridge will do fine."

"Sure, mom, I'll be back in a while." Phoenix walks out of the door and changes into his eagle form, and launched into the air to go hunting. He heads toward the mountain where he knows he can find something to catch. After circling high, he spots a partridge; he swoops down, grabs the creature in his talons, and carries it home. He lands in the yard and starts to cross the yard to dress out the bird.

"Phoenix, you should have gotten me up, so I could hunt with you," says Alana.

"Not this time, Alana, do you see that mountain there?"

"Yes, that's where I went hunting; it would take you at least two weeks just to get there."

"Show me, please."

Phoenix changes to an eagle then back to his human form.

"I can be a sparrow, owl, eagle, condor, and a Phoenix."

"I have never heard of a Phoenix," said Alana.

Phoenix stops dressing the bird he was working on and transforms into a small version of his bird form. It so shocked Alana that she shied away from him.

Phoenix transformed back into his human form. "Are you all right?" he asks.

"You caught me off guard is all."

Phoenix turns back to his task and finishes it. then takes it into the house to give it to his mother. She puts the bird on a spit and has her son turn the handle to keep the bird moving over the hot coals. Over the years, Phoenix has the speed down just so, and it cooks the bird just right.

"Phoenix, you keep that bird moving. Alana and I have some female things to do, and that'll keep you out of my way for the time being." Pam leads Alana out of the front door to the water trough.

"Now, young lady, remove your clothes and get into that tough."

"Why?"

"Because young lady, I told you too!"

Alana thinks about it and does what she's told. Moments later, she gets water poured all over her hair, and then she feels Pam scrubbing her down. The more Alana is washed, the more she protests. When Pam was satisfied, she let Alana out of the trough and helped her dry off; then, covered with a towel, Pam leads Alana back into the house to Pam's room with the door closed. Pam selects one of her dresses and helps Alana put it on. Then they move out to the hearth to dry and comb Alana's hair.

There was a knock at the door, so Phoenix answers it, and Dance Master is standing there.

"Come on in Dance Master; it's good to see you."

"Who's the young lady with your mom?"

"An important friend, her name is Alana. Come and meet her."

"Alana, meet Dance Master, he's my friend."

Alana looks up, "Are you the alpha male?" she sees the wolf in Dance Master.

Dance Master looks at her for a moment before he answers. "No, Phoenix, here is the alpha male."

Alana looks at Phoenix then looks back to the Dance Master, "he is not very imposing, is he?" says Alana.

Dance Master laughs, "No, Alana, he doesn't, someday we hope to fix that. On a serious note, Phoenix is the most powerful person we all know."

Alana turns to Phoenix, "Do I belong to you?"

"No, you belong to yourself, here you're free."

"What is free? I've been owned since I was born; I've been someone's property. I've never been free before."

"Alana, in my country, you're your own person, no one owns you, and the only ownership is between married people."

"Married, what is married?"

"Married is when a man and a woman want to live to gather and make a family they join, and it's for all their lives," said Pam.

"In my clan, women are not free to choose; they are forced into slavery as being the spoils of a fight, or stolen. I'm forced to clean, cook, and make children at the whim of the man who owns me. I get no say in what happens to me."

"Alanna, that'll not happen here; you have my word on that," said Phoenix.

"Mom, I must return to the southern kingdom to keep my word with the new ruler. Will it be alright to leave Alanna in your care until I return?"

"I'd be glad to look after her son. It's nice to have another woman here to talk to." Pam puts her hand on Alana's shoulder, tenderly.

Phoenix walks to the door and opens it to step out. Alana follows him.

"Phoenix, may I come with you?"

Phoenix places his hands on her shoulders and smiles before he answers her. "Alana, I can't take you on this trip, but on others, I will. You'll be safe here, I promise, and I'll be back. I think I'll miss you," smiles Phoenix.

"Are you sure you have to go?"

"Yes, Alana, I must go, I have to keep my word when I give it. I give you my word I'll return in a couple of months. Now I have to go."

Alana's face fills with tears. By this time, Pam is there to take her into her arms.

"Alana, he'll be back, in the mean time we can learn about each other."

Alana nods her head and lets Pam lead her back into the house. Phoenix launches into the air and circles the house feeling emptiness in his heart. Phoenix flies to his grandfather's house and lands in the yard to be met by his grandmother. She points to the smithy and returns into her cottage. Phoenix enters the smithy to see his grandfather hammering out a billet of steel.

"Grandfather! Do we still have some star stone left?"

"We sure do, son; it's over in that bin there," points Zeke.

"Thanks, I need to take a few with me to the southern kingdom. I have a promise to keep."

"That's fine, son, you brought it here, so take what you want."

Phoenix chooses three-star stones and shakes his grandfather's hand. "Oh, before I forget, you and grandmother should go see mom; she has a couple of guests you'll like the young girl Alana."

"We'll do that, besides your grandmother has wanted to go see your mother anyway."

Phoenix walks out to the yard and prepares to leave.

"Young man, you're not going to leave without giving me a good bye kiss, are you?" said his grandmother.

"I wouldn't dream of it," whence Phoenix.

With the kiss given and grandmother slaps his bottom, Phoenix smiles, realizing she's telling him she can still give him a spanking. Phoenix launches into the air and wings his way to the southern kingdom. It takes Phoenix several days to reach his destination, where he converts to an eagle mile out from the city and lands behind the smithy. Phoenix shoulders the bag with the star stones and walks into the smithy.

"Well, my friend, how fairs the kingdom?"

"Phoenix, my friend, I'm so glad you came. The kingdom is doing well; there have been a few incidents that took care of themselves."

"Can you tell me about them?"

"It appears that the three guilds don't like who you put in charge, and they tried to poison me, I turned the tables on them, and the guilty parties died of their own devices. Now they're scrambling to find three new leaders."

"Good! I can't afford to lose you. Before I leave to head north, I'll remind them of what I want before I leave."

"Did you bring the star stone you promised?"

Phoenix patted his bag. "It's right here, my friend."

"My friends call me Angus, and what may I call you?"

"My father's name was Todd; you, my friend, may call me that."

Angus holds out his hand and shakes Phoenix's hand. "I like that name," said Angus.

"Todd, I need to leave to deliver a repair job for a friend of mine. Would you care to come along?"

"Sure, how far away is it? I sure could use some food; it was a long flight."

"Stick with me, Todd. I'll see you get a delicious meal."

As they walk along, "Angus, do you have a wife yet?"

"No, not yet; why?"

"Have you considered someone from one of the guilds?"

"Todd, that would be a death sentence; they would think to get control of the kingdom through the girl after getting rid of her husband. I know that because I listened to the conversation from my perch in the great hall where they can't see me."

"I see, so I assume from the spring in your step we're going to see the girl you hope to win?"

"How'd you know Todd?"

"I worked in a smithy all day at the end of the day I'm usually dragging myself about unless something real interest was waiting."

"Know, wonder; you're the king. You're right, of course. Her name is Patti."

"Will she be Ok with feeding another person without warning?"

"We're about to find out, friend Todd."

Angus knocks on her door, and this beautiful woman opens the door. She has the reddest hair Phoenix has ever seen, and her green eyes almost shine, and the freckles enhance her beauty.

"Well, Angus, it's about time you returned my pot. Who's your friend who needs to close his mouth before he catches an insect?"

Angus chuckles. "Patti, this young man is named Todd. He just brought me some star stone, and he has had a long journey. I brought him here to get a good meal. Will it be alright?"

"Yea, both of you get in here."

"Angus, sit at your usual place, Todd, you sit there at my place."

"Aren't you going to sit with us, Patti?" asks Todd.

"I wasn't going to."

"Please sit with us; we need such a stunning girl as you to set the table off."

Patti gave Todd a look that said, that's a lot of bull.

"No, Patti, I mean it," said Todd.

Patti pulled down another place setting and sat close to Angus. She served up a tremendously hardy stew; it was excellent. Todd had two helpings. When it was done, Todd reached into his pocket, pulled out a gold piece, and gave it to her.

"Patti, that meal was worthy of a king."

"Now Todd, we both know it's not true; no king would eat such food," said Patti.

"We'll see. Now, Angus, you'll ask this woman to marry you; if you don't, I will."

Angus's face turns to beat red, and Patti stands aghast and shocked.

"No, who're you Todd, to be telling a man or woman for that matter to get married," said Patti.

"Well, Angus, what do you say?"

Angus's face turns even redder, he loosens his collar, and his mouth moves like a fish out of the water, opening and closing without saying anything.

"Angus, do you want to marry Patti here?"

Angus nods his head, yes.

"Well, man, get down on your knee and take her hand."

Angus does as he's told. "Angus, do you want to marry Patti?"

Angus chocks on the words. "I..."

"Angus, just say yes!" commands Todd.

Angus crocks, "Yes."

"Now, Patti, will you accept his request?"

"Yes!" and she pulls Angus to her and holds him. Is this what it takes to get something out of you?"

Angus just holds on to her, "Yes."

With a bit of anger in her voice, "what right do you have forcing people into decisions?"

"Remember a bit ago. I mentioned a meal fit for a king?"

"Yes, what of it?"

"I am King Phoenix."

"You can't be him, look at how you're dressed."

"I know it's not impressive, but it makes it easy to walk among the people to see how they are doing and if the people I have in charge are doing their job."

"You're really the king?"

"Yes, Now I need a place to sleep. Do you have a barn with hay?"

"No, your majesty, you'll sleep in my bed."

"Patti, under your roof, or in your yard, you're in charge, and I'll follow your orders. Now Angus and I will wash your dishes and turn in for the night, or at least I will."

"But!"

"Angus, do you want to wash or dry?"

The dishes are washed, and Patti puts them away. Phoenix gets a blanket and is shown where the barn is, and he turns in for the night. Patti and Angus spend the next few hours talking mostly about being married to each other. Morning comes, and Phoenix wakes Angus.

"I'll be at the smithy in an hour; it's time to make a grand entrance as Phoenix."

"I'll fly ahead to meet you there," says Angus. Angus changes to a swallow and flies back to his smithy.

Phoenix changes into a sparrow and flies north of the castle. Then changes to the Phoenix and flies over the castle to announce his arrival. As Phoenix lands, he is met by Angus and the new leaders of the guilds.

"Welcome your majesty!" says Angus.

"Thank you, Angus! May we go somewhere to talk?" asks Phoenix.

Angus leads the way to the smithy. The two men work the day away forging star stone. Phoenix forges a small wolf head, and Angus forges a dagger from star stone.

"Phoenix, this is great; after I sharpen and polish it, it will hold its edge; what did you make?"

"I'm making a wolf head necklace for someone I know. I hope she'll like it."

"Are you going to engrave it like the knife you carry?"

"Yes, but my grandfather engraved the knife, not I. I've kept my promise, and there is an extra star stone you can have. I'm going to make my entrance and departure. I have other places to go to."

Phoenix walks from the smithy, transforms into the phoenix, and screams out to get everyone's attention. Soon everyone fills the courtyard.

"I've been here, and I find something disturbing. I've learned that someone has tried to kill the person I chose to rule over you. I'll no longer tolerate this behavior."

Phoenix transforms into his human form and climbs the steps to where the three guild members are. Phoenix placed his hand on the wooden lintel of the door and branded his mark into the wood.

"The first rulers felt this brand on their faces before I banished them. In the next incident, I'll hold the whole guild responsible. Watch that block of stone."

Phoenix points at the block and reduces it to a small pile of rubble.

"If any harm comes to Angus, my new ruler, I'll take it out on the whole guild and reduce you to ash."

Phoenix turns to the three guild leaders and asks, "Do you understand?"

They turn pale as they confront Phoenix. "We understand your majesty!"

"Good, see that you remember." Phoenix launches into the air and hovers, and he carves his sign into the stone steps of the castle. "This is my reminder to you all."

Phoenix left his mother's home weeks ago.

Alana stood outside to watch Phoenix as he flew off, feeling sad and empty. This is new to Alana. She never felt this way before; all she ever felt was fear from her owner. Always fear and dread. What's wrong with her, she wonders. She starts to cry. Pam watches Alana from the window, then walks out to Alana and takes her into her arms to calm her down.

"What's the matter, Alana?"

"I don't know. What strange power does your son have over me? I feel so empty without him here."

Pam smiles, "Alana, you have fallen in love with my son."

"What is love?" asks Alana.

"It's difficult to explain; it can be great joy and happiness or cause great pain."

"I'm in pain now, Pam, will I get better?"

"Yes, I'm sure of it. Now come back into the house, and let's talk."

In the house, Dance Master was making some repairs to one of Pam's chairs. Pam directs Alana to Phoenix's room.

Chapter

42

"Alana, tell me about your life with the sea raiders."

Alana tells Pam what life is like as a slave to the sea raiders, how women were nothing more than livestock to be traded, sold, and used. Sometimes they were the spoils of war. You were not your own; you belonged to some man who could do what he wanted to you.

"I was carrying a child when we were attacked, and they wiped out the whole village. Me they captured and cut me open and took my child. Then they left me to suffer and die. I must have passed out, and your son found me. I asked him for mercy. Then he cradled my head and cried over me; I felt his tears as they fell on my face. I remember I reached up and touched his face. Then I passed out. The next thing I was here."

"Alana come with me; I want to show you something."

Pam led Alana into the kitchen, then Pam reached a small book from the shelf, placed it on the table, opened up to a page, and told Alana to read the Phoenix's legend. Alana turned the book this way and that way, then looked up.

"I don't know how to read."

"Here, I will read it to you," said Pam.

"The Phoenix is a great bird of fire, and he lives for a thousand years, then bursts into flame and is reborn from the ashes. The Phoenix can carry great weight. His tears can heal the sick or wounded."

"You mean when he cried on me, I became healed?"

"Yes, Alana, the thing is He didn't know that. He cried because he couldn't save you at the time, which caused him to cry. I'm glad he did."

"Then that's how he saved me?"

"Yes, now it's time to teach you how to read and write. In the morning after breakfast, you'll spend the morning learning to write."

Then chimed in Dance Master, "in the evening, I'll teach you to dance, and to dance with a sword."

"Now Alana, go wash your face; we have work to do, it'll help pass the time until Phoenix returns.

Alana learns to write her letters, and it goes fast in a month. She is reading every book she can get. Pam sits with her to help her pronounce some of the newer words. After lunch, Alana learns to dance with Dance Master; then, he teaches her how to dance with a sword. Alana becomes as good with the sword as Phoenix is.

During the mornings Alana and Pam were reading. Dance Master would run over to Zeke's smithy and gave him a commission to make another rapier for Alana like the ones he made for him.

"Dance Master, who is this sword for?"

"I'm going to give it to Alana as a type of graduation gift."

"She, like you, becomes a wolf, right?"

"Yes, she does."

"Ok, we'll both work on it. I need someone to pump the bellows, and Phoenix isn't here to help."

"I can do that."

"Good, Tell Pam and Alana you'll be helping me tomorrow all day."

"I will." Dance Master leaves to return to the ladies.

The next day at the smithy, Dance Master is waiting for Zeke to return from his morning flight, he's ready to put in a day of work. As he remains, Lisa calls him to the house to give him some tea while he waits. Then she asks some pointed questions.

"Well, now Dance Master, when are you going to marry my daughter?"

"I…"

"That's why you came to see her, isn't it?"

"Well, I."

"Take your foot out of your mouth. Both Zeke and I approve. Zeke can help you make a gift for her if you ask him. Now get out to the smithy Zeke just landed."

Dance Master walks out to the smithy expecting the same grilling he was getting from Lisa and was pleasantly surprised to see Zeke directing him to pump the bellows to heat the star stone. The rest of the day is spent forging the metal into a sword blade and then the hilt and guard. Now all is left is to weld it all together, polish, and sharpen the blade. Zeke also is going to engrave it special for Alana and provide her a sheath to carry the sword.

"Now, Dance Master, come to dinner with us."

"I should be getting back to Pam."

"You'll eat with us tonight. Pam already knows you'll be here for dinner."

"How can I turn down such an invitation?"

"You can't; we want you to know we approve of you marrying our daughter. If you return here tomorrow, we'll work on your gift for her."

"Alright, I will ask her tonight when I return. After all, Phoenix, as much as told me to marry her, I wouldn't want to disobey my king."

After dinner with Lisa and Zeke, Zeke brought a box and opened it to display several crystals.

"Pick one, and we can cut and set it into an amulet for you to give Pam. She likes the blue or red ones."

"How about this blue one?" asks Dance Master.

"Come back in two days, and we'll work on it. That'll give me time to finish the rapier," said Zeke.

Dance Master returns to Pam's house; all the way there, he rehearses what he will say to Pam. He knocks on the door, and Alana opens the door. Dance Master enters and sees Pam at the hearth. He walks up to her forgetting all that he was going to say. He takes her hands, drops to one knee in front of her, and croaks out, "Marry me?"

Pam is of two minds; she wants to jump up and down and squeal like a girl or break into tears. She stands there, composing herself and says, "Yes!"

Dance Master stands up, takes her into his arms, and hugs her. "That was the hardest thing I've ever had to say; thanks for accepting."

The whole time Alana watched, not saying a thing, and perceiving the wonderful thing that just took place in front of her. Pam watches Alana and walks over to her. "Yes, love hurts, but it feels wonderful to Alana. I think you'll find out about it yourself."

Alana believes she needs to leave them alone she returns to Phoenix's room. Alana can smell Phoenix all over the room, and she's glad she can at least have this much of him for now.

Two days later, Pam, Dance Master, and Alana travel to the smithy to visit Lisa, to give her the news. Dance Master goes to work with Zeke on his wedding gift. The women put their heads together and talk about the upcoming wedding, while the men work in the smithy.

They all get together for dinner and conversation and they talk late into the night. Pam and Alana retire to Pam's old room, and Dance Master retires to the smithy to sleep in the hay bed that Phoenix used when he slept there. In the morning, Zeke hands the sword over to Dance Master, "what do you think?"

Dance Master pulls the sword from the ornate sheath and wheels it about. "Zeke, this is one of the best swords I have ever held, perfect balance and weight. He flexes the blade. This is strong, as well."

"Then, it'll be a good gift."

"I love the wolf pattern you engraved on it. She'll be proud to own such a weapon."

The Dance Master called to Pam and Alana to return to Pam's cottage; the women hugged and passed kisses and promised to return for visits. It takes just under an hour to reach the cottage and start the day out with Alana reading.

Phoenix's several-day journey back to castle Phoenix from the south finds everyone in a flurry of activity, so Phoenix's arrival seems to go unnoticed, curious Phoenix enters the castle over in the corner of the throne room the queen and several people are having a conversation. Phoenix had a long flight, and is tired and hungry. A short time later, Phoenix found the kitchen.

"Chief, what do you have for a sandwich?"

"Majesty, what's a sandwich?"

"Follow my instruction, and I'll teach you. Cut two slices of bread about so thick."

"You mean like this?"

"That's great; now slice off a thin slice of cheese, then some meat."

"Will this do?"

"Perfect, now put down one slice of bread, then the cheese, the meat, and the last slice of bread. Now we have a sandwich. Now, if I could get some mead to drink, I'll be all set."

"Your majesty, may I use the sandwich for the festival?"

"Sure, do what you want, with the idea. Could you please get or send someone to get me some cold mead?"

"I'll get it and bring it to your room, sire."

"Thank you."

Phoenix retires to his room to sleep the day away; at evening, he dresses in some clean clothes, grabs his dirty ones, and takes them down to have them cleaned, and he joins in on evening meal. As Phoenix enters the dining room, he winds up being attacked by a blond-haired cutie with hugs and kisses, followed by Orion with a handshake and the queen with a hug and kiss from her as well.

"Sire, when did you get here?" asks the queen.

"This morning, but with all the activity, no one saw me, so I took advantage to get some food hence the sandwich and some mead, then I slept the rest of the day."

"May I bring you up to date, sire? It was advised to have a festival to bring prospective suitors for the children, so we're planning the festivities."

"How are you going to inform the outside world of this?"

"Well, brother, we were hoping you'd help us out there, you do travel to so many places," said Mary.

"Do you have the invitations made up?" asks Phoenix.

"Yes. I can have them here by morning," said the queen.

"Ok, send ten of the invitations to the west; I'll take the rest to the south and east."

"We'll do that, here's a copy of the invitation," said Orion.

Phoenix read it, "two months, that'll be a bit tight for the eastern towns. Question where are you going to put everyone when they get here?"

"We'll set up tents in the courtyard and just outside the walls of the castle," said the queen.

"Sounds like you have this well in hand, so I'll leave it to you to deal with."

Phoenix took Orion with him to go out to the village outside the castle walls to talk to the local people. Orion asked Phoenix why are they doing this walking about. Phoenix educated him that these are the people who will suffer the brunt of this festival and should be included in the planning of this festival. After questioning the people, Phoenix is satisfied that the people want to do this too, and Orion got his first good lesson on how to rule wisely.

"Phoenix, why do you take the trouble to talk with the common people?"

"Because Orion I come from what you call common people. Rulers tend to forget that the common people, is what makes the economy work."

"I don't understand."

"Ok, did you see these people when your father ruled this land?'"

"No."

Phoenix waved his hand over the area, "These people were slaves, they were run down and living in pigsties. What do you see now?"

"I see cottages, and the people seem to be happy."

"Good, a good ruler looks after the people, not the guild."

"The guild they're powerful, I see it."

"They are corrupt Orion, they goaded your father to attack me, they could've cautioned him, but didn't. They got the king's ear and filled it with hate and lust. My advice would be to trust yourself and not others for advice. A good place to start is with the common people."

"Phoenix, if the guild is powerful, wouldn't it be better to listen to them?"

"Ok, Orion, let's look at the numbers. Would you rather have three hundred people angry with you or a handful?"

"I suppose a handful."

"Me too. I can deal with the guild I already have, and if necessary, I'll deal with them here as well."

"How did you deal with them?"

"I threatened to kill them all if the ruler to the south was killed, and I gave them a demonstration of how I would do it, when I finished, they were scared."

"I need to tell my mother about this. The guild has been talking to her."

"I see. I'll set these guild members straight."

"Are we done here, brother?"

"Yes, we'll return. I have a long day tomorrow."

In the morning, Phoenix went to the guild house to have a conversation with them.

"I hear you're giving the queen advice; you'll stop it now if you continue, I'll stop it my way by killing you all."

"Your majesty, we mean no harm or disrespect."

"Yes, you do. You'll no longer consult with the queen; if you need to consult, you'll only consult to me, is that clear?"

"Your majesty, you…"

Phoenix rings them in with flames. "Is that CLEAR!"

"Yes!"

Phoenix puts out the fire. "One other thing, if anything goes wrong at the festival, I will hold you responsible and I'll kill you."

The guild members turn pale, "Yes, your majesty."

Phoenix leaves to deliver the invitations. Phoenix walks out to the middle of the courtyard and launches into the air as the Phoenix, screeching his thunderous cry. He's then gone to deliver the invitations to the kingdoms to the south and east of the castle. It takes a month to invite everyone to the festival. Everyone seems to be excited and willing to travel the distance. The last stop is the village east of the place where his mother lives to see his old dance partner and see how she's doing.

Phoenix lands in his bird form, and Brad, a friend, meets him.

"Hi Brad, how's Pam, your wife?"

"Very large with child, it may be twins, the midwife isn't sure yet."

"May I see her before I leave for home?"

"Please, come with me. If she knew you were here and didn't come and see her, she wouldn't talk to me for a year."

"We wouldn't want that, now would we?"

Phoenix is let in to see Pam at Brad's house, and she's excited to see him. "Phoenix! It's so nice of you to visit me."

"It's always good to see you, Pam, I was going to ask for a dance, but I see that's out of the question."

Phoenix sees the paleness of her face, and he leans over to kiss her. When a tear falls on her face, her color immediately returns to normal, and she seems more robust. "I must go. I have much to do Pam, I'll be back to see your new children."

"Thank you, your majesty; I'll look forward to it."

Brad walks Phoenix out the door and back to the square.

"Brad, what's wrong with her?"

"No one knows, they're saying they may have to cut her open to deliver the children."

"Brad, I think she'll be fine now."

"How do you know?" asks Brad.

"Trust me. If you have to deliver the children the way you said, send me a message, I can help."

"Yes, anything to save my wife."

"Bye Brad, I really must go, you know where my mom lives?"

"Kind of."

"Send someone who can fly; they'll find her house in that direction, points Phoenix.

Phoenix springs into the air to fly home. It'll be good to see Mom and Alana thinks Phoenix.

An hour later, Phoenix lands in the front yard of his mother's house; Phoenix just makes it to the door when an explosion of happy glees and two arms encircle his neck. All he hears is her saying; you're home. Phoenix wraps his arms around her waist and holds her. Phoenix feels strange holding Alana; it feels different, somewhat nice. Phoenix looks over her shoulder to see his mom and Dance Master standing there, smiling.

"What did I miss?" asks Phoenix of his mother.

Phoenix disentangles himself from Alana, but he holds her hand to keep her from going all entangled again. They all retire to the table to catch up on all the news. Phoenix tells them about the festival at castle Phoenix and how everyone is doing. Alana is excited about going to the festival. After a meal, Phoenix decides to get some sleep.

"Where are you going to sleep, son?" asks his mom.

"I thought I'd go to the smithy and sleep in the hay. I figure Dance Master will sleep next to the hearth."

"Sleep in your room Phoenix, I'll sleep on the floor next to you," said Alana.

"No, Alana, that's not the right thing to do, I'll be back in the morning."

"Your mother and Dance Master are to be married. Does that matter?"

"Only after they get married. Now be a good young lady, and I'll be back in the morning."

The whole time Pam and Dance Master are watching with a knowing smile, but not saying a word. They learned when Alana has made up her mind; she'll stick to it. They all walk out to the yard and watch Phoenix launch into the air and fly toward the smithy. Shortly Alana changes into a wolf and chases after him.

"I expected that; I hope my son will realize that she's not going to quit until they marry. In her way, she already owns him."

Pam and Dance Master return to the house and talk into the late hours about their future. Phoenix lets his grandparents know he's there and will be sleeping in the smithy. Phoenix lays down on his straw bed and falls into a deep sleep. An hour later, Alana shows up, and Lisa steps out to ask her what she needs.

"Where is my Phoenix?"

Lisa smiles and points to the smithy. "He will be at the far end." Lisa returns to her house.

Alana walks in softly so as not to disturb Phoenix's sleep; she curls up beside him and shares his blanket. With the fall of the night, she falls asleep. She feels her heart fill as Pam said it would with great joy being close to her man. In the morning, Phoenix wakes to find Alana asleep using his arm as a pillow. He's about to scold her and changes his mind. He realizes how pleasant it is to have her so near to him. He watches her and studies her face, the wolf colored hair and that pretty face, then her eyes open, and he is again taken in by the gold color of her eyes. Smiling, Phoenix leans down and kisses her. Alana looks at him wide-eyed, she has never been kissed before, and her arms snake around his neck to pull him down on her.

"No, Alana, not now. When we marry, not until then."

"You will marry me?"

"Yes, that's if you want to."

Phoenix gets up and pulls on his shirt. "Let's go find some breakfast, Alana."

When they step out, Lisa is there, waving them to come into the house. She has them sit down and feeds them breakfast.

"Grandmother, we should go to mom's house."

"No! Young man, you'll not. Your mother should have some time with her new husband to be."

"But grandmother."

"No, buts! You also need to spend some time with your future bride alone."

"I've not formally asked her yet."

"Then get to it, young man, you did just sleep with her all night."

"I didn't know she was there."

Armed with a spoon and a look that will brook no more nonsense, "Well!"

Phoenix gets up from the table, kneels before Alana, and takes her hand. "Will you, Alana be my wife?"

Her answer is immediate; she springs from her chair and tackles Phoenix knocking them to the floor with tears flowing and with her holding on to his neck. "YES!"

Laughing, Phoenix picks them up from off the floor. Grandmother applauds the couple.

"Your mother and Dance Master are going to marry in a few more days, why not you two as well?"

Phoenix turns to Alana, "What do you say?"

"Oh, Yes!"

"I need to work in the smithy today; I wonder if grandfather is back, yet I need some of his help."

Phoenix walks out to the smithy, followed by Alana; as he enters the door, he can hear his grandfather working to stoke up the fire in the forge.

"Grandfather, may I use your engraving tools?"

"What for a son?"

"I started this medallion teaching a friend of mine how to work star stone. I'd like to finish it."

Grandfather takes the medallion and looks it over. "Nice work, you know where the tools are."

"Thank you."

Chapter 43

Phoenix seats himself at the bench to start engraving greater detail into the wolf shaped medallion and Alana not asking any questions hoovers over Phoenix, trying to see what he's doing. Grandfather is watching and decides he needs some help.

"Alana, would you like to help me over here?"

At first, she doesn't want to be too far from her husband to be, then realizes she can watch him from the short distance. Zeke takes her to the bellows and shows her how to pump it to keep the fire hot. Zeke didn't need the help, but he could see his grandson getting agitated and so to head off a squabble, he put her to work to keep her mind busy and out of Phoenix's way. By the end of the day they are all covered in dirt from the forge, Alana was happy she got to help and remain close to Phoenix. Grandfather approaches his grandson, "Let's see what you've done?"

Phoenix hands over the medallion, and grandfather turns it over and looks at it from different angles, letting Alana see it as well.

"Son, you are doing very well. You could sell this for a lot of money. It nearly looks real."

That's high praise of his work from grandfather. Grandfather hands the medallion to Alana to look at.

Alana looks to Phoenix "this is so pretty; would you make one for me some time?"

Phoenix looks at her trying to deciding to give her the medallion now, or on the wedding day, he decides to wait.

"Yes, Alana, I'll make one for you."

Her face lights up with joy; no man has ever given her anything, except beatings, she can hardly wait.

"Grandfather, how is the meat supply doing? I think I'd like to go hunt something up to help with feeding us."

"We could use some meat. Your grandmother is about to start asking me to go scare something up."

"Great, Alana, and I can go get you some meat. Any preference?"

"Not really."

Alana looks to be in shock, "you'll take me hunting with you?"

"Sure, it'll be fun, come with me. Grandfather, we'll be back in a couple of hours."

Phoenix leads Alana to the center of the yard, and he changes to Phoenix the bird, scoops her up in his talons, and flies off toward the mountain valley. He changes back to his human form upon landing.

"Alana, you change into the wolf, and I'll change to my eagle form, I'll distract the deer, and you hamstring it, and I can cut its throat."

She agrees to the tactics, Phoenix changes to his eagle form and launches into the air to find the deer. While floating on the air currents searching for game, Phoenix eyes spot a bird that doesn't belong here; he only watches it for a few moments when he spies a deer. Phoenix circles the spot where he found the deer and waits until Alana catches up. She positions herself to wait for Phoenix to distract the deer. Phoenix dives down on to the deer and hits the deer in its face allowing Alana to run up and hamstring the deer. Phoenix changes to human form, and using his knife slashes the deer's throat.

"Alana, we work well together, good job!"

"Do you want me to gut and skin the deer?" asks Alana.

"No, it'll be easier to carry back as it is, then we can skin and gut it. Alana, did you see the sea bird as it flew by?"

"No, I was scenting the spoor looking for a deer, I saw nothing."

"It was probably nothing, let's return to grandfather with our prize."

Phoenix scoops up Alana and the deer and flies back to grandfather's house and lands in the front yard with Alana and the deer. Grandfather helps them carry the deer to the back of the smithy and hang it up on the rack so they can work with it. Alana using the knife that Phoenix gave her she starts to cut open the deer to gut it when Phoenix plucks the knife out of her hand.

"Did I do something wrong?" she asks.

"Not really, but if I let you get that dress covered in blood and guts, my mother would kill me."

"No, she won't. I'd not let her!"

Grandfather laughs, "He is right, you know, come with me. I'll give you something to wear that you can get dirty." He leads her into the smithy, and he finds some old clothes that should fit her well enough.

"Here, Alana, you can change your clothes in the curtained off area."

"Why?"

"It's just the way we are."

"It seems strange, in my village, the woman went without clothes most of the time."

She takes the old clothes and changes in them behind the curtain, and when she returns to the back of the shed, she helps to cleans out and skin the deer; Phoenix helps, and he takes the liver and heart to grandmother. After dinner, Phoenix stretches and proclaims a need to get some sleep. He wonders out to the smithy to his straw bed; he gives up on trying to get Alana to use his mother's old room. Both curls up on the blanket, and with a couple of kisses, they go off to sleep. In the morning, Phoenix wakes and watches Alana sleep, her face is so happy and beautiful. He realizes when they marry, he'll have to keep her with him wherever he goes. That won't be so bad, he thinks.

"Alana, wake up, it's time to get up."

She opens her eyes and smiles. "This would be more fun if we were naked," she said.

Phoenix's face turns bright red, and she laughs. Looking into his eyes, "I love you! I've never loved anyone before."

He leans over to kiss her, "Alana, I love you too! Now let's get up."

They head to the water trough to wash up for breakfast, and then for some breakfast.

The two enter the house to find Pam, Dance Master, and Lisa sitting around the table.

"I hear you propose to Alana sire," said Dance Master.

"Is it getting hot in here or is it me? Yes, I did ask her."

Alana turns to Pam, "can I marry him right now?"

"You could, but will you wait until tomorrow, there's much to do, and I could use your help."

"Oh, OK, I'll wait. What help do you need?"

"You'll spend the day with my mother and me to get ready for the marriage ceremony."

"The whole day? Will I get to be with Phoenix?"

"No, just us girls, it'll be work and fun, and the men can do what they do."

The women are swept up in all they want to get done. The men retire to the smithy to talk and wait. "Your majesty, do you have any fine clothes to wear to your wedding?"

"Not really."

"Can you fly us to the castle and back today?"

"I can, but I can't carry anyone going that fast."

"That's fine. I have some clothes for me, fly to the castle and ask the queen and Orion to help pick out some tasteful clothes."

"If I leave this minute. I might make it. Explain to Alana why I left."

"We'll take care of it."

Phoenix walks behind the smithy out of sight and changes into a falcon the flies off, hoping Alana doesn't see him go and try to follow him. Phoenix drops down into the valley then changes to the Phoenix, and he climbs into the sky to make up some time. As Phoenix climbs, he sees a sea bird again flying toward the direction of the castle. He ignores it for the sake of time. It's later than midday when he arrives unannounced, he flies into the throne room in his sparrow guise to see what's going on and he finds the queen alone. Phoenix drops down to where the queen is sitting.

"My queen, I need your help?"

She almost faints away at the sudden appearance of the Phoenix.

"Are you OK, my queen?"

"You shocked me out of a year's growth with that sudden

appearance."

"I'm truly sorry. I need your help. I'm to be married tomorrow, and I need a tasteful set of clothes to wear. Will you help me?"

"Majesty, you're getting married?"

"Yes, I'm sorry to let you know in this way. I'll be bringing her to your festival. I must warn you she is no lady, and she speaks her mind."

"Majesty, we will accept her and make her welcome."

"Thank you. Now I need a set of clothes."

The queen leads him to her husband's room and opens his closet, she rummages around and pulls out several sets of clothes. Phoenix selects the least gaudy of all the outfits.

Phoenix bundles the clothes into a bag and runs out of the room and the castle, calling back, "Thank you, queen, and tell everyone I give them my love and about my marriage."

Phoenix launches into the sky and sets out for home; he arrives in time for dinner, and he is scolded by his future bride for leaving and not telling her where he went. Alana was going to carry on for several more minutes. When Phoenix grabs Alana by the shoulders, then pulls her into a hug and soundly plants a kiss on her lips. He releases her, she steps back, then both hands go to her face, and she turns red-faced. It left her speechless, and she turns to runs off into his mom's old room.

"Is she OK?"

"She will be when she recovers from her shock."

Dance Master pats him on the shoulder. "I intend to file that bit of information away. It worked well to stop the squabble."

"I didn't plan it; it was just some that came to me."

"It worked, just remember it for the future."

"Well, gentlemen, let's retire to the smithy," said Zeke.

Phoenix saw something his grandpa never did before, Zeke took three tankards done from a shelf, then went to the back of the smithy and swept the floor and located his hidden door and opened it up and entered, he returned a few minutes later, with a jug. He poured all three tankards full of mead and passed them out. He watched Phoenix as he took a drink Zeke was disappointed that Phoenix didn't chock on the liquid.

"I've had mead before grandfather. Some of the kingdoms it's an insult not to partake. I'll tell you this. The first time I drank I did chock."

Phoenix pulls his clothes from his bag and hung them up to air them out and hopefully get out any wrinkles.

"That's some fancy duds, boy," said grandfather.

"I know, but it was the least pretenses of all the choices I had to choose from. I hope they'll work."

"Well, son, have you figured where you'll spend your marriage night?"

"What do you mean, grandpa?"

"Look at this, your mother and Dance Master will return to her cottage to spend the night, you're not going to want to stay here."

"I don't have any place else I can go, no wait; I'll go to the village near the east coast. There's an inn there where we can stay."

"Well, let's get some sleep, tomorrow promises to be busy," said Dance Master.

They turn in each picking his spot on the floor while grandfather hangs a hammock and crawls into it. During the night, Alana slips out of the house, goes to Phoenix in the smithy, curls up next to him, and goes to sleep. The next morning Phoenix is first to wake, and he sees Alana sleeping content beside him. He lies there watching her smiling; he realizes that he'll soon be her man and she'll be his woman. Moments later, his mother walks in to see everyone sleeping.

"Wake up, everyone. You, young lady, get into the house."

Alana hurries out the door, and Pam stands there looking down on the men with her fists on her hips.

"Your breakfast is on the stump, eat, and get dressed."

"Yes, mam." All three men say.

Phoenix is out the door; first, he's starving. Dance Master follows him; then, grandpa brings up the end. They finish the food laid out for them; then Dance Master pulls Phoenix back into the smithy to change their clothes. Phoenix's outfit has gold and silver stitching in interesting designs. Dance Master has some fine cloths. Both look at each other over and approve. While they are returning to the yard, they hear Zeke and Lisa talking, and she's scolding him to get dressed.

"Phoenix, a word of advice."

"Yes, Dance Master."

"Be sure to tell your bride how pretty she is."

"If you say so."

"I do say so. I spent my wedding night in the preverbal pig pen because I failed to take note of all the work, she did to get ready for the wedding."

"I will be guided by your advice, my friend."

It seemed to be an eternity before the women and grandfather emerge from the house. All Phoenix could do was look at Alana, she walked up to him and stood looking into his eyes.

Phoenix crocks out, "you are very petty."

Dance Master was having the same problem talking as Phoenix

was. The ceremony didn't take long, and the two couples were married. Dance Master and Pam retired to her cottage. Phoenix got Alana to change into a simple dress so they could travel. He picked her up in his talons and flew east toward the coast. It didn't take long to reach the village where he landed just outside of town, and they walked in. They entered the inn and get a room to stay for a few days. That night Alana instructed her husband on the finer points of lovemaking. All it did was increase his desire to get to know his wife even more. While he was in town, Phoenix and his wife paid a visit to Brad and his wife, Pam.

"You're here! What did you do to my wife when you were here last?" queried Brad.

"Why is something wrong?"

"No, she is as healthy as can be. Thank you!"

"May we see her?"

"Yes, by all means. Who is this lovely creature?"

"This is my wife, Brad. Her name is Alana."

"Her name is as pretty as she is."

Brad leads them into the house to see his very pregnant wife.

"Phoenix, you've come back to visit. I'm sorry I didn't greet you, then I was not feeling very well."

"It's alright Pam; this is my new wife Alana; we have a room at the inn and thought we would stop by and visit."

Pam takes Alana's hand. "Have you danced with him yet, he's quite good, you know."

"We have not had the chance yet, but that'll be changed soon," said Alana.

"He's a good friend I hope you and I can be too."

Alana smiles, "I think I would like that."

"Now, you two get out of here and go do some fun things together while you can."

Phoenix and Alana promise to return after the birth to see her babies. They leave the house, and Phoenix changes to his alter ego and scoops Alana up and fly to the coast. Once there they set down, and he changes back to a human so they can walk hand in hand down the beach.

"Phoenix promise you'll never leave me behind."

"Alana, you know I can't do that; things will come up, and I must go by myself."

"I guessed as much, will that be very often?"

"Not if I can help it."

"Thank you for that much; you do know I feel great pain when you're away from me."

"Alana, I feel the same way. It took me some time to realize this is love. I do love you. Here is your wedding gift." Phoenix pulls the medallion from his pocket and gives it to her.

"Is this the medallion you were working on?"

"It is, now, you must keep this with you always."

"I will, but why?"

"It's star stone, and when I work with it, the stone forms a connection with me, and I can follow it, so I'll know where you are."

Alana hands the medallion back to Phoenix, and she turns her back to him. "Please put it on me."

Phoenix puts the necklace on her and closes the clasp. She turns to face him.

"I have never received a gift as grand as this is. I'll keep it with me always."

They sit down to watch the ocean roll in and out when Phoenix sees sea birds that do not exist on this world.

"Alana, do you see those sea birds?"

"Yes, what of it, husband."

"As memory serves me, they are not from this world, but from the one, we left.

"Does it matter?"

"I guess not, only this moment matters."

"Husband, have you decided where we'll live after this?"

"No, I haven't."

"I have an idea."

"I'm listening, Alana."

"That valley we went hunting in seems like a nice place to live."

"That's not a bad idea. I'll have to build a house there."

"I know you can do that, and if you ask, your grandfather will help you."

"I'll bet Dance Master would help too if I ask."

"Good, now we just have to have a place to stay while you do the building."

"I can solve that too. I can get a tent to set up for us to use for a short time."

"I like it."

"You realize I'll have to leave you to do that."

"I can live with that husband."

"Good, we'll return tomorrow so I can go get a tent."

Chapter

44

In the morning, they leave to see his mother to let her know that Alana and he'll be going on to the castle for a time. After a few goodbyes, Phoenix and Alana set out to travel to the castle so Alana can stay with the queen and the twins while Phoenix purchases a tent for him and Alana to use while building a home in the hidden valley. It was late in the evening when Phoenix landed in the castle courtyard. Phoenix leads Alana up the stairs, and when they reached the top stair, the queen met them at the door.

"My majesty, I'm glad to see you, and who is this pretty young lady?"

"Queen this is my new wife, Alana. It's a rather long story, and right now, we need some food and a drink. Then some sleep all in that order."

The queen takes Alana by the arm and leads them to a table and calls for the chief, "Bring something for the King and his wife."

The queen sits down next to Alana. "You are beautiful; I hope we'll become good friends."

"I hope so too."

The food arrives, and some mead, Phoenix, and Alana eat their meal, when it's done Alana seems to drift off to sleep.

"Queen the tents you're going to use for the festival, would it be possible to get one for me to take with me. I'll purchase it from who makes them."

"No need for you to pay for them. We have some extra you can take one of them."

"Good, I'll be leaving Alana here for a few days so I can set up the tent for us to live in while I build our home."

"Good, then Mary and I can get to know Alana while she's here."

"Be careful queen, Alana is not what you would call a lady, she's a bit rough, so don't be shocked at what she says."

"She's a country girl?"

"It's more complex than that, if she wants to tell you about it, she will, if not be kind about it."

"We'll treat her well majesty."

"Thank you, we've been traveling all day, and it's tiring. We shall see you in the morning." Phoenix picks up Alana from her chair. Phoenix carries her up the stairs to his apartments to put her to bed. The next morning Mary hears that Phoenix is back, and she comes charging into his room and is brought up short. Never before has the king slept without any nightclothes on, and here, he is naked and with a strange woman. "Oh, no! I'm so sorry, your majesty." She runs out the door and slams it closed. Phoenix sits up and begins to laugh.

Alana stirs next to him, "husband, what's so funny?"

"My sister Mary must have heard I was here, and I usually sleep in nightclothes when she burst in here and saw me naked, and with a strange woman, it caught her off guard."

"Sister? You never told you had a sister."

"She is not my real sister, just someone I call sister. Now get up and get dressed, you'll have to meet several people here at the castle."

Phoenix and Alana get dressed, and they descend to the dining area where they're greeted by the queen, twins, and the guild. Phoenix is not happy to see the guild but says nothing. Alana knows the guild, she grabs Phoenix's arm, and he feels her tension.

"Good morning, your majesty, and to your lovely wife," says the queen.

The queen dismisses the guild members, so just the king and her family can have a conversation after the guild leaves. "Queen, why is the guild here?" asks Phoenix.

"They have been giving me advice for the up and coming festival. I hope you will attend."

"I have delivered your invitations to the other parts of the kingdom; you may get a lot of people here."

"Thank you, your majesty," said the queen.

"OK, Mary, before you bust a gut, what do you want to ask?"

"Who is that woman?"

"I am called Alana, and I'm his wife."

"His wife?"

"Yes, is that a problem?" asks Alana.

"No, I just thought he would never get married because he can't have children."

"I also can't have children." Alana stands up, opens the front of her dress, and shows her belly and the scar that runs vertically up it. "My child was cut out of my belly; I can no longer have children."

The queen looks at Phoenix, "I understand." The queen gets up and helps Alana close her dress and puts her arms around her.

"Child, I'm so sorry for your loss."

Alana, almost on the verge of tears, feels the love and concern from the queen. Alana likes the queen and, in time, will like Mary as well.

After breakfast, Phoenix leaves the castle to go into the town to make some purchases. He takes Alana to a dressmaker and commissions a leather outfit, and cloak for her to wear on their flights to keep warm. Phoenix locates a miller to buy some wooden boards to build his house. Then he finds a mason to cut some stone for the house foundation. Last, of all, he hires a team of wagons to deliver the materials to his grandfather's cottage. The whole time Alana is like his shadow. As they return to the castle, Alana stops Phoenix.

"I know that man; I've seen him in my village he was talking to my husband."

"Are you sure, Alana?"

"Yes, I cannot forget his looks or his smell; my husband gave me to him to use."

"Thanks, Alana." Phoenix changes to his alter ego, scoops up Alana, and flies off into the sky to locate a secluded place.

"Alana, I fear for the queen and the twins, and now you. I'll have to leave you here to take all the items to build our new house. You'll be here all alone. Can you protect them while I'm gone?"

"I can, my husband. Thanks to Dance Master, I know how to dance the sword."

"Good, we'll have to practice some time, the twins also know how to dance the sword, and I bet they would like to practice with you."

"I'll practice with them. You won't stay away, long, will you?"

"After the festival, I'll take us to our new home and we'll start building when we get there. I'll only be gone long enough to deliver the tent and materials I bought to the place where we'll build our new home."

"I miss you already, and you're not gone yet."

"I feel the same way, Alana. We can enjoy our time here, and in a few days, we will pick up your leather travel clothes, so we can be together more and keep you warm."

"I like that."

Phoenix returns them to the castle after they land, they head-on into the dining room to catch some lunch. After which Mary promptly monopolizes Alana and takes her to her bedroom.

"I want to apologize to you, your majesty, for barging in on you and my brother this morning and then the stupid question of you bearing children. Please forgive a jealous girl."

Alana hugs her and says, "It is OK, I know you love him and care about his wellbeing, and I can understand and forgive you."

Mary hugs Alana, then she stands back, "How long have you worn this dress?"

"A couple of days now, I don't have anything to change into."

Mary looks at Alana and walks around her. "Will you trust me?"

"About what?"

"Your clothes now come over here." Mary opens her closet, and it's packed with dresses.

Mary looks through her clothes and selects several of them to have Alana try them on. Alana not wanting to give any offense does as she is asked. After a time, she begins to enjoy trying on the dresses.

"What color does Phoenix like?" asks Alana.

"Now, let me see, as I remember, he likes to wear blue."

Alana selects a blue dress and tries it on. "That's its Alana; you look stunning in it. Now come over here, and let's apply some makeup."

"What's makeup?"

"It enhances your beauty. Mother always says use only a little; too much makes you look like you're trying to hide something."

Mary applies just a hint of blush and a bit of pink lip covering. "Now Alana take off those clothes; you need to take a bath, then we will put all this back on you. You'll knock my brother's eyes right out of his head."

"A bath?"

"Come along, you'll love it," said Mary.

They enter the next room, and the tub is full of hot water. Mary plunges her hand into the water and declares it's just right. Alana is ushered into it, and Mary scrubs her and washes her hair, using all kinds of sweet-smelling perfumes. After a bit, Alana decides this is a good thing; it feels good to sit and soak. Mary drags Alana out of the tub and dries her off, then leads her back to her room to dress her. A short time after the hair is dried and combed, Mary dresses Alana in the blue dress, applies the blush again, and just the pink hint to her lips. Then Alana puts on the wolf necklace Phoenix gave her.

Mary bows to her. "My majesty, you look wonderful."

Alana looks in the mirror and is not so sure, but she likes what she sees. Mary takes her by the arm, and they leave to go to the throne room, to show off the new Alana.

Alana enters the room, and everyone turns to see her, all Alana can see is her husband looking for his approval. He walks up to her and bows to her. "Would your majesty permit me to escort her to dinner?"

"Yes, husband." Alana thinks she will have to spend more time with Mary and the queen and become a real lady.

When dinner is over, Phoenix and Alana retire to their rooms for the night.

"Alana, I'll be leaving in a couple of days to take the tent to our new home sight, will you be OK?"

"With your sister Mary and the queen, I suspect I'll not be bored. Tell me the truth; do I look good in the blue dress?"

"You look beautiful in that dress. That is the truth. To me, you look good in anything, even that rag you were wearing when I found you. I have to admit; you nearly knocked my eyes out of my head."

"Mary said, I would. I'm going to have to get to know her and the queen better to become a lady."

"You'll have the time for it with the festival coming. Remember what I asked you, protect them while I'm gone."

"I promise."

"Let's turn in and get some sleep."

Alana has her husband undo the back of her dress and Phoenix thinks maybe she'll have to wait just a bit longer to go to sleep.

Two days later, Phoenix and Alana return to the garment shop to try on Alana's leather outfit and cape.

It doesn't fit without some adjustment to the outfit to fit Alana; she wants to dance the sword in it. With the refinement, they're to return in two more days. In the meantime, Phoenix flies the tent to the location where he may set up his new cottage. Phoenix goes to his grandfather and enlists his aid in selecting a sight for the cottage. They get to the location, and grandfather asks what his grandson has in mind. Phoenix suggests it would be nice to be close to the stream. Grandfather shows him he can't be too close, or the house will be washed away in the first spring flood. He recommends building upon that hill overlooking the stream; it's above the flood line and close enough to use the stream.

With the sight settled on Phoenix and grandfather set up the tent a little way from the build sight so it won't be in the way. They both fly back to grandfather's cottage.

"Grandfather, thank you for your help!"

"Thanks for asking son, I was hoping you would."

"Grandfather, in a few weeks, a wagon train will be here to make a delivery of the materials I purchased and sent ahead."

"Where do you want them to be put it when they get here?"

"Someplace out of your way, and then I'll fly it down to where we will need it. I'm going to see mom and Dance Master to ask him for his help when we're ready."

"I know he'll agree."

"I hope so."

"If you don't mind, grandfather, I'll need to use the smithy to build all I need for the cabin."

"Like what?"

"The usual things, iron for cooking and utensils, plates, pot, and pans."

Grandfather leads Phoenix into the smithy. "You mean that stuff over there?"

"Grandfather, I made that years ago as practice."

"You sure did, now you get to have it for your use. The rest of the stuff you need is right here. Dance Master and I built the rest of your stuff."

"I wish he were here so I could thank him."

"Give him a few minutes. Grandmother left to tell him you're here. He should arrive about now."

In walks, the Dance Master. "Hello your majesty, it's great to see you."

"Same here, Dance Master, and thank you for helping grandfather with making the plates and utensils for my home."

"My pleasure, my majesty."

"Dance Master, would you be willing to help me build my cottage?"

"I was hoping you would ask; you'll have to take me back and forth if I do come."

"That'll not be a problem for me."

"Grandfather, I'm going to carry this stuff down to the tent, so it'll be set up and ready to use, then I'll be back for dinner."

The men pull all the items out of the smithy and put it into a big leather bag. Phoenix changes to his alter-ego grabs the bag, flies down into the valley, and unloads it into the tent. As he is getting ready to leave, he sees a sea bird fly by. Phoenix changes to his falcon shape and follows the bird as it heads to the coast. Just as it gets ready to leave the shore and head out to sea Phoenix, the falcon pounces upon the sea bird to bring it down. Phoenix underestimates his strength and winds up killing the sea bird, and it falls into the surf and is lost.

Phoenix changes into the bird phoenix and flies back to his grandfather's cottage.

"Grandfather, have you seen any sea birds as you fly to the mountain and back?"

"No, but I haven't been looking for them either."

"Majesty, is there a problem?" asks Dance Master.

"I don't know. Something doesn't seem right. I feel it. How are you getting to the festival Dance Master?"

"Run, in my wolf form, why?"

"How about I carry you?"

"OK, we'll be leaving early enough to arrive a week early to the festival so we can get a place to stay and, of course, pick up my things and buy your mother some things she wants."

"Good, I'll be here to pick you up."

"I'll let your mother know."

"OK, now can we get something to eat, I'm starved and exhausted."

Dance Master runs off to his home, and grandfather and Phoenix enter the house to wash up for dinner. Grandmother lays out a good meal of rabbit and vegetables, which Phoenix wolfs down and washes it down with some mead from grandpa's stash. Then off to bed in the smithy. As Phoenix fell asleep, he wondered if Alana would be next to him when he woke. Grandmother had breakfast ready when he came in to wash.

"Grandfather wants to say goodbye to you before you leave."

"Alright grandmother, I'll slip out to go see mom and come back, will that be alright?"

'Yes, I'll let him know where you went if he returns before you do."

"Thank you." Phoenix leaves and flies to his mother's house in his falcon form to not draw any attention to himself. Phoenix lands in the yard, and his mother and Dance Master meet him at the door.

"I thought I'd say goodbye before I left, I've someone who'll have a serious fit If I don't return soon."

Pam hugs her son and thanks to him for being willing to carry Dance Master to the festival.

"You're welcome. I had best get back to grandpas. He wants a word with me before I go."

"See you in three weeks, son," shouts Pam.

Phoenix returns to his grandfather's cottage and finds him there.

"Oh, good, you're here. I saw one of your sea birds, and I followed him, and he launched out to sea, and I followed for a short distance and saw nothing."

"Thanks, grandpa, I need to get going so I can return to Alana."

CHAPTER

45

Phoenix launches into the sky and heads back to the castle; he'll be there late in the evening. Phoenix announces his presence and lands in the courtyard. The queen, Orion, and Mary, greet him at the top of the stairs.

"Where's Alana?"

"She'll be here shortly," said Mary.

"Another experiment of yours, Mary?"

"I'm trying to teach her to be demure, poised, and a lady."

"That's not a bad thing if she's exuberant and anxious."

"It's not proper for a woman to fawn over her man; she needs to control it and him," said Mary.

Mary turns her nose up and walks back into the castle, her mother just about bust a gut to keep from laughing. Orion comes down the stairs and grabs Phoenix's hand. "I've missed you, brother."

"I've missed you too Orion, have you learned anything more since I left?"

"I sure have, the common people are brilliant, you were sure right about them."

"Orion, I need to talk to your mother about some things. Can we talk later?"

"Sure, Phoenix, I'd like that, see you later."

"Queen is there somewhere we can talk without eyes and ears to get in the way?"

"Not here, majesty."

"Ok, don't take this wrong." Phoenix changes and scoops up the queen and flashes into the air and heads south to the last plowed field and sets down.

"Now we can talk," said Phoenix.

"I want to apprentice your son to my grandfather for two years so that he can learn some lessons he can't get here. He'll also learn to work with his hands. When he returns, you'll have a son you can be very proud of."

"I'm already proud of him, sire."

"Trust me, he'll be different, and he'll be a better ruler for doing it."

"I will consent."

"I want to do the same with your daughter; there is a kingdom to the south. I know the wife of a friend who would like help. She'll learn how to cook clean and manage a house and a business."

"I will consent. Now, will I get to see them?"

"Yes, when I make the trip there, you can travel with me to see them, and you can meet the people who'll care for them."

"I'm not sure I can thank you, sire, for taking my children away."

"You will in time. At the same time, you can have Alana to teach; she needs someone like you to show her statecraft."

"You would leave her here for two years for me to teach?"

"She won't like it, but yes. I'll come back from time to time to visit her. I'll miss her greatly."

"She misses you something terrible, if you don't go see her, she'll get sick, in a bad way."

"One last thing, there is something brewing, and it's not good. I'm trying to find out what it is. I hope I'm not too late in its discovery. Please be careful."

"I will. Now, sire, you must get back to your wife."

Phoenix scoops up the queen, takes her to the castle, and lands on the porch; there is a blur of blue as Alana latches on to Phoenix's neck in a tight hug.

"You came back for me."

"You bet I did."

"I'm sorry about not being demurred and ladylike."

Phoenix whispers to Alana. "I rather like this better."

Alana smiles and holds tighter.

"Honey, could you let me go until I get something to eat? I could eat a whole deer right about now."

Alana let's go but holds onto his hand to the table. The queen orders some food for the king. After the repast, the king and Alana retire to the bedchamber.

In the morning, Alana wakes before Phoenix to make sure he's there and not a dream; she shakes him awake.

"Good morning, husband! I like calling you that."

"I love hearing it. How'd you like a trip to the south? I need to go there?"

"I'll go wherever you want to go, husband."

"Good put on your leather outfit, we'll be moving pretty fast, and it'll get very cold."

Alana puts on the leather outfit and cloak, "I had them add to the outfit. See!” said Alana.

Alana had them sew a wolf’s head, much like her medallion, and at the top, she added the Phoenix emblem.

“What do you think?”

Phoenix walks up to her and touches the sewing. “I like it; it suits you.”

“When do we leave?”

“Right after we eat.”

Phoenix goes downstairs to the dining table to eat with the twins and the queen.

“I must take a trip south today, and I’m taking Alana with me. Do you need anything from me before we leave?”

“I thought you were going to talk to me, Phoenix,” asked Orion.

“I am. Alana ask the chief to make us a couple of sandwiches to take with us, have them wrapped up. Orion, come with me.”

Phoenix changes to the Phoenix form, scoops Orion up in his talons, and flies off straight up and heads to the west fast, the first empty field Phoenix sets down.

“I talked to your mother last night; after the festival, I’m going to apprentice you to my grandfather for two years. You’ll learn how to not only to work steel but also learn to rule wisely. What do you say?”

“You mean, I’ll learn to make knives and stuff?”

“Yes, mostly, he’ll teach you other things as well, and it’s hard work, see.” Phoenix shows Orion his hands to see all the calluses and the rough hands. Your arms will be stronger too.”

“I can hardly wait,” says Orion.

“I want you to keep this quiet, at the castle; there’re too many eyes and ears, that’s why I brought you out here. Now let’s get back.”

Back at the castle, Alana waits with her rapier and a bag of food and water. "Husband, I'm ready to go if you are."

"Bye, everyone, we should be back in a few days." Phoenix changes and scoops up Alana, and they head skyward heading west; when the get out of sight, Phoenix turns south and increases his speed, so if anyone is following, they'll soon be outdistanced. Phoenix takes two days to reach the southern kingdom. At the border of the kingdom, Phoenix sets down and changes to his human form.

"We'll walk from here Alana. I don't want to draw attention that I'm here."

Phoenix looks at Alana and sees she's struggling under the hot cloak and leather outfit. Here in the south, it's much hotter and humid, causing her to sweat.

"Alana, take off your cloak, and I will carry it in the bag; when we get to the inn, I'll get you a dress to wear."

A while later, they arrive at Patti's inn, and they enter. Alana is ready to wilt from the heat; Patti comes out from the back room. "Name your poison friend."

"We will have two tankards of cold mead and a room for two days."

"I can accommodate you…" Phoenix turns to face Patti, and her eyes go big with surprise.

"The name is Todd, and this is my wife, Alana."

"Pho… I mean, Todd right away."

Patti disappears into the back and comes back with two tankards to find Todd and Alana sitting at a back table.

"Patti, can I buy a dress for Alana here? The leather outfit is a bit too warm for here in this climate."

"Very well, Todd, Alana, would you follow me please."

Alana takes a drink of the cold mead and sits it down to follow Patti. Patti takes Alana to her and Angus's sleeping quarters. Patti closes the door and turns to face Alana.

"You're married to Todd?"

"Yes, he's my husband."

"You have to tell me all about it while you're here. Now take off your outfit, and I'll see what I have for you to wear." Patti rummages around and finds a few light dresses.

"Patti, do you have any dress in blue?"

"Not really, but this green one will set you off." Patti turns around to put the dress up next to Alana and sees her scar running up her belly.

"Oh, my girl, what happened to you?"

"I would rather not talk about it if you please."

"I understand," said Patti. Patti embraces Alana and is crying, causing Alana to cry too.

"Here we have to get you dressed and wash our faces. Here's a pair of shoes for you to wear."

"I thank you, friend Patti."

Both women walk out to the main room, and they find Todd and Angus enjoying a tankard of mead. Both men rise as the women approach their table.

"Alana, that dress looks good on you?"

"Are you sure, I thought you liked blue?"

"I do like blue, but I like other colors too, and this color looks good on you, now come sit down here next to me."

"This is the girl who stole your heart, Todd? She's very beautiful," said Angus.

"She is that and more."

Patti told Todd that all their stuff was in their room just down the hall and to the right. They continue their conversation until the local bully enters the inn, thumping his fist on the bar, "Ale barkeep!"

Patti calls up to the bully, if you cause any trouble, I will crack your head open like last time. He quits being so boisterous, Patti serves him his ale then returns to the table. After a few more drinks, the bully approaches their table, and he leans down to Alana. "Hey, sweet thing, how about you have a real man."

Alana was about to get up and knife him when Phoenix stops her. Phoenix stands up. "I would let her go with you if you were a real man." Phoenix pushes the bully away from the table.

Madden from the insult, the bully, takes a swing at Phoenix (Todd) dances out of the way. He was making the bully look like a fool in front of his friends. He charges Todd, catches him around his waist, and throws Todd to the floor. He is about to pummel Todd when Alana starts to pull her knife to stab him. Angus stops her and whispers, "watch!"

Todd plants his feet on the floor and shoves with his legs throwing the bully over his head on to the floor; Todd rolls up to his feet to meet the charging bully, with a solid punch to the bully's stomach, causing the bully to double over, and trying to catch his breath. Todd grabs the front of the bully's shirt and, with the other fist, delivers a blow to his jaw, knocking him flat to the floor, breaking a table, and a couple of chairs on his way down.

Todd fishes two gold coins from his pocket and hands them to Patti, "this should cover the damage and the room for the next two nights."

"You shouldn't have to pay for the damage; he should." Todd laughs, "it was a rather a good scuffle I enjoyed; it's worth the cost."

Todd sat down, and Angus let Alana go, and she scolds her husband for fighting without her, then she rounds on Angus for stopping her.

"You didn't tell me, she was a wild cat, Todd."

"She's not; she's a wolf. Be glad she didn't bite you."

Angus looks at Alana with some surprise.

"Patti, I need to have a private conversation with you."

"Ok, where and when?"

"Now, and we need to leave here, Alana will come with us in her wolf form, she will make sure we have a private conversation."

"Angus dear, watch the bar, we'll be back soon," said Patti.

The three of them leave the bar and head out to an open and plowed field. In her wolf form, Alana walks about sniffing the air looking for spies, then she causes one to fly up, and Phoenix burns it to ash.

"This must be serious!" said Patti.

"It is. I want to apprentice a spoiled little girl to you. The very one that was kidnaped to be taken here for the guild to have on hand to control me."

"Oh my, I remember. So why bring her here?"

"I have a couple of reasons. One the guild won't suspect who she is and leave her alone. Two, you can teach her how to be a commoner what it's to serve and not be served, she needs to learn how to cook, clean and manage things if she is to become a good ruler."

"No special treatment?"

"None, but one."

"That is?"

"She is to come here a virgin and be returned a virgin."

"I can protect her from the likes of the man you fought tonight, but I can't protect her from herself."

"I can accept that."

"I got the who, now for the when?"

"In a couple of months, when the festival is over."

"That works. I'll have a room for her."

"Will you need any money for her to stay?"

"You should know better than that, Todd. She'll work for her room and board."

"Good, that's all set. Alana, come back."

Alana returns to walk with the two in her wolf form; as they reach the edge of the plowed field, Alana hackles rise, and she is growling.

"What's wrong, Alana?"

The bully and two other men approach them with clubs.

"Todd, we're going to take both women now."

"Oh, I don't think so."

"Who is going to stop us?"

"I will show you." Phoenix changes to his alter-ego and lays down a wall of fire in front of the men. They all break and run except the bully. He just falls the ground cowering.

"Don't hurt me, sire."

Phoenix takes out his branding iron and brands the man on his forearm. "If I see you again, I will kill you. Now get out of my sight."

The man runs off, gibbering as if demons were chasing him.

"I'm sorry, Patti, I now have to change my mind about this apprenticeship."

"Why?"

"One of those men will say something about you and me and put Mary in danger if she were here."

"You're right. I'm sorry."

"I have someone else in mind. I'll talk to her."

All three return to the inn, and the next morning Phoenix, alone with Angus, show up at the castle to appear. That night at the inn, the men show up not to drink but to meet the king. For an hour, the king orders a round of drinks, and chats with the men, and then asks if he and his companions can have some space.

They assure the king no one will bother them. Phoenix returns to the table with Angus, and they have a conversation.

"As I recall, did you finish that amulet you forged?"

"Alana, show him your necklace."

Alana takes it out of her dress and shows Angus.

"This is exquisite! Could you teach me, sire?"

"I would love to, but I can't, I'm still learning. Now the man who taught me could teach you."

"Would he?"

"I'll ask him; I'm traveling that way when I leave here."

"Can you not stay longer, sire?" asked Patti.

"No, Alana and I have other things to do. I'm sorry this didn't work out. You would've been a good teacher."

"What will you do now?" asks Patti.

"I have someone else in mind to ask."

Phoenix turns to Alana, "It's time to turn in; we have a long couple of days starting tomorrow."

"Patti, I'll leave the dress in our room and the shoes; I thank you for letting me use them."

"You'll do no such thing; you keep them, I would be honored to give them to you."

"Thank you; I will treasure them."

Phoenix leads Alana to their room to turn in for the night. In the room, they begin to change for the night when Alana stops them.

"There is an intruder here."

Phoenix changes into an owl and perches in the rafters. After a few moments, he pounces on a rat in the corner of the room. Alana changes to her wolf form, and Phoenix changes to his human form. He picks up the rat by the tail. Alana changes back to her human form.

"Husband kill him. He is an assassin. I remember him from my village."

"Sounds like a good idea."

The rat changes into its human form and draws a knife; he was not fast enough; Alana ran him through with her rapier. "He was to kill us as we slept."

"Alana, are you up for a night flight?"

"Yes, husband, let's get away from here. I love your friends. But you have too many enemies here."

Chapter

46

Alana puts on her leather outfit and cloak then bags up her dress and shoes; Phoenix opens the front door and lets them out into the warm night. Phoenix changes to his bird shape, scoops up Alana, launches into the air, and strikes out to the northeast. When the night gives way for daylight, Phoenix sets down in a clearing, and Alana spreads her cloak for them to sleep on. Later, Alana changes into her wolf form and hunts up a rabbit for their meal; she returns to dress it and puts it over a fire when her husband wakes up and sits up to watch her.

"Good morning, wife."

"I thought you could use some food, so I caught a rabbit."

When it's finished cooking, Alana presents it to her husband, and he takes his knife out, splits it down the middle, and hands her half of the rabbit. Alana looks at her husband with wonder. No one in her life has ever divided the food equally with her or given it to her before feeding on his own first.

(What manner of man have I married?) She wonders. She takes half of the food and sits next to her husband to eat. At the end of the meal, Phoenix asks his wife if she's ready to continue.

In his Phoenix bird form, he picks up Alana and her bag and launches into the sky, heading toward his old home. If he's right, they'll be there the next day. Phoenix flies through the night, and when the dawn breaks, he sets down to get some rest. Alana was not tired. She slept through the night as she was in Phoenix's talons. Upon landing, Alana gives up her cloak for her husband to sleep on. In her wolf form, Alana runs off into the woods to locate some game for a meal when she runs on to a camp of men. Alana keeps out of sight. She listens to them and realizes this is a band of guild members. Why are they here? She wonders.

Alana decides to leave and warn her husband before they discover her. She returns to see that the guild has woke up her husband. She stays out of sight. Phoenix clears his head to see spears and swords surrounding him.

"My, who are you?" asks Phoenix.

One of the men slaps Phoenix across his face, "we'll ask the questions. Who are you, and why are you here?"

"My name is Todd, and I stopped for the night; I'm headed to the east."

The man slaps Todd again, "Liar! No tracks are showing you were traveling anywhere around here."

"I'm not surprised. I flew here."

"Liar!" slapped the man a third time.

"I'm getting a bit tired of being slapped."

"Think so, men tie him up, and let's take him back to camp."

Phoenix heard that he decided to go along to see what's going on. Alana backed off, and ran ahead of them to their camp, and found a place to watch and wait. The men get back to camp with the prisoner.

"What's this!" ask the leader.

"We found this person a mile in that direction; he claims to have flown in and stop to rest."

"We don't need prisoners. Kill him."

Hearing that, both Alana and Phoenix react. Alana attacks the man nearest to her; Phoenix burns the ropes holding him and the burns all the weapons, and most of the men leaving the man who slapped him and the leader.

"Now I'll ask some questions. Do you know who I am?"

"No!"

"I'm Phoenix, the king."

The men's eyes go large with fear.

"Now you know who I am, who are you?"

"We're sea raiders, working for the guild."

"Close enough for the who, now for the why."

"Were here to cause trouble and keep your people busy looking for us."

"I see, the guild is responsible?"

"Yes!"

"How many of your bands are there?"

"We don't know. We're not told in a case like us we get caught we can't reveal too much."

In her wolf form, Alana rips out the man's throat, who slapped her husband, and the leader looks at her. "I told you all I know. Don't kill me."

"I won't. Phoenix brands the man on his face with his Phoenix brand. I'm letting you go so you can tell the guild I'm going to destroy them." Phoenix cuts the rope and lets him go. Alana changes back into her human form.

"Husband, you should've killed him."

"You may be right Alana, let's get back to our camp and get our stuff and leave."

"Before we do, husband, take some food. You will need it to fly us back toward our destination."

Phoenix heeds his wife's words and eats the food roasting on the spit, then some water, and Alana leads them back to their camp to pick up their things; Alana notices the man they let go is following them.

"Husband, we are being watched."

"I hear him in the brush. It's time to go." Phoenix changes and scoops up Alana and leaps into the sky to continue their journey. A sea bird tries to follow not far behind them but gets left far behind as Phoenix increases his height and speed. The sea bird loses sight of them and turns back to warn the southern guild of what happened. Phoenix flies the rest of the day and all night to reach his grandparent's cottage.

Phoenix and Alana stumble into the smithy and to the straw bed at the back. They fall fast asleep; they sleep like the dead until grandfather wakes them with his hammering. Alana wakes up and waves to grandfather. Then she asks him not to do any more work until her husband wakes up; she explains he flew for the last two days. Grandfather agrees and retires to the cottage to let Lisa; his wife know they have company.

Late in the day, Phoenix wakes to find Alana gone, so he gets up and leaves the smithy to the water trough where he washes his hands and face. He stretches and grabs his shirt to pull it on. As his head sticks out the top of his shirt, he is knocked to the ground, and his face is covered with big wet kisses from a wolf licking him.

Laughing, Phoenix pushes Alana away. "Look what you did, girl, now I have to wash again."

Alana changes from her wolf form to human, and she is laughing too. Phoenix realizes this's the first time she has done so. It was nice to hear.

"Did you catch anything for dinner?" Phoenix takes his shirt back off and washes again.

"No, I was hunting something else."

"Did you find anything?"

"No."

"Let's go in and visit my grandparents; I see you changed into the green dress. You look nice."

Alana grabs Phoenix's hand, and they walk into the cottage, where dinner is ready. Alana being in a talkative mood, expounds on all that has happened to them and the band of men they encountered.

"Speaking of your band of men, I've seen a lot of sea birds flying through the valley, some heading east to the ocean, one or two to the west, and one to the south."

"Thanks, grandfather, you'll need to take care, there may be more raiding parties in the area."

"We will, son; I'll let your mother know."

"That will be an Ok grandfather; I'm going to go see her tomorrow."

"She'll be glad to see you both."

"Grandfather, would you be willing to apprentice a young man for two years as a blacksmith?"

"How much trouble will he be?"

"I don't think he'll be a problem; he'll be over eager if anything."

"Who is he?"

"He's the queen's son Orion. I want him to learn how to work with his hands and learn how to manage a business."

"That may be fun, and I can have him make his tools and such. I rather miss having you around to help me."

"If you are agreed, I'll bring him here after the festival."

"I agree. Now that the meal is over, let's help grandma clean up."

With the dishes cleaned up and put away, they all sit around the table and watch the fire in the hearth flicker and put out a warm glow; it makes one tired just watching. The grandparents wander off to bed, and Phoenix leads Alana out to the smithy to the straw bed. Early in the morning, it's still between the dark and the light of day; Phoenix wakes up and leaves Alana sleeping in their straw bed. He walks to the water trough and splashes cold water on to his face to finish waking up. As he's putting on his shirt, he spies a sea bird off in the distance. Phoenix changes into a falcon and wings his way after the sea bird. Then he knocks it out of the air with his attack.

'What is going on, why so many sea birds flying about? What is the guild doing?' ponders Phoenix.

Phoenix flies back to the cottage to find Alana waiting for him.

"What happened, husband?"

"I took out another sea bird."

"That's good and not so good?"

"How so, Alana?"

"It's good you stopped a message, but they'll change their route now."

"I see what you mean. Let's breakfast with the grandparents, and we'll go see my mom."

"I like that; it would be nice to see Pam again," said Alana.

In minutes, Phoenix flies Alana to his mother's house. Both

Pam and Dance Master greet them. After the greetings and a few cups of tea. Alana regaled them with what has happened with embellishments here and there in the story about the trip south.

"You say sea birds are flying east to west, and south?" asks Dance Master.

"Yes, I've seen them; in fact, I killed a sea bird just this morning flying by my grandparent's cottage."

"That's disturbing, when I was at the castle, I saw many sea birds fly in and out of the window of the guild, I thought nothing of it, but now it might mean more than I think."

"I'll need to think on this some more, I still need more information than I have," said Phoenix.

"I'll keep an eye out for people moving about this area; Pam can help me search."

"Speaking of my mother, I need to ask a powerful favor from you."

"What is it, son?"

"I want a certain young lady to learn to serve instead of being served. I want to apprentice Mary, the queen's daughter, to you for two years. Would you be willing to do that?"

"Why?"

"She is a spoiled brat, to be blunt, and she thinks that commoners are there to serve her, she needs to learn that she's the servant and not the other way around. After all, you taught me that."

"So, you were listening. Yes, I'll teach her, your majesty!"

"Mom, you don't have to call me that here in your home."

"I know, son, it's just fun to watch you get flustered."

"Gee, thanks! I'll bring her here after the festival in a few weeks, be careful when you travel there."

"We will; don't forget you're picking up Dance Master," said Pam.

"I remember. Now, if it's alright, I promised to take Alana to the sight were our new cottage would be."

"Can we come too?" asked Pam.

"Sure, I'll carry Dance Master and Alana, and you can fly, mom."

They all walk out to the yard, and Phoenix changes, then scoop up both Alana and Dance Master; it's a short flight and Phoenix slows so his mom can keep up as they wing their way to the valley. Phoenix was about to drop down on the clearing not far from the tent when Alana was pounding on his leg and waving him away from the area. Phoenix flew on toward the mountain when he sees three sea birds following him. He flies ahead and lands close to the brush. Alana and Dance Master change to wolves and vanish into the bush. Phoenix and his mom change into sparrows and fly into the brush to wait. The sea birds soar past them, and Phoenix and his mom change to falcons. The two birds flying by suddenly disappear in a cloud of feathers. Phoenix kills his target while his mother brings down her prey, and right there to assist her is Alana in her wolf form. The bird changes into a man thinking he can muscle Pam off him and kill her, until Alana sticks her muzzle in his face and starts snapping at him, causing him to stay still and not move. Pam relieves him of his weapons. Phoenix flies on to catch the last sea bird. Phoenix doesn't seem to be catching the bird in front of him, so he uses his Phoenix powers to burn the bird's tail feathers and wing feathers, causing the bird to crash into the ground. Stunned, the bird changes into a man and Phoenix removes his weapons, and then Dance Master appears at his side.

"Do you want to do the honors of questioning him, Dance Master?"

"I sure would."

Dance Master draws his rapier and waves the blade's point in the man's face. "Now, let's get some answers. I'll ask the question if you don't answer, I will start at your hand and work my way up your arm, then your other arm, legs and then I will make you into a girl, provided you live long enough, question why are you here?"

No answer, Dance Master stabs the man through the hand, and the prisoner screams in pain.

"Now, let's try this again; why are you here?" Dance Master places his sword on the man's wrist, ready to push it through the bone.

"We were told the make trouble and to take attention away from some grand plan."

"What grand plan?"

"I don't know; they didn't tell us."

"Who sent you here?" growls Dance Master.

"I can't. They'll kill me."

"Wrong answer." Dance Master shoves his sword into the wrist of the man, twisting it and breaking a bone. The man screams out, "The guild master sent us."

"Any question you want to ask sire?"

"How many men are here in the valley?"

Dance Master places his sword at the man's elbow joint and pricks him.

"Six, they're at the tent we found."

Phoenix takes out the brand and places it on his hand and then touches the man's right check and brands him with his mark. "Let him up. Now start walking to the sea, find a ship, and leave; never come back; with that brand, you're now hunted, and it'll be your life if you're caught."

Phoenix walks back to the women and the man they have captive. Dance Master takes his sword and stabs the man through his elbow so he can't fly. Phoenix pulls him up to his feet and asks him, "How many men are in the valley?"

"Six men."

"Your friend lied to me. He gave me a different number." Phoenix brands the man on his face and tells him to go catch his friend headed to the coast." Phoenix pushes the man in the direction of his friend.

Phoenix and the family head back to the tent, Alana and Dance Master as wolves and Pam and himself as sparrows. They spy out the situation and find seven men, not six; one of them is in a rat form guarding the outside are of the tent. Phoenix changes into an Owl and silently pounces on the rat killing it and leaving six in the tent. Alana and Dance Master approach the tent from the wooded side and wait. Phoenix changes back to a sparrow and flies into the tent's open door and sits upon the support beam, his mother follows him. Phoenix drops down into their midst and changes into a human before they can react, Phoenix burns two the men to ash. The man behind Phoenix pulls a knife and approaches him to stab him in the back. Pam drops down and assumes human form, and with the knife, she took from her first prisoner, she stabs him in the heart, killing him.

Alana and Dance Master charge into the tent and each takes a man down chewing on an arm. The last man tries to make a run for the door, and Phoenix burns him down in his tracks. Alana is struggling with her man, and he tries to pull his knife and stab her. Phoenix burns his hand with the knife, and as he screams, Alana rips out his throat. Dance Master changes to human form, draws his rapier, and waves it around the man's face, lightly touching his face.

"Now, I want some answers to my questions."

The man spits at Dance Master. "That wasn't nice," he stabs the man's hand to the ground. The man uses his other hand to pull his knife, and Dance Master takes it away from him and places it to the man's neck. "As I remember, your dagger is poisoned, now answer my question, who sent you?"

"No! I won't tell you."

"The guild master is going to be short, another assassin." Dance Master shoved the knife into the man's neck, killing him.

"Well, this was the place I wanted to build my cottage," said Phoenix.

"It is a nice place, husband, clean up the bodies, and I'll wash up the dishes, and we can make it ours," said Alana.

Chapter 47

The men move the dead bodies to a rock ledge, and Phoenix burns them to ash; Pam and Alana wash up the dirty dishes and put them back into the bag. Phoenix was telling Dance Master where the house will be built, and the smokehouse, with garden. Pam asks, "What about the smithy?"

"I'm sure grandfather will allow me to use his, when and if I need to."

"It's getting late, we need to get back," says Pam.

Just before Phoenix changes, "Husband, I want to stay here tonight."

Phoenix looks her in the eye and understands. "I'll be back soon." Phoenix scoops up Dance Master and leads the way home, followed by his mother. They fly over grandfather's cottage and on to his mom's cottage and drops off Dance Master. A quick goodbye and Phoenix wing his way back as a falcon so as not to draw attention. Alana has hunted down a rabbit and has it on her spit cooking it, waiting for Phoenix to return.

Alana hears men outside and decides to exit out the back of the tent. She changes into a wolf and watches the three men. Phoenix arrives to see the men reach the tent, and he changes to an owl; it isn't long, and he spots Alana. He drops down beside her. Neither says a word. Phoenix changes to his human form and heads to the tent. He's a bit irritated. Phoenix steps into the tent. The three men pull their knives and swords.

"I've had enough dropped your weapons, or you'll die where you stand."

They laugh and move closer to kill Phoenix. Before they take a step, all the metal knives and swords turn red hot, burning them. They quit laughing. They throw their weapons down and charge Phoenix in the hope to overwhelm him with numbers. A big mistake that he burns two of them to ash and the last one he beats nearly to death with his fists. He grabs the last man by the front of his shirt and pulls him close to his face.

"Who sent you here?"

The man looks into his eyes and sees death, and he then answers, "The guild master."

"How many more are coming this way?" Phoenix shakes him, and the man says, "no one we were the last."

Phoenix brands the man's face. "Fly back to your guild master and tell him I'll see him soon."

Phoenix drags the man out the door of the tent and throws him into the creek. "Now go before I kill you!"

Alana appears at his side. "We should leave. It's getting too populated," said Phoenix.

"No, husband. You are making this land mine. I'll not leave it; I will fight to keep it. Tonight, we'll be fine. While you were tending to business, I scouted the area. There is no one else near."

"You know, Alana, I forget how tough you are. I'm proud of you. Let's see how your dinner is."

They find it a bit overdone, but it's palatable, and they eat rabbit jerky and wash it down with water. Alana has Phoenix help her find some leaves and grasses to make a bed for the night. They curl up on their makeshift bed and watch the fire die down as they lay there in each other arms.

In the morning, they get up, and Phoenix says, "It's my turn to get something to eat." He runs out of the tent, changes into an eagle, and flies up high until he spots his prey a nice big salmon-like fish and so he swoops down and scoops it up and flies back to the tent. Phoenix takes the fish down to the stream edge, and with his knife, slits it open to clean it out and he shows Alana how to cook it.

After breakfast, they clean up the dishes and decide to return to the castle to get ready for the festival, and Phoenix wants a conversation with the guild master. They return to grandfathers so Alana can get her leather outfit. Then they go to Pam's cottage to pick up the Dance Master.

Ten miles from the castle, Phoenix lands and changes to his human form.

"Dance Master, I'm leaving you off here, so you can return unannounced I'll meet you in the field to the west of the castle. Something is going on, and we need to ferret it out."

"I understand, sire."

Phoenix changes and scoops up Alana and continues to the castle. The festival starts in the next two weeks, so preparations are well underway; some of the guests arrive early so they can meet the Queen, and possibly King Phoenix himself.

Over the two weeks, Phoenix meets with Dance Master out in the woods to discuss any findings. So far, I have gleaned nothing from the guild.

"Sire, I'm not able to get close to the stable of the smithy; when I do, everyone in the area leaves."

"When do they meet Dance Master?"

"About noon. Why?"

"You can't get in there, but I can."

The next day Phoenix disappears and flies out of the castle in his sparrow form and heads for the stable and flies up into the rafters to wait. It doesn't take long; a sea bird flies in and changes into a man. Soon a guild master and the blacksmith appear.

The guild master asks, "Have the raiders landed yet?"

"They'll be landing tomorrow morning."

"Good. Are the two assassins ready?" asks guild master

"The boy apprentice has been in the castle for a week and is not noticed. A woman is in the guild apartments and will also be ready to make her move if the boy fails."

"Do it tonight then," states the guild master.

"Right at the dinner hour, we'll poison the King and take over this kingdom."

"Do it well, assassin I'll be there to watch," replies the guild master.

They all leave. Someone has entered the stable.

Phoenix gets a message to Dance Master and tells him about the plot to kill him and that the sea raiders will be landing on the east coast. The guild is in on the whole thing.

"What should we do, sire?"

"Tonight, you get your men together and round up all the guild members quietly, and I'll deal with the assassins."

Dance Master does what Phoenix commanded, and they capture

most of the guild members and their families and put them into the dungeons. At the table, Phoenix and his guests dine, and the guild masters are there as well. They have a nice dinner, then the wine and mead are poured and passed out to everyone, with the king being last to get his cup. The boy assassin carries the cup to the king when Alana jumps up and grabs the boy by his neck.

"What's in the cup, lad?" she asks.

"Mead, my lady."

"You're a liar; I smell something else in the cup as well. Here take, a drink from the cup."

"But, your lady, it's the king's cup."

"He won't mind, now drink it or I'll kill you" as she presses her knife against his throat.

The boy drinks the mead, then pitches to the floor, and convulse until he dies.

The guild masters call for a guard to remove the boy and displays anger that anyone would harm the king. The guild master then indicates he has a gift for him, and the guild master calls for the woman waiting in the wing of the apartments. She comes out of hiding, and her beauty stuns every man in the place. The king intensely watches her as she approaches him. This makes Alana jealous.

"Come here, child," speaks Phoenix.

Alana hackles are raised, and she is ready to kill this adversary of her husband's affections. The woman approaches to within a few feet when Phoenix tells her to stop.

"Alana cut the woman's dress off."

Alana looks at the king and wonders what he is doing. This is not like him. Alana uses her knife and cuts the dress up her back, and it falls to the floor. As it hits, you can hear a tinkling sound of glass vials and metal. Phoenix gets up and picks up the dress.

"My, what are all these vials, and look all these needles. I wonder what would happen if you drank one of these or were scratched by one of your needles. Poison, perhaps?"

Alana's knife is now poised at the woman's neck. Through clenched teeth. "Were you going to kill my husband?"

The woman makes no sound. "Dance Master arrests the guild members in this room and takes them all to the dungeon; I'll deal with them when I get back. Alana, change into your leather outfit. We have a long flight to make tonight."

"Sire, what do you want to do with the woman?" asks Dance Master.

"Lock her up with the rest of the guild masters."

"Where are you going, sire?"

"Alana and I have a war to fight; the sea raiders will be landing tomorrow. I want to prevent that if I can."

"Do you need more help?"

"I don't have time, Dance Master; I have to fly all night to get there, and I can't carry enough people to make a difference."

"Then good luck, sire, I'll help the queen here then until you return."

Alana returns and is ready to go; Phoenix and Alana leave by the front door, and Phoenix, in his bird form, snatched up Alana in his talons and fly off toward the east to the coast. Phoenix flies up to the twelve thousand feet where it's cold and heads northeast, flying faster than before. They arrive at the coast in the north, and Phoenix sees the ships with rowboats loaded headed for shore. Phoenix sets the forest on fire and continues down to the south, stopping the raiders from landing, then flying back up the coast; he burns several ships giving the idea they need to return home, which they do. Phoenix flies south, then doing the same thing getting the raiders to turn tail and run.

Phoenix sets down out of sight of the village where Bard and Pam live. Phoenix relaxes his talons to release Alana. We will walk from here. When they get to the village square, a man drags out a woman and holds his sword to her throat.

"Lord Phoenix, I have heard much about you. Now leave, or I'll kill this woman."

"Then what would prevent me from killing you. Whoever you are."

"My name is Eric the bloody, and I'm going to take this land."

"No, it'll be over your dead body, Eric."

"Not so, Phoenix. Archers."

A wall of arrows comes at Phoenix, and he burns them in midflight. Then they launch another wall of arrows, and that wall is burnt to ash, then the archers are turn to ash. Phoenix turns to face Eric, and he turns the sword to red hot metal at the sword's hilt, causing Eric to throw down his sword.

Alana steps from behind Phoenix. "Still killing women and children, father?"

"Alana, is that you? Why aren't you dead? I cut your child from your belly myself."

"Let's say I survived, but you won't." Alana draws her rapier and approaches her father.

Eric shoves the woman to one side the woman runs to get out of the way. Eric picks up the sword with his other hand.

"Daughter, you do remember I can fight with either hand equally well?”

“I remember, father”

Eric is a slash and chop type of fighter. Alana is a dancer with grace and smooth efficient moves. For each slash and chop Eric makes, Alana dances away and leaves Eric with a cut. She cuts Eric all over and he is bleeding from several wounds. His next charge Alana opens his face with a nasty cut. Angered, Eric makes a final charge, and Alana ducks under the slash and comes up running her rapier through Eric’s throat up into his head. Eric drops his sword and clutches at Alana’s blade, and she pulls it out and steps back. Eric falls to the ground and reaches for his sword, and Alana kicks it away.

“No, father, you don’t get to die with a sword in your hand.”

The men watch as their leader dies, and they turn tail and make it to shore to sail away.

The woman Eric had held comes up to Phoenix. “They have the rest of the people at the manor house as hostages; they’ll kill them.”

“Where are they holding the people?”

“In the back courtyard.”

“I’ll go there, Alana. Take the woman and enter the front door. I’ll cause a distraction, and you should be able to enter,”

“Yes, husband.”

Phoenix changes into a sparrow, flies over the house and lands in the center of the courtyard. Before he changes, he sees where the guards are. Phoenix changes to his human form and burns the two archers to ash. Then the men with spears are next. The men with knives find them too hot to hold on to and drop them. Then the doors to the house are kicked open, to show Pam still pregnant, and Brad are held at knifepoint. Looking at his friends, they have been severely beaten; Pam looks like she's dying. Brad is beaten to the point his lungs have been punched, and he will die soon himself. Alana had entered the front door, the man holding Brad is stabbed through the heart, and he drops Brad as he falls dying to the floor.

Alana then puts her sword to the neck of the man holding Pam. "Move, and you die."

The man tries to stab Pam, and Alana is faster and kills him dropping Pam onto the floor. Phoenix rushes over to Pam and keels down and picks up Pam's head and puts it into his lap. The midwife looks at him after touching Pam's belly and shakes her head. Phoenix cries, and his tears fall on Pam a second time, and she wakes and reaches up to touch his face.

"I knew you'd come." She faints. The color of her skin is looking better, and the bruises are healing. His tears have worked. The midwife looks at Phoenix.

"Sire, what did you do? She and the children are getting stronger."

Phoenix carefully lays Pam down, and the midwives take over, Phoenix moves over to grab Brad's hand and looks him in the face. His tears fall on to Brad's skin, and his breathing is getting better, and his bruises are healing.

"Brad Pam is going to be alright, and so are the children."

"Thank you for saving us Phoenix, will you keep an eye on my family when I'm gone?"

"Hopefully, that won't be for a while, Brad. You're going to be alright."

Phoenix helps Brad up and into a chair; there is a flurry of movement around Pam, her water broke, and she's to deliver her children now. The midwives chase everyone from the room. To the men, it seems an age of time has passed. When, it was only thirty minutes, they hear the cry of one child, and moments later, a second child is born. The midwives bring out the newly born boys to show their papa. He almost faints. The woman finishes cleaning up Pam, and they have a door brought to put Pam on so they can mover her to her bedroom to recover.

The men remove the dead bodies from the house, then they clean up the floors. Pam is in her bed with her new boys, and her three daughters are there to see their new brothers. Alana stands there with tears in her eyes, knowing she'll never have another child. Pam sees her crying.

"Alana, would you like to hold one of my babies?"

"May I?"

"Yes, of course."

Alana carefully picks up the child and kisses it on his head, then the tiny hands grab her hair, and she smiles; she places the child back next to his mother and takes the child's hand.

"He's so small."

Alana cries, knowing she'll never have a baby of her own.

"Husband, we must return to the castle."

Chapter

48

Seeing the pain in Alana's eyes, Phoenix understands and leads her to the village square, and he transforms into his namesake, picks up Alana, and flies to their tent where they spend the night, resting and getting something to eat.

In the morning, Phoenix gets ready to change and leave. "Husband, may I stay behind here until you return?"

"Are you sure?"

"Yes, I need some time to myself."

"Then, yes. Once I take care of the guild masters here and in the south, I'll return."

"I'll be safe, her husband, return to me soon as you can."

Phoenix takes to the sky and heads back to the castle; he has some guild masters to deal with.

Alana decides to strip down to her undergarments and then changes to a wolf and takes off cross country to Zeke's and Lisa's house to pick up some of her clothes and return to the tent. It takes her four weeks to accomplish this. In the meantime, Phoenix sends the guild master under escort back to the east coast and gives orders for the ship to sail south and then wait for the rest of the guild to show up. Phoenix heads south, arrests the guild masters in the southern kingdom, and sends them packing with men to herd them to the south shore to catch a ship out of the country. Phoenix lands on the south coast to make sure all the guild members are on board. They left with orders never to return on pain of death.

Phoenix returns to the Phoenix castle and puts another escort together to take the twins back to his home. It takes two weeks to travel with Dance Master and the twins. Mary is dropped off with his mother, Pam, where Mary will work for her living under my mother's direction. Suffice it to say Mary was unhappy. After a few brow beatings for which my mother is great at, Mary complies.

Orion was the easiest to settle in. He was excited to get to work, grandfather was rather pleased with the boy, and they hit it off right away. With everyone settled in, Phoenix flies down into the valley to be with Alana. She was excited to see him.

They spent a few days playing about the property when Alana told her husband they needed to get the house built. By this time, Phoenix had moved the building supplies from grandfather's to here, so now they need to level the property to set up the foundation. It took a year to build the cottage, using help from Dance Master, Orion, and grandfather. Alana had her house in the valley. When Phoenix finished the place, he and Alana spent their time alone getting to know each other. Two weeks later, Phoenix tells Alana he needs to make a trip across the ocean and see what the sea raiders are up to; she can stay or come along if she wants to. He would be leaving in the morning.

Alana was ready to leave with Phoenix. She had dressed in her leather outfit, and when he was fed, they would be off. They took three days to fly across the ocean, and Phoenix set down near a stream where Alana caught a rabbit to cook, and plenty of water to drink. They found a sheltered area to spend the night. In the morning, they flew north along the coast looking for ships. When he saw them, he burnt them; Then, Phoenix turned south and did the same thing at the shipyards he found. Alana told her husband of a great river and that he would find many ship builders. Taking her word, he located and destroyed all he could see of the shipbuilding places. Then he turned to the woods and burnt them back a few miles to make it harder to build more ships.

Phoenix believes he sent his message loud and clear. He decides it's time to return home. He flies back toward the coast when Alana is pounding on his talon, and she points to the north. There's a fire. Phoenix turns that way and finds another village that has been sacked. Phoenix lands, and again he and Alana find devastation; people lie dead everywhere. It makes Phoenix heartsick to see what the sea raiders will do to their own people. Phoenix gets ready to turn the whole village to ash when Alana stops him. Alana starts turning her head one way then another; then, she heads deeper into the village as if she were looking for something. Then she finds it a newborn child lying next to her dead mother, and it must be hungry for it was crying. Alana handed me the child and ran off to find some food it could consume. She returned with some milk and a way to make it drinkable for the child. Alana feeds the child until it was full and ready to sleep. I walked around, checking for more bodies, and I found no one who was alive, so I burned the bodies and huts to ash.

Alana had rummaged around and found a baby pack to put the baby in, and then she found a water bag to fill up with llama's milk so we could transport the child back with us. The problem is no llama to milk; Alana didn't let that stop her; she knew where they could find a herd not far up the coast. We located a small herd, and a couple of the llamas had a calf. Phoenix set Alana down with the child and launched forth to scoop up a mother llama. Phoenix caught the llama, and it passed out from fright. It made it easier to milk her.

With Alana and a child wrapped up in Alana's cloak, Phoenix launched into the air, clutching Alana and the baby. It took three days to cross the ocean and land at Brad and Pam's village. Brad came out to meet them.

"Hi, Phoenix, to what pleasure do we owe for the visit?"

"We need to feed our baby."

"What? Your baby?"

"I'll explain later, we need some milk to feed the child, and a place to wash up."

"Whew! I guess so. Follow me." Brad led them to the back of his house into the courtyard; he asked for milk to be brought for the child and food for Phoenix and Alana. In the meantime, Brad had the baths set up with warm water. Once washed and fed, Pam and Alana wander off to Pam's room to get some clean clothes and clothes for the baby girl.

"I'm puzzled, friend Phoenix. I know you can't have children, so how did you and Alana have a child?"

"The child is a war orphan. I flew with Alana to the sea raiders' coast and burned their ships. On the way back, we found a village burning; we sat down to investigate. Everyone was dead, the child had been lying beside her dead mother, and Alana found the child there. No way were we going to leave it there."

"Oh, look out, Phoenix!"

Three girls pounce on Phoenix laughing and shouting. "Uncle Phoenix." Phoenix falls to the ground and wrestles with the girls tickling and laughing with them. When they settle down, can we see your new baby?" they ask.

"I bet if you go quietly to Aunt Alana, she'll be glad to show you her new baby."

The girls go running off to find Aunt Alana.

"Brad, do you have a place where Alana and I can bed down? I've been flying the last three days without rest; I'm nearly dead on my feet."

Brad leads Phoenix to a back room and has his staff change the bedding and darken the windows. Once in bed, Phoenix is sound asleep. It isn't long, and Alana is in bed with Phoenix, all curled up, leaving her baby with the nanny's watching the twin boys. Pam's girls take a turn holding the new born girl and playing with her under the nanny's watchful eye, and their sisters just ignored the twin boys. They were old news.

The next morning Phoenix and Alana get up and breakfasted with Pam and Brad.

"Phoenix, our fall festival is in a couple of weeks, and we would like to thank you for saving our lives again from sea raiders. Will you come?"

"Sure, Alana and I and a few of my friends would be glad to attend. Don't go to any fuss over us, please."

"Let us in our humble way, thank you, Phoenix."

"You would do us honor, by just having the festival."

"Ok, just the festival as we would normally do it."

"Thanks Brad. Tomorrow Alana and I must return home."

Phoenix and Alana spend the day with Pam and Brad; in the morning, Alana dressed in her leather outfit, and the baby wrapped in a leather backpack and the items Pam gave Alana for the child. They were ready to leave when Brad leads out a llama and gives it to them so that the baby can have fresh milk. Phoenix changes and scoops up the llama and Alana with the child to fly to the valley cottage, which is just a couple of hour's flight. Phoenix lightly touches down and lets Alana out then the llama. Alana holds the rope for the llama until Phoenix can take it.

Looking around, Phoenix realizes he'll need to build a stable and corral to hold the llama. Phoenix ties the llama to a nearby tree and set to work building the stable. With the llama at his home and Alana is happy taking care of the child. Phoenix flies to a farm close to the castle and purchases a wooden container and has it filled with hay for the llama, and Phoenix carries it back to his cottage and stores it away.

"Alana, tomorrow I would like to go check on my charges, they are nearing the end of their two-year apprenticeship, and I'll need to take them home soon. Would you like to go visit?"

"Yes, I think I would want to show off our new baby girl."

In the morning, Alana and the baby are ready to leave, but they don't need the leather outfit since the flight is only a short one. They land at grandfathers and are meet my grandmother. Lisa and Alana with the child steal away into the house so the two can fuss over the baby. Phoenix walks into the smithy to see Orion and how he's doing.

"Phoenix, I'm so glad to see you!"

"Granddad, how is your apprentice doing?"

"Look for yourself." Zeke shows Orion's work.

“Wow, Orion, this is great workmanship!”

Smiling from ear to ear, “That’s great praise from you, sire.”

“I see you made your future bride her cooking set up; who’s the other one for?”

“My sister, I hope she’ll like it.”

“I’m sure she will,” said Phoenix.

“How are you going to transport all this to the castle?” asks Zeke.

“I would carry it, but now I have Alana and our baby to carry.”

“What baby?” asks both Zeke and Orion.

“Let’s go to the house, and you can see for yourself.”

They retire to the house and see the women fussing over the child. “That baby!” says Phoenix.

Zeke asks, “how did this happen?”

“Is there any mead in the house?” asks Phoenix.

Zeke pours Phoenix and himself a tankard of mead, and Phoenix tells the story of how they found the child and brought it back with them. Zeke refills their tankards.

“Interesting smiles, Zeke, I now have a great-grandchild.”

“Have you told your mother yet?” asks Lisa.

“Not yet we’ll be leaving shortly to go see them; I need to check on Mary and see how she’s doing.”

“I hear she was a handful, according to Dance Master, and you know your mother.”

“I do grandfather, why do you think I chose her. How did it turn out?”

“You’ll have to see when you go to your mother’s house.”

“Alana, it’s time to go see my mother, let’s say our goodbyes.”

Phoenix launches into the air with Alana and the baby with the usual promises and travels to his mother’s house. Landing in the yard, he's met by Dance Master and Pam.

"Where's Mary?" asks Phoenix.

"She's here somewhere," said Dance Master. "What's this sire, a baby?"

Alana and Pam, followed by Dance Master, move into the house to visit so that Alana can show off her baby. After all the fussing over the baby, Mary comes in to see Phoenix and Alana. She's happy to see them but the baby gets all her attention.

"Mom, how is Mary doing? Is she learning?"

"Yes, she has learned to follow and do work. Not willingly at first, but now it has sunk in. she'll do well by her future husband."

"I'm glad; then it was worth it."

"I'll be taking them both back after the fall festival. Will you and Dance Master be attending the festival? Grandparents said they would."

The visit went off the way Phoenix hoped it would. Alana told the story of the child and how we now have a baby. Pam and Mary made a cold dinner, and we all ate; when we finished, I indicated we needed to get back home to milk the llama and feed and water it. With the goodbyes and hugs, Phoenix scooped up Alana and child and returned home.

"Alana seems to be happy, more so than when I first met her," said Mary.

"I think your right Mary, but I can only imagine what it would be like to lose a child the way she did. How empty you feel knowing you lost your child, and can never have another one," stressed Pam.

"Now that you mention it, I believe your right. I'm happy for her now she's happy."

"What are we going to take to the festival?" asks Dance Master.

"Oh, that's right, Mary, what should we make to take with us?"

The women put their heads together to come up with an idea; it'll mean they'll have to walk the two days instead of flying. They'll have to carry several items with them, and Dance Master suggests that he rent a llama from the farmer a day's run from there so they can pack all their stuff, food and blanks and such. Pam flies to her parents to let them know what they're doing, and Lisa decides to bring some food for the festival too.

Chapter

48

They decided to make a family trip out of it. Phoenix and Alana will fly directly there, and then Phoenix will fly home each day to tend to the llama until the festival is over. Everyone is received, and the people who bring the food they get it to the main square where tables and fires were set up. The air is filled with music and people talking. That evening when everyone is stuffed from all the food, the music is struck up, and couples start dancing. Alana turns over her baby to a nanny to watch, and she captures her husband from some other girls. She won't let him dance with anyone else except his mother, grandmother, and Pam, his friend. Orion has a lineup of young girls to dance with. Mary has a line of suitors, and she dances with all of them.

The festival ends, and everyone leaves in droves, Phoenix with Alana and their child leave for home, and the rest of the family return on foot for the two-day walk, leading the llama with their possessions. Back at home, Zeke, Lisa, and Orion collect their items and walk the rest of the way home.

The next day Phoenix leaves Alana at home with the child, and he travels to castle Phoenix to let the queen know the children will be returned to her within a week. Then off he flies to make his rounds to the other villages and towns. Before he leaves, Phoenix sends a wagon to Zeke's cottage to pick up the items Orion forged, and then swing by, to pick up the things for Mary at his mother's cottage and return them to the castle.

At the end of the week, Phoenix meets everyone at Zeke's cottage after the usual good buys and hugs; Phoenix scoops up the twins for the flight back to the castle. Phoenix lands with the twins. The queen is there, and with a great display of affection. That night the three didn't come down for dinner; Phoenix ate alone. In the morning, the queen came down to breakfast; she walked up to Phoenix and kissed him on the forehead.

"Thank you, sire! You have made my children better than they were. Mary may not think so, but I see how she has changed toward the staff here. I could've wished I had you for a mentor in my younger life."

"You're welcome, but it worked out for me as well."

"How so?"

"I now have a brother and a sister I can count on to be good rulers in the future."

"Sire, you have left me with another problem."

"What would that be?"

"You took away our blacksmith with the guild masters, and now we don't have one."

"You may."

"You mean Orion?"

"Why not, he's capable."

"He's my son."

"Have you looked at the items he has made for his future bride? Or the items he has made for his sister?"

"No."

"You should."

The queen looks at Phoenix for a few moments and sees he means what he said. She heads upstairs to see her son, and she asks him to show her the stuff he made. He informs her that they are being shipped in and that he would be glad to when they get here.

"Is Phoenix still here?"

"Yes, he's at the dinner table."

"Good. I want to talk with him." Orion changes his clothes and races down to the dining table.

"Phoenix, do you think you could talk to the blacksmith and see if he'd let me use his forge once in a while?"

"That sounds like a good idea here. Eat your breakfast, and we'll both go see the blacksmith."

The queen shows up, and Orion tells her "Phoenix and I will go see the blacksmith and set up permission to use his forge."

The queen starts to say something, and Phoenix shakes his head no. She smiles and says, "Sounds like a good idea."

Phoenix and Orion walk to the blacksmith's smithy with breakfast done, only to find it empty, and from the look of it, not being used.

"Orion, I exiled the blacksmith with the guild members; he was one of them, so your castle has no blacksmith."

"Then how will I be able to work here?"

"What's going to stop you?" asks Phoenix.

"I don't know all that I need to know to run this smithy."

"Then take what you know and learn more. From time to time, I can help you."

"You mean you want me to be the blacksmith?"

"No. what I mean is if you want to be, you can be the blacksmith; you have to choose."

"You mean, I have a choice?"

"Yes! You know enough to start, and you have the tools and knowledge to give it a go as your own business. Over time you'll get better."

"Then I accept. I like making things with my hands."

"Then, as your king, I give you this smithy as your own."

"When can I start?"

"Anytime you like," said Phoenix.

Phoenix and Orion look around and find a ledger of jobs, a backlog of repairs, and some fabrication pieces.

"Looks like I have some backlog work that's way behind; I best get the forge started."

"Here, Orion, I'll start the forge. Otherwise, it'll take a while to get it up to heat." Phoenix using his power lights up the forge and brings it up to temperature right away.

Orion locates the first repair job in the ledger, and in a couple of hours, he and Phoenix repair the plow. Then turn to make other repairs. Late in the evening, Orion and Phoenix return to the castle to wash up for dinner. Orion regales the queen and sister Mary about what they did in the smithy. The following morning Orion puts up the sign that the smithy is open for business. Soon people start showing up to pick up or make sure the new smith is aware of the repair work that needs to be done.

With Phoenix's help, all if not most of the repairs are taken care of. Orion loves the work and wants to make this work on his own. The next day Phoenix has Orion put up the closed sign so they can take a trip. Phoenix takes Orion to a quarry where he can get his materials for making his metals. They approach the businessman in charge and order Iron, coke, and coal. To be delivered to castle Phoenix to the smithy. Phoenix pays the men some gold coins, and they promise to return in three days.

Phoenix returns Orion home, and visits one more day and returns home to Alana the next day. Orion is happy to have opened the smithy. His mother is impressed at his work. Mary is also a wonder; she goes to the kitchen to cook dinner, she makes some biscuits for her stew, and the chief is very impressed. Then Mary makes a batch of cookies, and the chief has never had this before and wants to learn how she does this. The queen becomes more impressed with her children and thanks to Phoenix for the last two years in her heart.

Orion has just put his metal in the clay crucibles and has them in the forge to make some ingots for future use in his work. As he is pumping the bellows to heat the forge, a young girl carrying a few pans and a large pot stumble into the smithy. Her red hair is much like a haystack piled on her head, and the green eyes you would swear they glowed even in the dark, and the freckles across her face. What shocked Orion was her language? It's not like he hasn't heard the words before, but just not from a girl. Orion almost breaks out laughing but decides to hold it in.

"Young maid, what might this humble blacksmith do for you?"

She drops the two pans and a pot. "Can you repair these?"

"Let me see what kind of repairs." Orion picks up the pans and pot and places them on his table. He turns the items over and over a few times and tells the girl he can repair the pans, but the pot is beyond repair. He can fabricate a new one if she would like.

"How do I know your quality will be any good?" said the girl with her hands on her hips.

"Well, you could ask around to my past customers, or I can make a new pot, and you will see for yourself."

She tries to see fault in that statement but can find none. "When can I get my pans, and how long to make the pot?"

"You can pick up the pans tomorrow after lunchtime; the pot will take less than a week."

"I'll be back tomorrow." She starts to turn to leave when Orion stops her.

"I need your name for my ledger so you can get your items back."

She looks at Orion, trying to see if he is trying to make advances to her, she doesn't see that intent in his face or eyes. "Irish. My name is Irish."

"Irish. Nice name. You can pick up your pans tomorrow."

Orion looked the pans over and decided a process for his repair; he heated the pans to red to yellow glowing, then he drift-punched each end of the cracks to keep them from cracking further, then he placed the pan on the clay block and heated some metal until it was molten. He poured the metal into the cracks and let them cool. Then he reheated the pans and forged welded the new metal to the pan.

In the morning, Orion sanded the excess metal off the pans, and they looked as good as new and ready for use. A little before noon Irish showed to collect her pans.

"These look almost new; how much will it cost?"

"For those two coppers, and we'll be settled, the pot will be at least six coppers."

Irish weighs what he said and agrees to the price. She pays him the two coppers and will pay the other six later. "If the quality of the pot is anything like the pans you repaired, it'll be worth it."

Then Irish stopped at the door, look back at Orion, and watch him as he works; each move is graceful and smooth. His bow, come to think of it, was also graceful. She clears her throat and asks, "What is your name?"

Without looking up, he says, "I'm called Orion." Orion then turns back to what he's doing.

Irish smiles and runs off to her home. Irish is a bit perplexed Orion didn't make a pass at her like most boys. She begins to wonder if he even likes her or is, she just another job waiting to be done. Then Irish admonishes herself. He's just another boy. She waits all week like she's sitting on pins and needles. The morning of the day when she can pick up the new pot, she appears at the forge just as Orion opens.

"Good morning Irish, your pot is not done yet; I'll have it finished late this afternoon."

"Is it alright if I wait here for it, I promise to stay out of the way?"

Orion points to a bench, "Sit there, and you'll be out of the way." Irish plants herself on the bench to watch.

She watches Orion's every move as he finishes heating and hammering her new pot to shape; then, she watches him heat the pot to a glowing yellow color, then he puts it into a sand pile to let it cool.

Orion turns to Irish, "would you like something cool to drink?"

"Yes, it's very hot in here."

Orion goes to the smithy's back, opens a door in the floor, disappears down the steps, and returns with a pitcher of water from an underground spring. Orion hands Irish a cup and fills it up.

"Orion, why did you put the pot on the sand?"

"To make all the stresses in the pot normalize in one direction, then I'll heat treat it and put on a handle, and it'll be complete."

"Sounds so complicated."

"It's not really, just something to be learned. So, Irish, what do you do besides cook?"

"How do you know that I cook?"

"Well, let's look at the picture, you brought me two pans to repair, and a pot that needed to be replaced, you're a girl, a pretty one at that. Most girls I know do the cooking."

"My dad does the cooking, and he has been teaching me to cook; what do you mean I'm pretty?"

"I meant no disrespect; you look pretty. If you don't cook, what do you do?"

Irish turns red, and she can feel the heat in her face. "I shepherd our sheep."

"I see a girl of many talents," grins Orion.

"I'll have you know blacksmith I can do many things!" says Irish with her fists on her hips.

"Oh, it's time to take the pot out of the sand." Orion turns away from Irish, pulls the pot from the sand, and places it back in the fire to heat it. Leaving Irish spluttering and confused about her argument.

"I see that your red hair is a true statement about your temper Irish."

Irish stood there, her mouth opening and closing like a fish out of water. Her temper is getting hotter by the minute. Orion takes a page out of Phoenix's book and walks up to Irish and plants a kiss on her lips. Her eyes go very wide, and her temper subsides. Irish can say nothing; she's in shock. Orion decides to file that bit of information away for future confrontations; it seems to work very well.

Orion turns away from Irish and puts the pot into oil and brine to cool it off, and he works to attach the handle to the pot. The whole time Irish is just standing there watching him astonished that he kissed her. Irish is beside herself, and while Orion worked on attaching the handle, she ran off home, leaving the pot behind. Orion finished the pot and turned to Irish to see that she's no longer there. Orion decides to close the smithy and see if he can take the pot to its new owner. Orion queries a few people to where the new people with the girl with red hair might live. Eventually, Orion locates the cottage where Irish lives. He steps up and knocks on the door, and a man opens the door.

"Good evening sir, I have brought the pot that Irish has

commissioned. Is she here?”

“She is, and what’s your name, blacksmith?”

“Orion.”

“Orion, my name is Bryan, please come in.”

“Thank you, and here is the pot.”

Bryan takes the pot. “Nice job that’ll last a very long time, you’re very good.”

“Thank you.”

“Oh, yes, I owe you six coppers said, Bryan.” He walks to a box on the far side of the room to get the money to pay Orion.

“I’d best be getting back to the smithy; it was nice to meet you, Bryan.”

“Orion, what did you do to my daughter?”

“Irish has quite a temper, she was in the middle of a tirade, to get her to stop, I kissed her.”

“That’s all you did; just kiss her.”

“That’s all, if I have given offense, I’m sorry.”

Bryan starts laughing. “Where did you learn that trick?”

“From a friend having a similar problem with a woman, he kissed her, and she stopped yelling.”

“What happened?”

“They got married.”

Bryan starts laughing all over again. Bryan claps Orion on the shoulder. “You haven’t given any offense; you had best be run along, I suspect I’ll be seeing you again soon.”

Orion changed into his panther form and sprint for home; at the castle, his mother was eating dinner, Orion took his place and served himself.

“I see sis is cooking dinner again; she likes to do that, doesn’t she?”

"Yes, Orion, she does like to cook. What's your problem, don't you like your food?"

Orion was picking at his food. "Something happened in the smithy today. I was finishing a new pot when the customer came in to take it home, and we got into a conversation, which set her off on a tirade, and I kissed her to stop it, and it did."

"I hope you don't do that to all your female customers," said the queen.

"No, this girl has no husband. For some reason, she wanted to argue, and I didn't. So, I followed Phoenix; when he and Alana start to argue, he would kiss her, and the argument would stop. Why not it worked."

"What did this girl do after the kiss?"

"She was speechless, and when I turned my back on her to take care of her pot, she left."

"She didn't do anything, just leave?" asked the queen with a knowing smile on her lips.

"She just left, so I took her pot to her, and I met her father; I explain what I did, and all he did was laugh."

"Orion, go to bed, I promise this will resolve itself in time."

"Are you sure? It's confusing right now. All I can think about is her. All that red hair stacked upon the top of her head like a haystack. The green luminescent eyes and the delicate freckles across her face."

"You'll have to introduce me to her sometime."

"Yea, sure, mom." Orion heads upstairs to get a bath, then into bed.

Mary was passing through the dining area on her way to bed when she hears.

"Son, you have it bad," snickers the queen.

"Mom, what's wrong with Orion?" asks Mary.

The queen looks up. "Oh, nothing really, he's fine."

"What does he have that's bad?"

"It's nothing serious. In time you'll see it for yourself."

"Ok, if you say so." Mary continues her way to bed.

Miles away Dance Master and Pam find they are expecting a child of their own. By this time, Alana's child is about six years old and giving mom and dad a hard time. She doesn't want to learn to read or write and other things. All she wants to do is play. That year at the festival, Alana's child was old enough to go with some of the children, and when it came time to play some of the games, she couldn't participate because she couldn't read, write, or even do numbers. The worst came when it was time to dance, and no one would dance with her because she didn't know how to. The other children teased her so severely that she started learning all she could so she wouldn't be humiliated again when they returned to next year's festival.

When she was learning, she found a whole new world opened to her. She wanted to know more and more. She would even go with Phoenix to the smithy to learn how to forge metals. When time permitted, she would visit Pam and Dance Master to learn how to dance and sword dance. She borrowed Pam's book of names to look up a name. She chose the name Raven. Then one morning, watching Alana change to a wolf, Raven changed into a Raven; she could also switch to an Otter, which might explain why she always wanted to play.

"Well, young lady, your mother told me you had had your name day, what name did you pick?"

"I chose Raven as my name, father, see!" Raven changes to a Raven and fly's off and back.

"Do you have any other animal changes?" asks Phoenix.

"I can change into an otter," and she changes into an otter with black fur. She scampers about being playful.

Raven changes back into a human and asks Phoenix what he and mother can change into.

"Raven, I can change into a few birds, none of them a raven, your mother can only change into a wolf."

"If you're my parents, shouldn't I be able to change into what you can?"

"Raven, we're not your blood parents," stated Alana.

"Then, where are they?"

"Your father and I found you after the sea raiders destroyed your village. Everyone was dead. Your mother hid you, and I found you," said Alana.

"Then you're not my real parents?"

Phoenix placed his hands-on Raven's shoulders. "We're your father and mother; no one could love you more. Your true parents died, and your mother tried to save you."

"Are you sure they're dead?"

"Very sure," said Alana. "I smelled your scent on your dead parents. Then I heard you crying and rescued you."

Alana opened her dress and showed Raven her scar up her belly, "a sea raider tried to kill me, and he removed the child I was going to have, and killed the child, leaving me for dead. Your father there saved my life. He cannot have children either. You came into our lives and filled a void. We're sorry about your parents, but we celebrate that you came to us." Alana turns away and is crying.

"Thank you for telling me the truth." Raven walks over to Alana,

"Mother, it's ok. I love you."

Alana grabs hold of Raven and holds her tightly to her, and both girls are crying, and Phoenix embraces them both.

Chapter 51

Dance Master and Pam have had their child, and it's a boy. Phoenix had stopped by to see his new baby brother. He tells Alana about it, and they must go see the baby. After all the fuss, they all return to the daily grind at home. Phoenix makes his yearly trips to visit his kingdom and explore this land. Phoenix has flown to the far north where the polar Icecap is. Then Phoenix flew to the far west and finds an ocean. Then Phoenix follows the coast south to another icecap then back towards the southern kingdom. Phoenix stopped in a jungle on the equator he perched in the treetop as a falcon. All night long, he could hear strange noises and decided to explore in the morning. He changed to his sparrow form to get down to the forest floor. Phoenix dropped down through the trees and flew around. He almost became a meal for a strange plant.

As he flew among the trees, Phoenix, in his owl form, his wings make no noise as he flies through the forest. He lands to get his bearings when he spots a group of people and follows them, staying out of sight, and they lead him back to a small village. Phoenix perches up in the trees and watches the villagers below. He sees something that catches him entirely by surprise. A girl and two men were off to one side, and the two men changed into frogs. One bright blue shot through with a bit of red, the other frog, was bright green with some yellow and black markings, and both frogs postured in front of the girl until she picks one, the blue one. The two go off into the woods by themselves.

In the back of Phoenix's mind, he was trying to remember something about the bright colored frogs. The people who brought them to converge with came from South America. Several brought frogs with them. This was during the time Randy was into making more reptile people or amphibian people. Then a creature came charging out of the woods; Phoenix had never seen it's like before and was getting ready to stop it before it could cause any harm when one man got it to charge him, and he leaped up into the air and onto its back. Then he jumped off, and the creature came to a halt and died.

Then it hit him, the poison dart frog people. He needs to go to see his friend Angus and look at his library. Phoenix decides to leave these people to themselves and look in on them from time to time. As it turns out, the guild found these people a little time before Phoenix. Their first contact resulted in several deaths when they realized touching these people's skin was death itself. This gave them an idea for killing their foe the Phoenix.

Phoenix flew up out of the trees, changed to his phoenix form, and flew to the southern castle to consult with Angus's library. Phoenix flew in as a flacon to Patti's inn. He changes to his human form and enters the inn.

"Hi Patti, is Angus around?"

"He's at his forge. Would you like a drink or something to eat?"

"Yes, to both, do you have an open room? I've been flying all night, and I could use some shuteye.

"I'll get you that drink and food, and then make sure your room is ready."

"Thank you."

Patti delivers on her promise; the mead is cold, and the food is delicious.

After some sleep, Phoenix wakes up, and it's very early in the morning, and everyone is still asleep. Phoenix dresses and slips out of the inn and heads for the castle. Then he locates the night watch and has him show him to the library. Using his power Phoenix lights the candles in the room so he can read the books. The shelves are full of books, where to start. Phoenix wishes someone was about to help him look for the book he needs to look at. Then in walks the scribe who manages the library.

"Who are you, sir, to be in Lord Angus's library?"

"Not that it means much, I'm King Phoenix, and I need to read the book Randy wrote about the people he converted, and the book on the tribes that broke off and went into different directions."

The scribe's eyes went very wide, "Your King Phoenix!"

Phoenix claps his hands to get the scribe's attention. "Do you have the books I mentioned?"

"Yes, Sire!" and the scribe still stands there in shock.

Phoenix places a hand on his shoulder. "Look, I'm not that impressive, but the two books I need are. Please get them for me."

The scribe springs into action. He goes to the last bookshelf, climbs a ladder, pulls a book out, and brings it to the table for Phoenix to look through. Then he stands there, tapping his chin as if trying to remember, then the goes to the nearest bookshelf, and at the bottom, he pulls the other book out and places it with the first one.

"Is there anything else I can get you, sire?"

"Now that you mention it, a cool cup of mead and some bread, meat and cheese. Thanks."

The scribe runs off to the kitchen to get what the king asked for.

Phoenix opens the book of conversions and looks up the people who came from South America and converted with poison-arrow frogs. Fifteen people were transformed with the frogs, about an even split of females and males. That answered part of the question. Phoenix opens and skims through the next book until he came to the people who were the poison dart frogs.

Randy wrote about these people. They were a danger to others. One poison dart frog male wedded with a cat female, and she died during the wedding night poisoned from touching the skin of the man. The next incident was not much better. A birdman wedded a female dart frog, and he died during the wedding night, but the female conceived, and her child was able to fly, and her poison was not as intense, you could touch the child, but you got ill. The poison dart frog people decided to split off and go south and were never seen again, until Phoenix stumbled on them.

The scribe returned with the food and drink. "Sire, did you find what you were looking for?"

"Yes, I did, you'll need to add to this part of the book, I have found the poison dart frog people in the southern jungles."

"You did. We all thought they died out."

"They didn't; I want to put into the book not to go looking for them. I know where they are, and I want them left alone."

"Yes, Sire!"

Phoenix sits back, drinks his mead, makes a sandwich with the meat and cheese, and consumes it with gusto.

"Sire, is there anything else I can do for you?"

"What's your name, scribe?"

"I'm called David Sire."

"David, I want to thank you for your help; when I finish this, I'll be talking to Angus then head north to castle Phoenix."

"Sire, if I may talk freely?"

"Sure, David."

"Sire, you should sit with a scribe and give us your history and all you've done. It'll be a history we can keep."

"David, I'll keep that in mind. Maybe I'll sit with you and have you write it. It was your idea after all."

"I'd be honored, Sire."

Phoenix finished his meal and sets off to find Angus; he passes through the throne room then out to the smithy where Angus is firing up the forge. "Good morning Phoenix!"

"Angus, good morning to you! Have you seen any new people here at the castle?"

"No, sire, are there any new people?" asks Angus.

"Not that I'm aware of, Angus. I just came back from the south seas, and along the coast, I have found fresh signs of the sea raiders landing."

"That means the guild is trying to come back," stated Angus.

"That would be my guess, and all my rulers will be targets."

"With you topping the list, sire."

"Just be careful, Angus, they'll have a plan, and you'll be the first target."

"I'll be the careful sire."

Having given his warning, Phoenix leaves and heads north to castle phoenix to see the queen and then head home. At castle Phoenix, Phoenix gets a warm reception from the queen and the twins. During dinner, Phoenix tells of his adventure to the south and that he fears the guild is going to try a comeback, and Phoenix wanted them to be on guard. After dinner, Orion pulls Phoenix aside and asks him if he would come to the smithy.

"Do you want me to come formal or informal, Orion?"

"Informal brother, I have something to talk about. It's important, and you may meet someone."

"Sure, Orion, when do you want me there?"

"In an hour?"

"I'll be there."

Things had progressed between Irish and Orion, and Orion wanted to get permission from Phoenix to marry her. Orion wanted her to meet Phoenix, his brother, and friend. Phoenix meets Orion at the forge.

"Now, Orion, what's this all about?"

"I have met a girl, and I'd like you to meet her and get your approval."

"I've been hoping you'd find someone; you have my approval."

"Brother, there's more to this than the girl."

"Oh, tell me!"

"Bryan, her father, wants your approval, for my mother and me."

"You and your mother?"

"Bryan wants to marry mom; she'd say yes if you approve, she realizes she would have to give up being the queen."

"I see, said Phoenix with a serious frown, let's go see these people."

"Brother, when you see mom, call her Beth, nothing else."

"Beth, I have always wondered what her name was. Let's go."

Phoenix follows Orion, and they take an hour to hike to the cottage where Bryan and Irish live. Orion knocks on the door, and the Irish answer the door; when she sees Orion, she is a blur of red as she jumps into his arms. Phoenix smiles, remembering Alana and him. After the show of affection, Irish realizes they're not alone, and she jumps back from Orion, all red-faced and awkward.

"Orion, you didn't tell me just how beautiful she is." Phoenix takes hold of her hands and smiles at her. She pulls her hands back and invites them into the house.

Phoenix follows Irish into the dining area, where she stumbles through the introductions of her father, Bryan, and Beth.

"It's kind of you to want to meet with me, Orion and his mother are good friends of mine. I hope we can become good friends as well."

"We can, what are you called?"

"My best friends call me Todd."

"Todd, will you approve the marriage of Irish and Orion?"

"Done! Is there another approval I need to give?"

"There is Todd; I want to marry Beth here and make her my wife."

The queen looked hopeful at Phoenix. Phoenix stairs at the queen for a long moment and sees she wants to marry Bryan. Phoenix holds out his hand to Bryan.

"Your temper won't be a problem, will it, Bryan?"

Bryan gets his meaning and tells Todd that it'll not be a problem.

"Good, I give my approval for your marriage. I do need to talk to Beth alone outside for a moment."

Phoenix and Beth walk outside, and they walk a short distance from the cottage.

"Are you ready to give up being the queen?"

"Yes Sire, I am. I see what you've done to my children and how happy they are, and I want it for myself."

"Good! I have a replacement for you already."

"Who?"

"Mary will replace you. She's ready."

"What if she wants to marry?"

"I'll cross that bridge when the time comes."

"Then, it's alright if I marry Bryan?"

"I think so. He seems to be a good man; I like him."

"Let's go back, Todd, and celebrate."

"Lead the way, Beth."

Phoenix and the queen return to the cottage to celebrate the up and coming marriages. That night back at the castle, Phoenix talks to Mary.

"Mary, your brother, and mother are going to be married, which means your mother will be stepping down as queen. She'll still live here, but I want you to take over as queen here."

"I can't be the queen; I don't know how!" cried Mary.

"Sure, you do, my mother taught you how to rule."

"No, she didn't; she taught me how to run a house, not a kingdom."

"If you look at it, there's no difference, you use the resources that you have and get them to do the work, while you control the resources."

Mary considers what Phoenix is telling her and realizes she can rule in her mother's place, and she can tap her mother's experience and the Phoenix himself.

"Alright, brother, I'll do it."

"Good in the morning we'll tell the people you're the new queen regent, and I support you all the way."

In the morning, Phoenix turns into his bird self, makes a display, and screams out in thunder to get everyone's attention. In two-hours, everyone assembles at the castle to hear what the king has to say. Phoenix proclaims Mary is the new queen regent, and her mother has stepped down for reasons of her own. Now everyone is to go to Mary for any disputes.

"Let me make one thing clear, that all disputes previously settled by the queen regent will stay that way! You may bring Mary new ones. Remember, the scribes have recorded all previous transactions."

Once all the excitement dies down, the castle settles back to duty, as usual, Mary is getting the hang of being the new queen.

"Brother, did you know I was going to be the queen regent?"

"No, not at first. Your brother could've been chosen too, you know. I just wanted people ready to step in in case it was necessary."

"I see, if I'd been married, would you choose someone else?"

"Not necessarily, your mother wanted to be just a wife to Bryan, not his queen. Bryan would have felt subservient to your mother, and he wouldn't have liked it. So, she stepped down."

"If I marry, will I stay the queen?"

"That will be up to you; we can discuss this later. Now you need to find a dress my mother gave you, and we need to go see your mother and brother get married tonight."

"They are getting married tonight?"

"Yes, so we need to dress down and go see them."

Chapter

52

Phoenix dresses in his usual garb that most commoners wear, and Mary dresses in one of the dresses that Pam had to help her make. Mary meets Phoenix in the dining room. Phoenix has a small bowl with some dirt in it, and he applies just a little to Mary's face.

"This should make you less a princess, and more a commoner. The chef made us some cookies for us to take with us."

"You think of everything."

"I try, but sometimes I make mistakes too."

Mary and Phoenix walk to Bryan's cottage to meet her brother Orion's new wife and her mother's new husband. Phoenix (Todd) introduces Mary as Beth's daughter and Orion's sister. With hugs and kiss all around, and handshaking. The ceremony doesn't take long, and Todd breaks out the cookies he brought along.

"Mary, did you make these cookies?" asks Orion.

Thinking quickly, "Yes, do you like them?"

"You know I do," responds Orion.

"Mary, could you teach me to make cookies? I've never heard of them before," said Irish.

"Tell you what Irish, after everyone is settled in, I'll be glad to show you how to make them."

Irish hugs Mary and both girls will soon become fast friends. The night is upon them, and Todd with Mary, Orion, and Irish head back to the castle, at the castle gate Orion and Irish head to the smithy. Phoenix heads Mary past the castle gate, and they wait a few moments to give Orion and Irish a chance to get inside. Phoenix then leads Mary back to the castle and up into the castle itself.

"Why, did we do that, brother?"

"To keep your identity secret for now. You can reveal yourself in time."

"Thanks, this may come in handy in the future."

"It works for me; I dress down, and I can go to an inn and get drunk with the people. I manage to learn a lot from time to time."

"Phoenix, I have something I want to talk to you about in the morning."

"I see you have a flair for the dramatic Mary. In the morning, it shall be. Now I need to see your scribe in the library to bring one of the books up to date."

They separate, and each goes off in different directions. Mary heads up to bed, and Phoenix heads to the library.

"Scribe, are you here?" calls Phoenix.

A few moments later, a young man stumbles into the doorway rubbing his eyes.

"You called sire?"

"Yes, I need the book of the people breaking up into tribes, you do have that book?"

"A moment sire," the scribe goes to a shelf, climbs a ladder to the top shelf, and brings down a book. "Is this the book you seek sire?"

Phoenix opens the book and locates the place in the book he is looking for. "Yes, here it is. The poison dart frog people still exist; they live deep in the tropical jungles to the south. I want that noted here, and they're to be left alone."

"Yes, sire. It will be written. May I ask how you know this?"

"Personal experience, I've seen them."

"An eyewitness accounts. Sire, you're a wonder. Can I write your history?"

"Maybe, I promised a scribe in the southern kingdom David is his name, that he could write it. Now, if you like, you both can work on it."

"I would like that. Thank you, sire. I'll write that account in the book of tribes."

"Good night, scribe."

"Sleep well, sire."

In the morning, Phoenix meets Mary at the dining table for breakfast. "Well, sister, what did you want to discuss with me?"

"I was thinking, you travel to all the places you govern, and it takes such a long time to visit, it had occurred to me, we could locate and build a place central to everyone, and the rulers or representatives could meet there to give and or get information or news once a year."

"Excellent, Mary. I've had this in mind myself a few times, but situations made me forget."

"I have a map of some of the kingdoms you could fill in the missing information, and we can then try to pick a place so everyone will not have to travel extreme distances."

"Ok, let's see your map."

Mary brings out a large map that doesn't show the west or southern coasts, nor the polar regions. Phoenix adds to the map and shows all the villages and towns, not on the map omitting the poison dart frog people.

"This is not quite accurate, but it's the best I can do for now," said Phoenix.

"Brother, how do you know about the coasts to the south and west?"

"I've been there. In time, I plan to send people to map out the coasts and make a more accurate chart."

"If it's alright with you, brother? I'll set up the new meeting place based on this information."

"I'll leave that in your hands to set up the meeting place, and the way to communicate to the other villages and towns. I might suggest using people who can fly."

"Great idea. Do you have any other suggestions before I start, brother?"

"Yes, I made a couple of seals with the Phoenix mark. You can use this to send messages to other rulers, and they'll know it's from me, and that you are speaking for me. You'll get fewer arguments that way."

"I'll keep it safe; brother and I'll use it sparingly."

"I trust you, Mary. I must return home; I haven't seen Alana and Raven for over six months. I miss them."

"Have a safe journey, brother."

Phoenix kisses Mary on the cheek and leaves for home. Later that day, Phoenix flies over his home's valley and screams in his thunderous voice to let Alana know he's home.

As Phoenix lands, he finds two blurs, one black and one gray and black, filling his arms. Phoenix loves his family and loves it when they show how much he was missed. They settle down and tell each other about the adventures they've had. Phoenix hangs on every word. When he tells his tale, it seems much like the last story he told from his previous trip. Phoenix omits his find of the poison dart frog people, wanting to keep them secret for their own sake.

Phoenix tells Alana that Orion and the queen have met and married this last trip. She seemed interested, but Raven was very excited; she had heard of them but had never seen them. So, she begs to be taken to the castle for a visit. Alana agreed, and Phoenix decides it would be a good idea for reasons of his own. It was settled they'd leave in two days after Phoenix visited Zeke and his mother, who by this time has his new baby brother.

Phoenix collects his wife and daughter and flies to Zeke's cottage and visits for the day and spending the night. Raven slept in Pam's old room, and Phoenix and Alana spent the night in the smithy at the back in the straw. Now that Raven could take care of herself, Alana turned her attention back to her husband, and she didn't like to be too far away from him, so she stayed by him as much as she can. The next day saw them at Dance Master and Pam's cottage with Zeke and Lisa following on the wing. Raven changed to her namesake and flew on ahead. She loved seeing her baby uncle.

Dance Master met them in the yard and welcomed everyone; Raven had dashed into the house to see the baby. Raven hugged Pam and then over to the cradle to pick up her uncle and hold him. Alana came in, and she and Pam hugged and kissed one another by way of greeting, followed by a big hug from her son Phoenix.

"Hi, mom, how's my brother doing?"

"Raven bring the baby here so your father can see his brother," said Pam.

Raven gives up the child, and Phoenix sees his baby brother for the first time. When all the fuss has died down, Phoenix pulls the family together to ask some questions. Phoenix tells them what he suspects about the guild.

"Has anyone seen any sea birds flying around anywhere of late?"

No one answers his question, or they indicate a no answer.

"In the south, I've seen signs that the sea raiders have landed on the vacant shores; they've even built some huts. I've seen no one living there."

"You think they are going to come back after you told them not to sire," asks Dance Master.

"Yes, I do. They want power, and when I came on the scene, I destroyed that power. They want it back and will do anything to get it."

"We'll keep an eye out for them, sire, but how will we contact you?"

"Funny you should ask that my new queen (Mary) is setting up a communication network to all the villages, towns, and castles. When she's finished, you could reach me in a few days no matter where I am."

"That sounds great, son, when will it be ready?" asks Dance Master.

"I don't know yet, she just started."

"So, when did Mary take over being a queen, and what happened to her mother?" asks Dance Master.

"About two weeks ago. Her mother was married and stepped down as queen, and her brother Orion also married and took over the smithy at the castle. I put Mary in charge, and she came up with the communication network, and she's working on a central meeting place for all the rulers to meet once or twice a year."

"Sounds like Mary is going to be a good ruler," said Pam.

"You should know mother you taught her."

"I taught you also, son."

Phoenix laughs, "Yes, you did."

"Dance Master, would you come and walk with me?"

The dance master looks at Phoenix for a full minute, responding, "Yes, Sire."

Both men leave the house and walk away from home. Then Phoenix changes and scoop up Dance Master and flies off to a place in the valley where there are no trees or brush, just grassland,

"What do you want to talk about, sire?"

"Have you ever heard about the poison dart frog people?"

"No, I haven't."

"They exist; I found them in the deep south while exploring. They're very dangerous. One-touch will kill a person or animal who's not a frog person."

"I thought that was a myth?" queried Dance Master.

"No myth, I watched them kill a large bull-like creature who charged their village, and a man in a loincloth jumped on the creatures back and stayed there until it died. Then I saw two men and one girl they were trying to entice the girl to mate. They changed into frogs with electric colors, and she chose one and went off with him."

"Did you meet with them, sire?"

"I was going to but, they spoke a language I couldn't understand. I decided they could rule over themselves."

"Why are you telling me this, sire?"

"So, you can be wary, my friend."

Phoenix returns them to the cottage to find that Zeke and Lisa had returned home. Alana thinks it best to be returning home too. Phoenix scoops up Alana and flies back to the valley, followed by Raven when they land at home.

"Raven, go catch a nice fat fish for our dinner," says Alana.

Raven files off to the stream, changes to her otter form, and isn't long catching two big fish for dinner. She then hikes back to the cottage a mile away.

"Husband, what did you say to Dance Master when you two left?"

"Have you heard of poison dart frog people?"

Alana frowns in thought. "I've heard something when I was a young girl in my father's house. They were a people the assassins were looking for, and at the time have not found. They may have died out."

"They didn't die out. They moved deep into the southern jungles."

"Then, you have to keep them hidden or kill them, husband."

"Why do you say that Alana?"

"The guild will use them to kill anyone in their way, especially you my husband."

"I suspect we may already be too late, Alana."

"You're probably right, husband. You should kill the entire guild."

"You may be right, but how do you tell a guild person from a regular person?"

"I can tell a guild person from others; by the way they move. I was raised among them."

"We leave for the castle in the morning Alana, will Raven be going?"

"We can ask her; she should be here shortly with dinner."

Raven enters with two nice sized fish all cleaned and ready to cook; she spits up one of them and flays the other to be cooked in a pan.

"Raven, how would you like to go with us to the castle Phoenix?" asks Phoenix.

"Really! You'll take me the castle?"

"Yes, it's about time for you to meet some friends of mine."

"When do we leave?" asks Raven.

"Tomorrow, we'll leave in the morning after breakfast."

CHAPTER

53

Alana fishes out her leather outfit and cape. "Raven, you'll need to change to your otter form tomorrow so I can wrap you in this cloak for the flight."

"Can't I just fly along as a raven?"

"Actually, no, you couldn't keep up; what'd take you three to four days to fly your father can do in one long one."

"Then why the leather cloak, if it's a short flight?"

"At the speed, your father travels, it gets very cold, you'll find out tomorrow."

That night Raven can't sleep, with the new adventure before her, while Alana and Phoenix fall asleep right away. Way before sunrise Raven flies to the stream, catches another large fish, and brings it home to get it on the spit for breakfast; she's anxious to be on their way. Breakfast ends, and Alana dressed in her leather outfit and cloak, Alana has Raven change into an otter form, Alana picks Raven up, and wraps her in her cloak. Phoenix scoops them up and flies off to the castle, at the end of the day, Phoenix flies to the castle courtyard and releases Alana and Raven.

"I see what you mean, mother, I'm freezing, can we get to a fire?" pleads Raven.

"This way, ladies." Phoenix leads the way into the castle. He gets the chef to make sandwiches for them and puts Raven next to the hearth to warm up. Mary shows up after being informed Phoenix has arrived with guests.

"Brother, you have returned so soon."

"I returned for a couple of reasons, Mary, Alana wants to visit, and we brought our daughter Raven to introduce her to everyone."

Mary crosses over to the hearth and takes Raven's face in her hands, "My, you're a beautiful girl. We'll have to get to know each other better, Raven. Brother, how long will you be here?"

"I'm not sure, Mary, can we have our usual apartments, and one for Raven?"

"Raven can have my old room, and your apartments will be ready in an hour, will that be alright?"

"That'll be fine, your highness," said Alana.

"Mary, we need to talk in the private room," states Phoenix.

"Is tomorrow a good time Phoenix?"

"It will; I also have others to visit and a garment maker to enlist."

They turn in for the night; everyone sleeps even Raven; her father's flight was taxing due to the cold. In the morning after breakfast, Phoenix and Mary go to the private room to talk. To make sure it's private, there is nothing in the room but stone walls. With no furniture to hide anyone however small. So, they must stand or sit on the floor. They both pass information about the guild. Phoenix fears that they're back. Mary confirms those fears as she hands him a note. (There is a guild member here, be wary. A friend.)

"This is why I'm here."

"You mean you knew of the note, Brother?"

"No, I've seen signs in the south that they may be here. Alana may be able to flush them out. That's why I came back."

"When do we hunt them down?"

"Alana has already started and moving about here today to visit people will let her see more people who may be from the sea raiders or guild."

"Let's get back to your family, brother."

Alana and Raven wait at the hearth finishing up a tart made of peach-like fruit.

Alana, Raven, are you ready to go, I have a few things to accomplish, and you need to go with me."

Phoenix leads them to the smithy to visit Orion and Irish. The reunion is well received, and Raven was most of the conversation until Irish reveals that she'll be having a child. Then Alana and Raven whisked her off to a corner to talk. Orion and Phoenix walked to the far side of the forge so Orion could pump it up, making noise.

"We have eyes and ears on us, brother, be careful what you say."

"Do you have any star stone left?" asked Phoenix.

"Not very much; how much do you need?"

"Let's see what you have."

"Will this do, brother?" as Orion holds up a stone that is the size of a small marble.

"It's perfect for what I need, may I use your forge to work it, say tomorrow?"

"I'd be honored; may I watch you forge it?" asks Orion.

"I'll see you tomorrow. By the way, congratulations on your child."

"Thank you, brother, and I look forward to watching you tomorrow."

Phoenix pulls the women away from Irish. They move on into town; they stop at a garment shop where Phoenix commissions a leather outfit and cloak for Raven like her mother's, and he also purchases a couple of dresses for Alana and Raven. Phoenix leaves the colors and styles for the women to pick. After the dickering and the choices made, the women strip down to their underclothes to measure them for their clothes.

Phoenix leads the women out of the castle. Out to the backside of the cultivated fields to Bryan's cottage. Phoenix reminds Alana to call her friend, "Beth, not your highness." Bryan meets them at the door of his cottage.

"Hi Bryan, is it ok to come for a visit?" asks Todd (Phoenix)

"Yes, please come in."

They enter the cottage, and Beth is working at the hearth, making a meal for her and Bryan. When she looks up to see Phoenix and his family, she rises and walks up to meet them. Beth hugs Alana and is introduced to Raven for the first time.

Beth takes Raven's hands and holds them apart, "My such a pretty young maiden," causing Raven to blush.

Beth turns back to Alana and Phoenix and asks the question, "Why are you here?"

"Have any new people shown up lately? I suspect the guild is going to try for a comeback," explains Todd.

"We've seen no new people lately, but now that you mention it, Bryan and I have seen some activity out in the woods where we heard our sheep. They stay out of sight like they are watching us."

"Bryan, would you show me?"

"I can, is it important?"

"Very."

Bryan changes into a fox and Alana changes to a wolf, Todd changes to a sparrow, and Bryan leads the way from the cottage and cuts across the pasture in the tall grass, followed by Alana and Todd. They reach the woods after an hour, and Bryan leads them on into the forest for a distance. Then Bryan stops and changes back into a human; Todd does the same, and Alana stays a wolf. Bryan points in the direction he and Beth saw animals and humans moving about.

"Ok, you Bryan and Alana, stay here. I'll be back." Todd changes back into a sparrow and flies up into the trees and then flies along the direction Bryan indicated. Phoenix sees the tents set up, and he flies to a small flock of local birds looking for insects or seeds to get close to the ground and see if he can hear what is being said. No one is speaking, and Phoenix watches; the guild master steps out of his tent, and he sees the brand on the guild masters face. Phoenix drops down, changes to human form, and grabs the guild master by the throat.

"I warned you!" and Phoenix burns him to ash, then turns his attention to the guard. The guard is frozen in fear. Phoenix brands the guards face. "Tell your masters, I know you're here, and I'll burn you all. You'll leave my kingdom now and never come back."

Phoenix throws the man to the ground. Then transforms into a falcon and flies off in the opposite direction from where Alana and Bryan wait. Phoenix returns to where Bryan and Alana wait, "We need to return to your cottage. The guild is here."

Back at the cottage, Todd explains what happened in the woods and asks Bryan and Beth to go live with Orion and his wife for a time. You'll need to move your flock to another location, if possible. The guild will kill anyone they see out their way, and I'll be watching them to make sure they leave.

"Todd, are you sure we should go to the castle, smithy?" asks Beth.

"Yes, Beth, I do!" said Todd.

Bryan starts to protest until Beth places her hand on his shoulder. "Husband trust my friend, he has been fighting the guild for a long time, and he means to save not only our lives but Orion's and Irish's life as well."

"They wouldn't touch them," states Bryan.

"Yes, they will, and all the nearby neighbors, too," said Todd.

Bryan, Beth, and Raven return to the castle and go to the smithy. Beth has Raven go tell Mary to come down here as well. Raven flies off to do what she had been asked to do. Soon Mary and Raven show up at the smithy. They're ushered to where Irish is.

"Beth, what's so urgent that you sent for me?" asked Mary.

"The guild is back, and your brother thought you'd be safer here."

The women move to the smithy's back area where the living area is to visit Irish and keep her calm. Bryan and Orion are near the forge like they were keeping guard. Beth decides to see if the men would like something to eat. Bryan missed his meal when Phoenix showed up, and they ran off. Beth enters the forge area when a man materializes from the low shadows (he was in a rat form) he throws a knife at Beth when Bryan interposes his body in front of Beth and takes the knife in his right shoulder, he falls. Beth starts running toward the assassin as she changes into a black panther. She flashes across the floor, knocks the assassin down, and rips out his throat as he readied a knife for someone else.

Beth changes back into human blood, running down her face onto her dress; she returns to her husband, cradles his head, and pulls the knife out of his shoulder.

"Raven, come here, child!" calls Beth.

"Yes, Beth!"

"Can you find your father and bring him back here?"

"Yes."

"Please, get him, child, only he can save my husband from the poison, please hurry!"

Raven flies off in the direction of Bryan's house, passes over it, and heads into the woods; she feared she wouldn't be able to locate her father until she flies up to the top of the trees. Off in the distance, she sees her father's Phoenix form laying waste to the forest about him as he fights the guild. Raven flies straight to Phoenix and circles his head a few times, and he realizes who it is. Phoenix transforms back into his human form.

"What's wrong, Raven?"

"Bryan is dying, and Beth sent me for you."

Phoenix reaches into a pocket, "Here, take this back with you and pour this on the wound and he'll recover. Now I have to go after your mother."

"Father, you both be careful."

"We will now hurry, or Bryan may die."

Raven flies off toward the smithy and Phoenix heads south following the sea raiders and the guild. He soon locates the trail; Alana has left a few sea raiders with their throats ripped out as markers. Phoenix catches up to Alana in his falcon form and watches the sea raiders. It takes a while and a lot of distance to kill them all. There was a small army of fifty raiders and a hand full of guild members, all burned to ash. Phoenix changes into his Phoenix form and flies back with Alana to the castle when they have finished. They arrive back at the castle, and Bryan was on the mend. Bryan had been near death until Raven poured the vile of liquid on Bryan's wound.

Beth hugs Phoenix, "Thank you, sire, for saving my husband."

"Why did you call him sire, Beth?" asks Irish.

"I guess it's time to introduce you to everyone," said Beth.

"This is King Phoenix, his wife Alana, and daughter Raven. Mary is now queen regent; my son Orion is a prince. I was queen regent."

Irish stands there dumbfounded, and her eyes wide open in shock. "I…"

"It's ok, Irish; I didn't want anyone to know. The only responsibility I wanted was to be a good wife to your father, not to the whole kingdom."

Irish looked to Orion, her husband, "Why didn't you tell me?"

"I asked him not to tell you, Irish, for your safety," said Phoenix.

"What right, do you have to interfere in our lives?" said Irish with some heat.

Orion steps between Irish and Phoenix. More to protect Phoenix than Irish. "Because wife, he's our KING! And you will obey him!"

"What right does he have to…"

Orion kisses his wife soundly to slow her down, "Because he saved my life years ago, and if you think about it, he just saved everyone's life today, including yours and our baby."

"I, Oh. I'm sorry, your majesty."

Phoenix laughs a good hardy laugh and pulls Irish into his arms. "Irish, you're a treasure. You may question me anytime. However, you may not always like the answer." Irish is looking up into his eyes when Phoenix plants a kiss on her forehead and lets her go. Irish looks sheepish and stays silent.

"Irish, you can never say anything about this; if you do, you and your family will become targets for assassins or kidnappers."

"Yes, I understand."

Mary turns to Phoenix, "How did you save Bryan form the poison?"

"You can find that answer by reading about the myths of the Phoenix, the bird," said Phoenix.

After the excitement dies down, everyone retires to the castle, with orders to have guards posted around everyone's sleeping quarters. That night alone in their sleep chamber Alana tells Phoenix about Beth's condition.

"Are you sure Beth is pregnant?"

"Yes, husband, I can tell by her scent."

"Does she know?"

"Not yet, but she will soon."

CHAPTER

54

In the morning, Phoenix flew back to the burned-out camp. Then flew along the path he had burned, killing the sea raiders. So, he could scout for more. In his falcon form, he wasn't seen from the ground. Phoenix spotted a couple of men, so he flew on and changed to a sparrow and returned to watch the two men.

"I see you ran into the Phoenix; we told you not to move too fast."

"We didn't, somehow we were spotted, and it got back to Phoenix and his witch wife."

"We best head south, the last team has found what we were looking for, the poison frog peoples."

"You found them where?"

"In the deep south, they killed seven of our men before we realized how they did it with just a touch."

"So, we can use this against Phoenix and his people."

"That's the idea, we have to communicate that to the poison frog people, or we'll use a more direct persuasion to get their help."

The men turn and head to the south; they transform into sea birds and fly off. Phoenix lets them go, and he returns to the castle. He explains he must leave everyone behind to travel south. The poison frog people are in danger, and he needs to help them. Alana wants to go, and Phoenix says no, he needs to travel fast, and the poison frog people are dangerous you can't even touch them.

Phoenix has never denied his wife before, but now is not the time to take her, he needs stealth and speed, and she'd slow him down. Phoenix leaves that day and flies as fast as he can to the south to the very spot where he had found the huts on the south beach; there were a couple of ships that Phoenix burned to ash, then the huts and the men in them. Phoenix then changes form to the falcon and flies to the village where the poison frog people live.

A few weeks before, the sea raiders located and captured the poison frog people. They took a beautiful young girl to take to the southern castle to use her as an assassin to kill the ruler, Angus. Phoenix locates the village and changes to a sparrow, which allows him to get closer to the village huts. It takes him an hour to discover all the raiders and guild members. Phoenix sees what they are doing to the poison frog people. They had them in a hut ready to set fire to them if they didn't follow orders.

Phoenix set about destroying the weapons for the sea raiders; all weapons were burned to ash or slag. The men close to the torches suddenly were turned to ash. Phoenix, in his human form, stood in the doorway and gestured to the poison frog people to come out, and then he showed them their tormentors no longer had their weapons. The poison frog people then took their revenge and killed all the sea raiders. Phoenix, in his human form, stood back as the frog people walked up to him. Phoenix held up his hands to show he had no weapons, and he meant no harm.

An older man stepped through the crowd, and he held up his hands. He spoke in the Mayan language. Phoenix shook his head no, then he spoke in the standard language, and Phoenix addressed him.

"Yes, I understand, are you the only one who speaks this language?" asks Phoenix.

"Yes, I'm called Renwick. I was a sea raider. I was shipped wreck a hundred years ago on the south coast, and found this place. The other four people who were with me tried to conquer these people, and they all died. I didn't try to hurt them. I tried to stop my shipmates to no avail. These people saw that, and didn't touch me, so I'm alive today. They are mostly peaceful people unless provoked."

"I, see. I've been watching you from time to time and thought it best to leave you to yourself. I'm the ruler of all this land more for protection than anything. I just destroyed the ships at anchor and the contingent of men on the beach. I'll leave you now and return to my castle."

"Please, listen. They've taken a young girl from us to use as an assassin; they intend to kill a couple of kings with her. Would you bring her back to us?"

"I'll have to build a cage for her; or I won't be able to carry her."

"I can help with that, sire." Renwick hands Phoenix a vile; this contains an antidote to their poison. When you drink it, they won't be able to poison you. See, and Renwick touches one of the people. You see, I found a plant that counters their poison." Then Renwick touches Phoenix, and nothing happens. "This has allowed me to live with them without mishap, I even have a wife, and it's our grandchild that was taken."

"I'll do what I can to return her. Does she talk normal language?"

"Yes, Sire."

"Good, here I have a gift for you. If someone gets sick or wounded, pour the contents of this vial on them, and they will heal. I had best get started. Two guild men are returning this way; I suggest you had better get ready for them."

"I'll tell them sire; we'll deal with them," said Renwick.

Phoenix flies up out of the trees in his sparrow form, then changes into his Phoenix form and flies to the southern kingdom to meet with Angus. Phoenix flies over the castle and screams out in his thunderous voice to get everyone's attention. Phoenix lands on the front steps of the castle and transforms into human form. He doesn't have long to wait for Angus appears from his smithy.

"King Phoenix, to what pleasure do I owe this visit?"

"Do you have someplace we can talk in private?"

"Follow me, sire." Angus leads them into the castle and up into a sealed tower, and a guard was posted at the stairs to keep people away. "Sire, we can talk here."

"The guild has plans to assassinate you, with a poison from the frog people, I want to take you and Patti away from here and take your place. I'll explain all when I've finished returning the young lady to her people. For now, I need for you to trust me."

"I do, Sire, what do you want us to do?"

"Gather a few things, and we're taking a trip, you and Patti. Get her and return. We leave as soon as you get back."

Angus does as he told and brings Patti back with him; Phoenix has them wrapped up in a leather blanket; it will be a cold trip. Phoenix launches into the air and carries them north to his grandfather's cottage. They arrive late the next day. Phoenix lands in the yard and Zeke and Lisa come out to greet them.

"Well, grandson, what brings you and your friend here, and where are Alana and Raven?"

"Zeke, this is Angus and his wife Patti, this is my grandmother Lisa. Grandfather, I brought Angus here so you could teach him how to engrave."

"I know that tone of voice, son, what else?"

"They are endangered at the southern kingdom, so I brought them here for their protection."

"Then we'll make them welcome. Is this the Angus you told me about?"

"It is, and he's an excellent blacksmith."

"Then we'll have a lot to talk about."

"Come every one dinner is on, and we have enough for everyone," said Lisa.

After the meal, Phoenix leaves for the long trip south to the southern castle. Unburdened, Phoenix could cut the journey by a third and arrive quietly at the castle. Then take up residence and let everyone know he's here. Phoenix gets a good night's sleep and a large breakfast in the morning, and then he opens the throne room to take the audience. A few landowners show up to ask for more land and if the crown will allow it. Phoenix grants the requests if it doesn't infringe on someone else land.

Late in the evening, a delegation shows up consisting of four men and one young girl.

"Sire, a delegation from the south comes to cement an alliance with their city-state."

Phoenix takes the antidote he was given by Renwick and washes it down with some water.

"Send them in."

The scribe shows them in and announces them.

"You're the delegation from the south city-state. I didn't know there was such a place."

The man in charge bowed. "There are a few towns in the south we're but just one such place, Sire, and we wish to cement relations with your kingdom. We brought a young girl for your harem."

"I don't have a harem, so what good is she to me?"

"Sire, it would be an insult to our ruler if you don't accept her."

"So, girl, what's your name?"

She doesn't speak; she acts like she doesn't understand.

"Sire, she doesn't yet speak our language. She learns fast."

"What's her name?"

"We call her Wonder."

"Wonder, please come here."

The girl hesitates, but walks up to Phoenix, but keeps her hands to herself, knowing how dangerous she is to him. Phoenix takes her hand and can see the excitement in the eyes of the man in charge.

Phoenix smiles, "Wonder, you really are a wonder to behold. You and your people are now safe," whispers Phoenix.

"What's wrong, sire, you should be dying or dead; she's poison to touch."

"Let's test it out. Guards capture these men."

One man tries to pull his sword to kill both the girl and Phoenix; then, Phoenix burns him to ash. The others stand still and don't move. The guards take their weapons.

"Girl, your family is safe; Renwick gave me an antidote for saving their village, and soon as we deal with these men, I'll take you home."

The girl walks up to the man in charge and slaps his face, his mouth opens, and he dies before he can say anything. She does the same to the other two men; then she turns back to Phoenix.

"Sire, thank you. Renwick told you I knew your language, when will you take me home?"

"Will tomorrow do?"

"Yes, where do you want me to sleep? After all, I am full of poison, and I don't want to endanger others."

"If you like, you may sleep within my room, I'll be there too, and we can leave in the morning."

"You'll be there. I am a maiden, not a woman."

"Fear not, I have a wife, and she would cut my throat if she even though I had those intentions. Besides, I couldn't change into a bright colored frog to impress you."

"You've been watching us. Thank you for letting me touch the men; they killed my younger brother. Then they kept me in check by holding my people hostage."

"I didn't know of your brother, but your villagers I did, and they are safe. That's why I took Angus's place as a ruler. So, I could save you."

"Let's get some sleep. It'll be a hard trip to your home," said Phoenix.

In the morning, Phoenix wakes the girl and sees she is fed, and then packs up some food and water. Phoenix wraps her in a leather skin and then scoops her up into his talons and flies back to her village. It takes a couple of days; then, they fly a bit further south to land in a clearing. On touching down, a curtain of arrows comes flying at them, which Phoenix burns to ash, and then another curtain comes toward them. Phoenix gets mad and burns the forest all around them, killing twenty sea raiders.

The arrows stop. The shouts of pain and agony sound off, and Phoenix fearing the worst rushed into the wood to find that the poison frog people are touching the leftover raiders. It was the raiders he heard dying, not the villagers.

Renwick steps out of the undergrowth, and the young girl went running up to him. "Grandfather!"

"There, girl, are you alright?"

"I'm fine, they didn't touch me, and king Phoenix brought me home."

"King Phoenix?"

"Yes, grandfather, this is king, Phoenix."

Renwick looks to Phoenix, "does this mean you're our ruler?"

"In name only Renwick, I only assert my rule where it's needed. Looking around, I see no need to interfere."

"What does that mean?"

"It means I'll not take charge here, from time to time, I will visit, only to see if I need to help like today. I have made it clear to my people to leave your people to themselves."

"I had heard that before, in the sea raiders' country, when the government was taking over and made slaves of us all."

"I don't know what I can do or say to make you believe me, Renwick, except that I give you my word."

"I have had that before, too," said Renwick.

"Grandfather Phoenix has been watching us for some time. He described our mating practice to me at the castle when we stayed in the same room."

"He, what?"

"Grandfather, he didn't touch me. He kept his people and me safe by keeping me close to him. He brought me here, did he not?"

"He did at that."

"Then, grandfather believe him."

"I will believe you king Phoenix."

"I need to keep two men and no more, down near the coast to keep a lookout for the sea raiders. These two men will be fliers, they'll report to me. They don't need to come to your village. Now, if the sea raiders land again, would you like one of them to warn you?"

"You put me in a tough spot, sire."

"How so, Renwick?"

"You force me to make a choice. If I accept your help, what other conditions do I open my doors to? On the other hand, it would be nice to have time to get my people to safety."

"This has to be your choice Renwick; I'll not force you. I intend to protect my kingdom so my men will be placed where they can inform me of my enemy."

"I'll accept your rulership, if the raiders land, I'll want to know," said Renwick.

"It will be, as I've said. I'll give my orders to the flies not to enter your village unless giving you a message or warning you of the sea raiders. If they come on their own and you kill them, I'll not hold you responsible."

"I can ask for no more than that sire." Renwick sticks out his hand, and Phoenix takes it and shakes on the deal.

"Renwick, did you manage to save your grandson?"

"Now that you mention it, it's that little tadpole standing right there wide-eyed looking at you right there."

Phoenix stoops down and says, "Well, young man, it's good to see you." The boy hides behind his sister, and she takes his hand and leads him over to Phoenix.

"It's ok; he's the one who saved us all." The boy smiles but keeps his distance.

Phoenix stands up and tells everyone he'll be back some time. Then he changes into a sparrow and flies up above the trees and changes into Phoenix, the bird, and thunders out his voice, then flies off toward the north. Phoenix flies to his grandfather's cottage to check on Angus and Patti and see if they're ready to return home. It's late afternoon when Phoenix lands in the yard, and no one even notices that he's there yet. Phoenix walks into the smithy and finds Angus etching metal with the tools he had to make under Zeke's tutelage.

"I could spend another month here learning what you have to teach me," said Angus."

"That can be arranged," said Phoenix.

"Sire, you've come back," as Angus embraces Phoenix in a bear hug.

"I see you missed me. How are you doing, grandfather?"

"I'm glad to see you grandson, tell us all about it."

"Before I regale you with the adventure of peril and such, let's go to the womenfolk, and while they make a meal, I'll tell the whole story. Then I won't have to repeat it."

After dinner and a tankard of mead, Phoenix sets back in his chair, nearly falling asleep, when Angus shakes him awake. "You promised to tell us your adventure."

"Where to begin." Phoenix regales them with his quick flight to the south, then to Angus bring him and Patti here. Then all about the young girl from the poison frog people and then the battle with the guild and sea raiders. At the end of the story, Patti chimes in, "You best omit the pretty girl in your room for the night when you tell Alana your story."

"You got that right; she would rip out my throat with her teeth."

"You know sire, you are smarter than you look," states Patti.

"Patti, you should not talk that way to your king," admonishes Angus.

Everyone laughs, and Patti says, "I can talk to Phoenix, anyway I want."

Phoenix sits next to Patti, so he circles her waist and pulls her close to him, and he plants a kiss right on her lips, and she turns red and shuts up.

"Patti, if I were not married, I'd take you away from Angus for my own." Then he lets go.

"I'm exhausted. I'm going to fly home and get some sleep. I'll be back in the morning."

Phoenix tells everyone good night and flies to the valley to his cottage. He sleeps the sleep of the dead he was so tired. Late the next morning, Phoenix returns to Zeke's cottage well rested. Grandmother meets him in the yard with a sandwich and tells him that Zeke and Angus are working in the smithy.

"Good morning," said Phoenix around a bite of his breakfast.

The men just grunted and went about what they were working on. Phoenix chuckled and left to visit with the women. The day was languid and lazy, this is something Phoenix, needed. No fights, no decisions, and no life or death trials. That evening Phoenix told Angus and Patti they need to leave in the morning. Phoenix told them they would go to castle Phoenix for a visit; then, he would return them home. In the morning, Angus and Patti are ready for the flight to castle Phoenix.

Phoenix changed to his bird form, scooped up Patti and Angus, and flew off to the west; late in the evening, Phoenix lands in the courtyard and leaves off his passengers. Phoenix changes to his human form. A grey streak shoots down the stairs from the top of the stairs and knocks Phoenix down to the ground covering his face with a wet sloppy tongue. Laughing, Phoenix tries pushing Alana to one side so he can get up. "I missed you too, my wife."

Alana changes to her human form and hugs her man. Mary shows up at that top of the stairs with Raven, who stand there demure and aloof, trying to act like ladies. That is until Phoenix and company reach the top step. Then Raven breaks down and latches on to her father.

"I see Mary is trying to make a lady of you."

"I missed your father."

"I missed you and your mother; what we need now is some food and drink and a place for the southern ruler and his wife for a few days."

Mary calls one of the stewards and gives him instruction for the food and another to make up a bed in one of the apartments upstairs. Phoenix regales everyone about what happened; Phoenix omits sleeping with the young girl in his room. He decides he'd tell Alana later alone. Over the next day's Phoenix returned Angus and his wife to the southern kingdom.

Chapter

55

As Phoenix travels, he carried Alana with him everywhere until she gets too old to travel from that time forward everywhere Phoenix went Alana stayed home. Over time, Raven married Dancer, and they took over the cottage of Pam and Dance Master.

The average life span of a Chimerian is three hundred years. The Phoenix life span is one thousand years. When Phoenix buried his grandparents and his mother with her husband, he also buried his heart, Alana. Alana, he buried on the mountain they could see from their cottage, where no one could disturb her grave. During the next three hundred years, Phoenix charted his entire kingdom's continent and gave copies to the rulers of the southern and northern kingdoms and the central meeting place that Mary had set up. The communications network she put in place helps to head off a couple of invasions by the sea raiders and the guild.

Over time, Phoenix even made charts of the sea raiders' continent to keep them from building too many ships. He placed that map information in the northern kingdom only. Phoenix still visits all the villages and towns once a year. He even calls on the poison frog people from time to time to give them news and see how they're doing. Phoenix kept his word to David the scribe, and he let him write his history, then David the scribe died. Phoenix gave Joan at the northern kingdom the manuscript to continue the history, and she recorded all that occurred for the second three hundred years. When Joan lay dying, she handed the manuscript to me, her son Hector.

During the last four hundred years of Phoenix's life, when he was not protecting the kingdom from the sea raiders, he would take down rulers and set up new ones when that ruler wouldn't follow Phoenix's mandates. Phoenix made many enemies from within and without the kingdom. Phoenix grew old, grey-haired, and worn looking, but he still had his vitality and strength. The vultures were waiting for the King to die so that someone among their number could rise up and take charge.

Phoenix spent most of his time at Zeke's cottage because of the smithy. He let his place in the valley go. It was too painful for him to visit there. Then one-night, Phoenix came to my son and me to carry us from castle Phoenix to Zeke's cottage to be witness to his final act. He was to fly to the mountain to die. His funeral prier was ready. One of two things would happen either he'd be reborn as in the legends, or he'd die and be with Alana.

"Hector, my old friend, and your son Raymond I'm going to that mountain, you should be able to see the fire from here. Wait three days. If I don't return, you may go live your lives. Make sure you give me three days. If the legend is correct, I may be back."

"Good luck, sire."

Phoenix flies up to the mountain, lands on his funeral pyre, sets it on fire, and burns up with the wood, and everything turns to ash. Hector and Raymond see the fire, and they whisper their goodbyes to their King. They return to the cottage and settle in to write what happened in the book, with hope the legend is right, knowing that the wars that'll start that will destroy this kingdom.

Hector waits, and each morning he'd watch the mountain hoping to see the Phoenix return. On the third day, both Hector and Raymond watch the mountain. They are hoping against hope that Phoenix would appear. They get tired of watching, and just as they turn to gather their gear, Raymond sees a flash of light.

"Father, see that?!"

"See what, Raymond?"

"That father, it's the Phoenix!"

The Phoenix flies from the mountain toward Zeke's cottage with a thunderous cry, and he lands in the yard. Looking regal in his new golden body with fire shimmering about his body. At first, the Phoenix doesn't seem to know the scribe Hector, then Phoenix changes to his human form, and he looks not to be much older than Raymond.

"I remember, Hector, I remember."

"Sire, you need to reappear at all the castles and towns before war erupts."

As I lay down my pen, the Phoenix's next thousand-year reign begins, and my son Raymond will record it during his time here. This is where my writing ends, and Raymond's begins.

The End for now.